SOMETHING IN THE BLOOD

SOMETHING IN THE BLOOD

J. G. Goodhind

Severn House

This first world edition published in Great Britain 2007 by
SEVERN HOUSE PUBLISHERS LTD of
9–15 High Street, Sutton, Surrey SM1 1DF.
This first world edition published in the USA 2007 by
SEVERN HOUSE PUBLISHERS INC of
595 Madison Avenue, New York, N.Y. 10022.

British Library Cataloguing in Publication Data

Goodhind, J. G.
Something in the blood
1. Hotelkeepers - Fiction 2. Missing persons - Investigation - England - Bath - Fiction 3. Murder - England - Bath - Fiction 4. Detective and mystery stories
I. Title
823.9'2[F]

ISBN-13: 978-0-7278-6520-5 (cased)
ISBN-13: 978-1-84751-019-8 (trade paper)

All Severn House titles are printed on acid-free paper.

Typeset by Palimpsest Book Production Ltd.,
Grangemouth, Stirlingshire, Scotland.
Printed and bound in Great Britain by
MPG Books Ltd., Bodmin, Cornwall.

One

'Murder, robbery and any other kind of mayhem must be kept at bay in this fair city, my dear girl; hence your appointment.'

Hannah Driver, called Honey by those that knew her best – except her mother who revelled in being different about everything – eyed Casper St John Gervais with incredulity. He was elegant, eccentric and terribly effete, but was he also a little mad?

'Why me?'

'Your experience, my dear girl.'

'I've never been a policeman . . . woman,' she corrected.

'We – the association – just want you to act as liaison point between us and the police. You know, my dear girl, how a city's reputation can affect tourism. Crime must be swiftly and effectively dealt with. Anyway, besides you having an interest in bed occupancy, I understand you used to work with criminals.'

'I worked for the Probation Service – as a Senior Clerical Officer.'

'Precisely my point.'

'Casper, that means I used to type Social Enquiry Reports, a compilation of circumstances and excuses as to why the client shouldn't be banged up and the key thrown away.'

Casper had a very aquiline nose, very thin at the bridge and widely flaring at the nostrils. When he fixed his gaze on her, his eyes seemed to close together, like a pince-nez perched on his nose. His nostrils flared into black chasms.

'But you're all we have, my dear girl. No member of the association has that kind of experience. And think of the good you could do . . . Hmm?'

She only vaguely remembered agreeing to it. Bath Hotels Association had been holding their annual AGM when Casper had made the suggestion. As usual the stuffy bit was followed by a bit of a party – quite a sizeable party in fact.

A well-known wine importer had supplied the drink, and a local caterer the food. Honey had done the unforgivable; arrived early and had to sit through the AGM. The bulk of the membership didn't arrive until the meeting was over. A few glasses of Australian Shiraz had helped alleviate her boredom. She might have fallen asleep. She hadn't snored – at least she didn't think so.

Casper had taken advantage of the situation. He'd whispered something in her ear. 'I guarantee that the Green River Hotel will benefit if you agree to this.'

Some semblance of that promise had stayed with her. Upgrading a few bedrooms at the Green River had left her with a chunky overdraft. Running a hotel in a beautiful city was not a bed of roses. Roses had thorns and Casper's promise had poured like honey into her ear. Drat!

Lindsey, her daughter, who was far too mature for her age, offered consolation when she told her.

'Relax. Consider the positive side. It could add a pinch of spice to your life. You need to get out more.'

Honey watched as Lindsey cleared down the bar and locked up.

'Are you going nightclubbing tomorrow night,' she asked her.

Tomorrow night, Thursday, was Lindsey's night off.

Her daughter shook her tawny head. 'No. I'm going to a concert at the Abbey.'

'Pop?' Honey asked with a hopeful lifting of eyebrows.

'No. Medieval tunes for lute and lyre.'

'My, you are such a wild child. When I was eighteen . . .'

'You were irresponsible.'

'Who told you that?'

'Grandma.'

'She's a bright one to talk . . .'

Lindsey kissed her forehead. 'I'm off to bed. Now don't

worry. Like I said, you could do with a little pinch of spice in your life.'

The little pinch of spice came at the wrong time. Honey loved auctions, especially when there were antique clothes up for grabs. Today there'd been plenty.

Collecting clothes from the past helped her keep sane. Musing over who might have worn those gloves, that button-up boot, that lace-trimmed chemise made her forget that the laundry service had mislaid two dozen tablecloths, or that the honeymoon couple in room three had done irreversible damage to the bedsprings.

She had a small but interesting collection of lace mittens, silk stockings, garters plus some very interesting underwear. Today she had hit the jackpot and would have gone one better, then Casper phoned.

'Your first case,' he said. His voice was like tin on the end of the phone. The auction ran full throttle around her.

'OK,' she said, one eye on the auctioneer and the Victorian corset that was up for grabs: all whalebone and laces and made for a waist of less diameter than a modern thigh.

She was almost salivating.

'Where are you? Are you close by?'

Honey looked around her with furtive intent. Should she lie?

'The truth, dear girl,' said Casper as if reading her mind.

'I'm in Jollys' Auction Rooms.'

'Good. Be here by eleven thirty.'

Here meant his office. The phone pinged like a bouncing bullet. He wasn't taking no for an answer.

And what about the corset?

'Gone!'

She waved at the rostrum.

'Sorry madam. You're too late.'

Blast! It had been such a pretty little corset, red satin edged with black lace. Definitely French. Definitely provocative.

'But not for you,' she muttered as she pushed her way through the dealers, the curious and the bargain hunters.

She glanced at her watch on the way out.

First she had to settle her bill and collect her purchase. They were large; so was the price.

'Not for you, are they, hen,' smirked the cashier.

Alistair was huge, hairy and Scottish.

'Yep! I'm making a tent.'

'Once outside she shoved the Victorian bloomers into her Moroccan leather bag. They'd been listed as having once belonged to Queen Victoria – hence the price. The bag was copious, but the bloomers were more so. A sliver of cotton knicker leg fluttered like bunting between the gaping leather.

The sun came out as she passed the Pump Rooms turning the elegant façade the colour of honey. Inside a quartet was playing Handel to those taking tea out of real crockery with real tealeaves and real cream oozing from Scottish scones and sugar doughnuts. The music drifted on the air, but did nothing to soothe her slightly savage breast.

Missing the corset rankled. Red satin! And over a hundred years old! Now how rare was that?

Drat Casper St John Gervais! If he hadn't insisted she meet him at eleven-thirty *precisely*, the corset would have been hers.

They would have fitted me.

Well, ten years ago they would have. She smiled to herself. Call yourself voluptuous rather than slender, dear. There again, wasn't everybody's waist way beyond the Victorian eighteen inches?

Bath city centre was busy, but it was June and only to be expected. Baskets bursting with geraniums adorned the fronts of offices, banks and shops. Wisps of variegated ivy and purple aubrietia fluttered from lampposts. The elegant buildings forming Regency crescents and squares turned cowslip yellow when the sun came out.

Month after month the tourists flocked in from all over the world to gape at the Roman Baths, eat the massive buns on offer in Sally Lunn's Teashop and have their pictures taken in front of the Abbey, in the heart of the Royal Crescent or at the end of Pulteney Bridge.

The tourists were the city's lifeblood, the fertilizer that had caused a flowering of aged and listed buildings to convert to hotels, restaurants and guesthouses.

By the time she got to Hotel La Reine Rouge, an elegant edifice overlooking Pulteney Bridge and within walking distance of the Roman Baths, it felt as though she'd weaved her way through every nation in the world.

The La Reine Rouge was even more elegant inside than out, thanks mainly to its owner/manager's exquisite choice and eclectic mix of antiques, colour and sophisticated lighting.

She patted the arm of a turbaned statuette, one of a gloriously crimson, black and gold pair guarding the entrance. 'Hi chaps. Is the boss in?'

Neville, a real, live chap with bleached blond hair and wearing a burgundy waistcoat with a gold watch chain answered her question.

'He's waiting for you, sweetie. He's got his manicurist with him. He's terribly tense you know what with everything that's been happening.'

She gasped. 'Happening? You mean he's broken a nail?'

He threw her a sideways sneer. 'You're a very naughty girl, Honey.' His attention returned to the trio of white lilies he was placing in a tall, green vase. They didn't seem to fall the way he wanted, so he picked them out and started all over again.

'Only when tempted. But then, Neville, I hear you can be naughty when tempted.'

Neville blushed. 'Stop teasing me, Honey. You do it on purpose.'

The long-case clock standing on a thick Turkish rug chose that moment to chime the half hour.

The flowers were behaving badly. 'Oh bother!' Neville's vocabulary was as delicate as his appearance.

Honey raised her eyebrows. It was Neville who sounded terribly tense. Casper never was, but he was always beautifully groomed, she thought with a grimace. She looked down at her fingernails. The varnish was chipped. What else could she expect? Being the boss meant filling in when the dishwasher broke down or chambermaids didn't turn up. Tucking her arm through the handles of her bag, she hid her fingers in her pockets and made her way along the thickly carpeted corridor and down the stairs to Casper's office.

At one time the wine cellars beneath La Reine Rouge had stretched the whole length of the basement. After the builders had finished the basics, Casper had turned the area into offices for himself and his staff, papering the newly plastered walls with expensive hessian in rich sienna. The furniture was a mix of minimalist settees, Georgian breakfronted bookcases and ethnic artwork. Oh, and clocks. Casper loved clocks. They were everywhere: wall clocks, grandfather clocks, grandmother clocks, skeleton clocks, carriage clocks – all ticking away together. They even chimed together. Casper insisted they all chimed together in unison. He hated untidiness.

'Come in, my dear.' His voice rang like the sharp chime of one of his clocks.

The manicurist was buffing the smallest finger of Casper St John Gervais's right hand when she entered. He waved the woman away once that was done. 'Another day, another finger job,' he said with a demure smile.

The manicurist hurried out – no doubt on her way to Neville, who would settle the bill. Casper's patrician sensibilities prevented him from doing anything so plebeian as *physically* dealing with money.

He was sitting in a honey-coloured leather chair behind a mahogany desk that might once have belonged to Tennyson or Wordsworth. Casper loved items with provenance, a proven history and famous connections. He loved auctions as much as she did, though his preference was for mahogany chests of drawers rather than the cotton type with two legs that she favoured.

She smiled at him and brought on the flattery. 'You're looking as lovely as ever, Casper.'

'Thank you my dear.' Casper was the prima donna of the catering industry and adored flattery. He sounded like Noel Coward at the height of his success but looked like a rather muscular version of Randolph Scott.

Whilst she stood there, he brought out a feather duster from a drawer and proceeded to flick it at the imagined dust the manicurist had left behind. Casper hated dust and dirt. His hotel, his office and his person were immaculate.

'I trust you have heard the news, so I will not go into detail except to say that your services are required much earlier than one could possibly have anticipated.'

'Well, actually, I've been so busy . . .' She didn't get chance to explain that the dishwasher had thrown another tantrum or that a couple from Leicester had climbed out of the window that morning without paying their bill. Drat! – if only she'd put them on the third floor. That would have foxed them.

Casper ignored her and was holding forth about the meeting of Bath Hotels' Association the week before. 'As you may recall, the meeting took a unanimous decision to appoint a Crime Liaison Officer, someone who could deal with the police on their level and keep the rest of us informed. In view of your credentials, it was agreed that you were the right person for the job.'

'Yes, a little paperwork, a few meetings with the police, and some room occupancy,' she added brightly.

'I think the problem brought to my attention this morning needs a hands-on approach.'

She felt her face tightening as her eyebrows rose up into her hairline. Was that exciting facet to her life really going to happen?

'Hands-on? What exactly do you mean by that?'

Having secreted the feather duster in his top right-hand drawer, he used his elegant fingers to flick at an imaginary dust spot on his shoulder – too small a spot for Honey to see even though she narrowed her eyes.

'I mean, my dear, that a little detective work would not come amiss. I think you'd be quite good at it – better than the police, in fact. You know how slow they can be, shackled as they are to European guidelines and the Court of Human Rights.' His face stiffened with seriousness. 'I – we – want results, Honey. Fast results.'

In her mind she saw herself knocking on doors just like

the police did in their hunt for witnesses, hunting down muggers in their lairs – probably in neighbouring Bristol. The tingle of excitement melted at the thought of confronting big bruisers with muscles the size of beer barrels.

Her protests were sudden, strident and heartfelt. 'But Casper, I have a job . . . I've got a hotel to run and I don't really think—'

'As you may recall,' Casper was saying, 'we all agreed that crime was the greatest threat to visitor numbers. This honey-coloured city, this haunt of Jane Austen, Beau Brummel and . . . and . . .' He looked up at the ceiling in his search for another famous name.

'Jane Seymour?' said Honey in an effort to help him out.

He frowned. 'Did she live here? I never knew the Tudors graced us with their presence.'

'Not Henry the Eighth's wife. I meant the actress – you know: Doctor Quinn, Medicine Woman?'

He gave her a Paddington Bear type of stare, hard and vacant. 'As I was saying, someone with your background . . .'

'I was nothing very . . .'

'There are perks, of course. You do recall me telling you that?'

Her jaw stopped where it was, her mouth half-formed around a word.

'Yes. You did say so.'

Her heart thudded in her chest. Was this the answer to a dream? She certainly hoped so.

'As I outlined to you, it's only fair that the time you put into this should be recompensed in some way.'

He opened a leather-bound folder lying on his desk. 'I most definitely recall you saying that a block booking had been cancelled and you had rooms to let. Could you find eight rooms for more or less immediate occupation?'

Her voice resumed normal service. 'When?'

'The tenth?'

'Just a minute.' It was hard to keep breathing. Her fingers were all thumbs. This was a result, the type that put money in the bank. Without thinking of the consequences, she heaved her extra-large shoulder bag on to the leather-topped desk.

'Off!' Leaping to his feet, Casper reopened the right-hand drawer and brought out his feather duster. His face was a picture of wounded indignation. 'Do you realize this desk was once owned by Lord Berkeley?'

Not Wordsworth or Thackeray!

The feather duster had a strong enough head to sweep her bag on to the floor, but not before the nebulous knickers had spread over the desk.

Casper's raised eyebrows looked in danger of sliding upwards over his shiny forehead. He pointed a trembling finger. There were broad gaps between each word.

'*What – are – those?*'

Honey muttered vagaries about them having belonged to Queen Victoria and being a collector's item, '. . . and where the bloody hell is my diary!'

Whilst she rummaged, he picked them up. Eyes poker wide, he held the waist strings between finger and thumb, peering through the centre of what must have been a singularly draughty garment.

'Sorry, Casper. I can't seem to find . . . Ah! Here it is.'

Her mind was on business, and this was serious business – especially as far as room bookings were concerned. Once she was all set, she faced him.

It was hard not to laugh. With a look somewhere between distaste and true blue respect, Casper let the bloomers fall on to the desk, his delicate, white hands remaining at shoulder level.

'What utterly dreadful items! They're big enough to form the mainsail of a decent yacht!'

'So what were those dates?'

Sighing as though life had become terribly difficult, he repeated them.

Honey checked her diary. The tenth had a thick, ugly line crossed through it. Someone had cancelled, and at this time of year she could have sold that room over and over again. 'No worries!' Her face was flushed. Her pulse raced. 'How many did you say?

'Eight rooms. All singles, mark you.'

Singles! Only two thirds of the normal price, but hey, beggars couldn't be choosers; and she was certainly a beggar, thanks to the upgrading of the attic rooms and a deaf bank manager.

He passed her the letter and booking form. 'Here you are. As I said, I think it only fair that you should gain something from these extra duties. We must not allow crime to rise in this city as elsewhere in the Western world. We have an image to maintain.'

'Not to mention a bank balance and a lifestyle,' Honey muttered, still scribbling in her diary.

'Exactly. People expect certain standards. Ambience, good service and the standard of personal safety one would associate with . . .'

He studied the ceiling as he searched for the right word.

'Disneyworld?'

'Exactly! Therefore, a Crime Liaison Officer can only be a good thing.'

'Oh, I agree.'

Of course she did – now. She wasn't quite thinking on the same lines as he was. Filling up eight rooms in one fell swoop was fantastic. The alternative would have been to accept lower-priced guests from the Tourist Information Office, and even then they would only come in dribs and drabs.

After folding the forms inside her diary, Honey grabbed the escaped undergarment and stuffed it back into her bag. 'So who's been mugged, diddled or been sold a duff budgie?'

A puzzled stiffness came to the face of the chairman of Bath Hotels' Association. Street cred and slang were low on Casper's need-to-know list. If anyone could truly look down their nose at you and make you feel you'd been peddling your body on the street all night, Casper could.

'I'm not sure you're entirely aware of the seriousness of the situation.' His tone of voice was as sonorous as the clock in Reception.

Honey felt warm. She'd made a good bid at auction, the dishwasher man should have finished repairing the blasted machine by the time she got back, and the rooms she'd envisaged staying empty or selling cheap were full again. It was just a case now of doing this job Casper had landed her with. Surely her first assignment wouldn't be too difficult?

'So what's the problem?'

The way Casper lowered his eyelids so that she couldn't read his thoughts sowed the first seeds of worry in what had initially seemed a very fruitful morning. 'I'm afraid an American tourist has disappeared. Not from one of our more refined establishments, mark you. For some odd reason he chose to stay in a bed-and-breakfast on the Lower Bristol Road.' Casper said the word 'bed-and-breakfast' as though he were spitting out broken teeth.

No matter. Honey didn't care. She held on to that warm feeling and shrugged. 'Are we sure of that? Couldn't he just have gone home early or done something unusual like visiting Wales?'

'He left his luggage behind.'

'Oh.'

'And his passport.'

Steepling his fingers, Casper leaned forward. His tone was low, almost secretive. 'Let's look into this ourselves, shall we? – before we go to the police.'

'I don't think that's a good idea.'

When he threw her a warning look, the eight people in eight rooms melted away to nothing.

Her teeth hurt when she smiled. 'On reflection, I think you're quite right. I'll see what I can do.'

Two

Casper was OK about her checking things back at the Green River Hotel before pursuing the case of the missing tourist.

Anna, a Czech girl, was running Reception.

'Everything OK?' asked Honey.

'Very good, Mrs Driver. Are you OK?'

'Yes. I've become an amateur sleuth.'

'That is very nice for you. Does this mean the hotel gets an extra star?'

No, it was not some kind of quality rating, but Honey couldn't be bothered to explain. 'And I've bought Queen Victoria's bloomers.'

Anna's big brown eyes were totally *non comprende*. Honey sensed she would have preferred the hotel to have acquired another star. It would probably look better on her cv.

'Never mind.'

Honey marched to the kitchen and was welcomed by the sound of the dishwasher gyrating with water. Great! – that meant she could get on with a few things before paying a visit to Ferny Down Guest House, the bed-and-breakfast where the American tourist had chosen to stay. She glanced furtively at the dishwasher. It was always breaking down. She lowered her voice in case the blasted machine heard her and chose to be contrary.

'Done?' she asked Smudger Smith, the chef.

'Done,' he said without looking up.

He was poking around in the tray of fresh meat just delivered by the butcher. He had a thing about marbling: steaks without the right amount of fat threading through them were only fit for the pet-food trade, in his estimation.

The dishwasher continued to burble like a bonny brook.

Honey sighed. 'Thank God for that.'

Smudger glanced over his shoulder. 'Your mother's here.'

'But not for that,' she muttered, her feet already sprinting for the bar.

Her mother had her own flat at number 2, Squires Mews just behind the Theatre Royal. That didn't stop her turning up unannounced and mucking in. Sometimes she was a help, but most of the time a hindrance.

'Hannah!'

Her mother was one of the few people who still called her Hannah, but only when she had something serious to say – or at least something she considered serious.

She made the bar area just in time. The tap tap of kitten heeled shoes moved unrelentingly in her direction.

'Hannah, come out of that den of iniquity. I want to talk to you . . .'

'Sorry, Mother, but I've got some important business to do on behalf of the Hotels' Association.'

The door at the back of the bar formed a quick escape route. Although a Catholic, her mother had a Methodist aversion to alcohol – probably because her husband, Honey's father, had had such a liking for it. She never entered the bar.

Lindsey did. Lindsey, Honey's daughter, was replenishing the fruit juices. She grinned.

'Grandma's heard about you becoming a private detective. She thinks you might get involved with a policeman and end up drinking in bars all night.'

Honey grimaced. 'I already drink in bars *most* of the night. I run a hotel!'

'Grandma says she reckons you're no good at finding suitable men. She reckons she's going to find you one.'

Honey lowered her voice. 'Your grandmother's idea of suitable is someone with broad business interests and the personality of a hamster.'

Lindsey smirked. 'And yours is . . .?

Honey gave a 'don't know' kind of wave of her hand. 'I can go with broad shoulders?'

'A good starting point.' Lindsey's voice dropped to a whisper. 'Go on. Make your escape. I'll make the excuses.'

Honey kissed the soft cheek. 'Did I ever tell you that you're the best daughter in the world?'

Lindsey pretended to think about it. 'Only when I don't ask you for a pay rise.'

'That's my girl.'

'But you never call me that at three in the morning when I've been out clubbing.'

Honey threw Lindsey a long-suffering look.

'Mmmm!' She ruffled her daughter's tawny crop. 'It's just that you don't do it often enough.'

The door slid silently shut behind her, the car started first time, and although it was parked in a tight space, necessity honed her driving skills. She pulled out and headed for the other side of town. Things were looking good.

It was midway through the afternoon, so the traffic wasn't too bad. She kept to the inner-circuit road, skirting the city and sweeping towards the Wellsway, then bearing right and immediately left on to the Bristol Road.

Heavy-engineering works, scrapyards and devastation had once lined the road on the side fronting the river. They'd since been replaced by swank apartments in former warehouses, smart offices and landscaped car parks. The other side of the road was unchanged – lined with Victorian villas, some advertising bed and breakfast.

Ferny Down Guest House was one of these. Someone had followed the kerbside-attraction rule. It wasn't that downmarket. Hanging baskets full of purple, mauve and pink flowers hung from ground floor to guttering, obscuring the dirt-streaked façade of Ferny Down Bed and Breakfast. She found a parking space wedged between a van advertising carpet cleaning and a truck belonging to the City Council.

There was no garden as such at the front of the guest house. A low brick wall enclosed a frontage of red glazed tiles. The distance to the front door was no more than two yards. The door was plastic, totally out of sync with the Victorian brickwork.

She rang the doorbell – heard it echo inside. There were other noises, but not the sort associated with someone coming to answer the front door.

Stepping back, she looked up at the windows. Like the door, they had plastic frames and were double-glazed to keep out traffic noise: so much for keeping things in period.

The door remained steadfastly closed.

Grunting sounds, the sort struggling men make when they're lifting something heavy, came from the alleyway between Ferny Down and the house next door. Well she didn't have all afternoon. Back she went, turning right, then right again into the alley.

Three men were manhandling an old chest freezer out of the back gate.

'Careful with my fence,' one of them said. This had to be the proprietor. She'd memorized the details. His name was Mervyn Herbert. Good looks and dress sense were not on his list of priorities.

Overweight, but not obese, he had the worn-out look of someone trapped in a routine he didn't want to be in.

'Mr Herbert?' She ducked to one side as the men carrying the freezer squeezed out through the gate.

His eyebrows beetled when he looked her up and down. 'You from the Council?'

'No – Hotels' Association. I came to see you about your little problem.'

For a moment he looked as though he wasn't sure what she was talking about.

Sensing he wasn't keen to air his carelessness in public – i.e. losing a paying customer – she mouthed the words, 'Your missing guest.'

There was a wary look to his eyes when he nodded. 'You'd best see the wife. Come this way, if you like.'

Once the freezer was on its way to the council truck and the local landfill site, she edged her way around the path, carefully avoiding a pyramid of stones that appeared to form a rockery.

Mr Herbert pointed to a plastic-framed conservatory.

Through the misted glass she detected a blob of colour moving in a chair.

'She's in there.' Mr Herbert seemed more intent on the antics of the men with the freezer than he was on her. ''Ere!' she heard him shout. 'Go easy with that!'

She wondered why the men who collected disused domestic items needed to go careful with something obviously discarded. Perhaps because it still belonged to the owner until it was out of sight?

Mrs Cora Herbert saw her, got up from her chair and with a jerk of her head and a hissed command, beckoned her over. 'You from the Association?' Her perceptiveness was surprising.

Honey managed a smile. At the same time she took in the too-tight T-shirt, too-tight skirt, black shiny tights and uncomfortably high-heeled shoes. Mrs Herbert was mutton trying to be lamb.

They shook hands. 'Yes. I'm Hannah Driver. Everyone calls me Honey.'

'Oh! That's a nice name. Yes, I like that.' Cora Herbert looked impressed, almost as though she wished she'd thought of the name herself.

'Are you American?'

'My father was.'

'I thought you were,' she said, beaming from ear to ear. 'I bet you look like him.'

'I can't remember. He died when I was young.'

Cora's face crumpled with sympathy. 'Accident, was it?'

'You could say that.'

It had been an accident he had met a twenty-two-year-old model at a business do. It was hardly an accident that he'd lusted after her, divorced her mother then dropped dead on honeymoon.

Honey took in her surroundings. She'd seen better. A half-drunk cup of coffee sat on the table. So did an ashtray containing cigarette stubs stained with pink lipstick. The room reeked of tobacco. Holding her breath was out of the question. She'd keel over.

'My den, where I can do what I bloody well like,' said

Cora Herbert as if guessing what Honey was thinking, shooting her down before she raised an objection. 'Are you dry?'

'Sorry?'

'Do ya wanna cup of coffee?'

The thought was almost sickening. Café Latte was one thing. Café Nicotine was another.

'No, thanks.'

When she left here she'd stink of stale tobacco. Her hair and her clothes would need instant washing. Dry-cleaning bills and suede skirts came to mind. Today she wore linen, thank God. She got out her notebook and a pen – first requisite of a decent detective. 'So this American . . .'

'Mr Weinstock. At least that's what he said his name was. But that isn't the name on his passport, nor the address he gave us.'

'Didn't you check his passport details against the address given when he checked in?'

Without so much as a bashful blink, Cora took a cigarette from a packet and lit up. Thankfully, she turned away when she exhaled. 'What for? He paid me cash up front.'

'Ah!' Honey nodded. No point the taxman checking Cora Herbert's records. The passport details had not been entered and neither had the money.

'How long did he stay?'

'A whole week!'

Cora Herbert's tone was the oral equivalent of rubbing her hands together. Her face glowed with satisfaction.

'Unusual for a bed-and-breakfast.'

'A guest house! We are a guest house,' Cora Herbert snapped, sending whorls of smoke escaping from her mouth.

'Sorry.' Such were the sensitivities of guest-house landladies, Honey reminded herself. 'Still – a good booking. Few Americans take that long to look round.'

The golden triangle: London, Stratford-upon-Avon, down to Bath and back to London – that was the norm, and all done in two weeks, with Oxford thrown in.

Cora shrugged her naked shoulders against the gleam of see-through plastic bra straps. 'Whatever. He paid and that was it.'

'So his things are still here?'

Cora made a hissing sound through her teeth. 'Ooow, no. I had to clear the room because I had bookings, you see. It's in storage. I'll have to charge him, of course.'

'Of course.'

Cora Herbert, she decided, let nothing stand in the way of business. Every penny counted.

'If he's still alive, that is.'

'Well I can hardly charge him if he's dead.'

'Of course not.' Honey rebuked herself for having misjudged the woman.

'If he is dead, then I'll have to send the bill to his family.'

Back to square one!

Now burning only an inch or so from Cora's yellow-stained fingertips, the cigarette was stubbed out. A second or two and a little nail-biting later, another one glowed red between sequined fingernails.

Honey's eyes flitted to the garden. The rockery was incongruous, but all the same, she longed to sit on its pinnacle whilst drinking in the air.

She pulled herself back to the job in hand. 'Did he do much sightseeing?'

Cora narrowed her eyes against the rising smoke until they were just slits shaded by thick mascara. 'I suppose he did, though I didn't like to pry. I asked in a general kind of way, and he answered in a general kind of way.'

'Any particular places?'

'Well, the Royal Crescent, of course, and the Baths, but I think he went a bit further afield too. Came home by taxi three days running. Handed the driver over roughly thirty quid each time. I saw it.'

Honey agreed that he must have been visiting somewhere outside the city to attract that size of taxi fare: the American Museum at Claverton Down, or even pretty little Bradford-on-Avon? 'Its Saxon church is especially fine,' a Berkeley professor had told her. He'd also related a potted history of the Berkeley family and the castle situated halfway between Bath and Gloucester. He'd looked supremely satisfied on seeing her turn green at some of the gorier details.

'Was it the same taxi-cab company each time?'

Cora nodded. 'Busy Bee. The car was black.'

'What about your husband?'

'What about him?' The tone was sour, the eyes hard as pebbles. No love lost there, then.

'Did he speak to Mr Weinstock?'

'Might have done. He was always asking for crushed ice.' She laughed. 'The look on Mervyn's face when he was bashing them ice cubes with a rolling pin – enough to commit murder they were. Why can't he have bloody cubes like everybody bloody else? he used to say.'

Crushed ice. Honey knew from experience that Americans loved crushed ice. It could be annoying when nothing else would do and other guests were making demands. *Still, we aim to please*, she thought.

'I know your husband's busy at the moment, but I would like a word with him.'

Cora got up and poked her head out of the conservatory. 'MER – VYN!' Her voice was loud enough to wake the dead.

'No chance,' she said, coming back in. 'He's been so-called helping the council blokes to take that freezer. Must have got up a sweat and decided a few pints were needed.'

'He's gone to the pub?'

'Yeah.' Cora screwed up her nose and took another puff of her cigarette. 'It's a home from bloody home as far as he's concerned.'

Honey narrowed her eyes, partly against the damned smoke and partly because she was making a mental list of all the questions she should ask. She wrote down his name along with a note to question the taxi driver should Mr Weinstock not turn up. She smoothed the page flat with her hand. This was all very satisfying. Wasn't sleuthing à la Agatha Christie based on a process of elimination? Now what did those detectives on TV do?

It came to her in an instant. 'Can I take a look at his things?'

Cora got up from her chair. 'I don't see why not.' She led her to a cupboard beneath the stairs. 'There they are.'

Two holdalls, one smaller than the other but neither of them very big.

'Great!' She leaned forward, meaning to drag the bags outside.

An indignant Cora stopped her. 'No need to do that and mess up my hallway. I've got guests coming.' She said it as though she were the Royal Crescent Hotel and expecting a presidential cavalcade, not a gang of spotty backpackers.

Before Honey had chance to ask where she could take them, Cora pushed her in. 'There. I can't shut the door without locking it, but you'll be all right. You've got a light. Give me a knock when you've finished and I'll let you out.'

Stephen King horror stories came to mind. She couldn't quite recall one about a mad landlady locking an unsuspecting amateur sleuth under the stairs, but that didn't mean it wasn't possible.

After settling her nerves and giving her thudding heart a severe talking-to, she hunkered down and got on with it.

Nothing unusual about the clothes: typical non-iron stuff that anyone with any sense would take on a long-term vacation.

The flight documents and passport were in a see-through plastic zip-up. That alone was worrying, though not unusual. Most people carried their passports around unless they had access to a safe. Only upmarket hotels had safes.

'So I would take my passport with me if I was staying in a place like this,' Honey muttered to herself. 'But you didn't . . .' Her voice trailed away. So why leave it? Unless he hadn't had time or unless something bad, very bad had happened . . . The picture in the passport showed a strong-faced man with fair hair. His name was given as Elmer John Maxted, age 43, eyes blue, height 6 feet 1 inch, weight 210 pounds.

'You're a big man, Elmer John Maxted,' she muttered, and frowned. 'Now why call yourself Weinstock?' Her eyes flitted over the address – somewhere in California – and dropped on the space reserved for occupation, fully expecting something mundane like 'insurance salesman' or 'realtor'. Far from it!

Holding it up to the bare light bulb, she reread the details on a receipt for travel insurance. Her heart skipped a beat.

'Let me out,' she shouted, hammering on the door. 'Let me out!'

No sound from the hallway on the other side of the door. Wherever Cora Herbert was, she wasn't close at hand.

Honey dug her cell phone out of her pocket and tapped Casper's number.

'Casper. I know you won't want to do this, but you have to call the police.'

He played a few excuses as to why he shouldn't and asked why she thought he should.

'Look, he's left his passport here . . .'

Casper questioned what was the big deal about that?

'Casper, no one leaves their passport behind in a bed-and-breakfast. But there's something else. His name's not Weinstock – it's Maxted, and he's a private detective.'

Three

'The police are making enquiries.'

'Is that all?'

'My dear girl, the man has only gone missing. And that, my dear, is more or less what was said to me. They said give it one more day. If he doesn't turn up, then they'll put out a nationwide alert.'

The case of the missing tourist had run up against the buffers. She was disappointed. This had seemed like a *real* crime case; the police had tagged it routine.

On top of that the weather forecast took a nosedive.

'It's June, for goodness sake!'

The weather god took no notice of her outburst. The rain started at five that afternoon.

Thursday, and Lindsey's night off, and she was presently hogging the bathroom. The fallout from all manner of scented soap, shower gel and shampoo was drifting with the steam out of the bathroom window.

Honey was sitting outside beneath a two-hundred-year-old canopy. Its metal roof, the original colour turned to the mottled green of aged copper, ran the length of the private patio. Clematis and other plants climbed the fretwork supports. The patio area it covered was further divided from hotel guests by bushes and more plants climbing over a sturdy mesh of wire and stone pillars. She settled herself on a wooden bench. Like the roof, its framework was also of iron and painted white. As she fondled the lion heads forming the arms, she wondered how long before her career in amateur detection restarted.

The sound of the running water coming from the bathroom ceased. Accompanied by a cloud of steam, Lindsey came out wearing a bathrobe and a towel around her wet hair.

'I suppose you'll be late tonight.'

'Tonight? Certainly not. Expect me at around three. You want me to enjoy myself, don't you?'

'You said you were going to a concert.'

Lindsey's voice was muffled by towel and wet hair. 'Mother, I'm trying to appear wild, just as you want me to.'

'You are going nightclubbing?'

Lindsey replied through fronds of wet hair. 'After the concert.'

Honey smiled. The young social scene in the city of Bath was second to none. Trendy wine bars rubbed shoulders with the Theatre Royal, pubs, restaurants and clubs that partied till dawn. Lindsey was part of that scene, but with reservations. Goodness knows where the culture vulture genes had come from.

'Anywhere nice?' Honey asked, trying to sound laid-back and modern – even unconcerned. It was far from easy.

Lindsey rubbed vigorously at her hair. 'It depends on my friends.'

Who was she going out with? Honey sipped at her drink. Dare she ask?

'Three men friends,' said Lindsey before she had chance to ask.

Three men and going to a night club. Trying to sound laid-back and modern flew out of the window. Mother Hen took over.

'Now look, if you must go clubbing, keep in a crowd and don't let these guys take advantage, and make sure you get a taxi home.'

'Taxi's are expensive.'

There was a sense of déjà vu at that statement. Now where had she heard it before? Her response was also familiar. 'I'll reimburse you.'

'Mum! Stop fussing. The guys are great pals and are not going to rape me. Stop treating me like a child. I'm eighteen, for God's sake!'

Honey's mouth dropped open as the truth dawned. 'Gosh. You sound just like me.'

Lindsey's eyes echoed the smile playing around her mouth. 'And you sound just like—'

'Hold it right there!' Honey held up her hand, palm facing her daughter. 'I apologize for sounding like my mother. Go out, get drunk, get laid, but don't bring any trouble home.' She kissed her daughter's cheek. 'Just take care of yourself.'

'I will.'

The old coach house they lived in was situated at the end of the long, paved courtyard to the rear of the hotel. There were two bedrooms downstairs plus a bathroom. The upper floor, which had once held hay and barley for the horses, now boasted a fitted kitchen and a spacious living room. A stone fireplace graced one wall of the living room and two huge A-shaped trusses supported an exposed apex ceiling panelled in Canadian maple. The panelled ceiling was the reason Honey had created bedrooms on the ground floor and living space upstairs. The view was good. So was the ceiling, when you were lying flat on your back, staring into space.

Kicking off her shoes, Honey lay back on the yellow-leather settee and eyed with affection? – yes, affection – her collection of corsets, silk stockings, and beautiful garters festooned with ribbons, flowers and even tiny birds made of real feathers. Pride of place went to the copious bloomers. Like her other favourite items, the bloomers were safely framed behind glass and hanging above the fireplace.

Framing them had to be done swiftly, before an uninformed member of staff assumed the voluminous expanse of cotton was a tablecloth.

Honey grinned and raised her glass. Poor old Queen Victoria. She'd turn in her grave if she knew that someone could actually contemplate setting a plateful of English breakfast on her drawers!

End of the day – the best time. She poured herself a glass of wine. There was something about a good wine that made one see more clearly, when in fact, by reputation, it should make one's thoughts fuzzy.

First, the question of Elmer Weinstock: was he merely missing? Was he here on a secret mission? Or was it merely that Mervyn Herbert had smashed his last load of ice and decided to smash Elmer's head in along with it? On the other hand, perhaps there was some other reason that wasn't yet quite clear.

Never mind. At least her rooms were full. Dear old Casper had sent more business her way. She toasted herself.

'Honey Driver. Five-star hotelier, world-famous beauty and famous detective.'

A little over the top, but there . . . 'Give it time,' she said with a sigh and closed her eyes – when she dreamed she was wearing a deerstalker hat, toting a magnifying glass and smoking a pipe.

Four

It was Saturday night, pouring down and gone one o'clock when Loretta Davies, Mervyn Herbert's stepdaughter, left the Underground Club, which was subterranean, and close to the river.

'Gettin' a taxi?' shouted one of her friends, tottering on the edge of the pavement and hanging on grimly to her boyfriend, who was impatient to be away and screwing her in the privacy of some shop doorway.

'You must be jokin'. I'm skint now, ain't I!' The shouted reply was drowned in the drumming of the downpour.

Whatever else her friend shouted back was drowned too. Both the girl and the young man faded into the darkness between the high buildings.

Loretta pulled the collar of her jacket up around her face as best she could. It was plastic, black and shiny. The rain hammered on it before running off in sheets like it would off a tin roof. The mac was also short, her skirt shorter and her black tights sodden from the thighs downwards. Wisps of hair clung wetly to her face and water dripped from her eyebrows.

Passing cars muted the sound of her DM's splashing on the glossy pavements. Headlights glanced like the beams of a lighthouse through the teeming rain. Streetlights and headlights lessened once she left North Parade. She kept the gardens on her right, aiming to make her way across the road near Bog Island, an old Victorian lavatory that some quirky soul had changed into a nightclub at one time. As she bent her head against the driving rain, she cursed the night. Her footsteps bounced off the walls in narrow alleys. At times it seemed as if an army was following her – or at least one person, possibly more. She shivered inside her raincoat and dug her hands more deeply into her pockets, glad when she finally emerged into a rank of Regency houses.

Square panes in Georgian windows were shut tight around her and curtains drawn. Fewer cars flashed by, most sensible people already being home in a warm bed with a warm body. Even the shop doorways were empty, fumbling couples defeated by the wind-driven rain, their novice explorations saved for another time.

Empty echoes, lonely street lights and heavy rain: wetness and darkness took the night as their own. The rain hammered so hard and loud that she could no longer hear her own footsteps. She didn't hear his.

A shadow came alive. She was startled when he stepped out in front of her until she saw who it was.

'You!'

Mervyn Herbert had deep-set eyes. His teeth were yellow. 'Nasty night.'

Loretta was far from pleased to see him. 'Mervyn, stop following me!'

He slipped a hand into his trouser pocket and brought out a twenty-pound note. 'Here you are. I expect you could do with it.'

She hesitated, her gaze bouncing between his face and the money. She snatched it and stuffed it into her pocket.

'Thought you'd need it. You always did like a pound note, didn't you, girl?'

She didn't correct him and say that there was no such thing as a pound note, only a coin. The money always came in useful.

'I've got the car.' His smile was wide. 'Come on, sweetheart. I'm only doing my duty as a loving daddy.'

'You're not my daddy!' Her exclamation bounced between the buildings.

The light from a street lamp picked out Mervyn's yellow teeth as he smiled. 'We're still family. It's a lousy night.'

The rain trickled into Loretta's eyes and down the nape of her neck. She asked herself whether she could cope with him. The rain increased and lightning lit up the sky. Yeah! Yeah! Sure she could.

'All right.'

She was still shivering when she slid into the front passenger seat of the five-year-old Ford 'family' car. Family! That was a laugh. Her mother told people she'd been a child bride. She could hear her mother now: 'My Loretta's seventeen. I know I don't look old enough, but I was very young when I had her. Only eighteen myself.'

Hogwash! Her mother had been well into her twenties, but denied herself those extra years, just as she denied the extra inches around her hips and thighs.

She turned as she fastened her safety belt. The rain was unceasing. The streets seemed empty.

The headlights of a passing car picked out a figure amongst the shadows. She sucked in her breath, saw him stare, then turn and run.

She jumped when Mervyn patted her knee. 'Everything all right, sweetheart?'

She smacked his hand away. 'Keep your dirty paw to yourself!' She eyed the greyish complexion of the man sitting beside her. He'd made an effort to comb a few strands of hair across a hairless skull. The result was comical rather than complimentary. A sliver of hair slewed over his face. He pushed it back, a red blush of embarrassment creeping up his grizzled throat.

Loretta laughed out loud. 'Crikey,' she said, firmly asserting the old saucy self. 'You're getting to be a right slap-head, aren't ya!'

His knuckles whitened as his hands gripped the steering wheel more tightly. 'Saucy cow! One of these days . . .'

'One of these days what?' She laughed openly and loudly. 'You'll do what, Mervyn? Nothing! I'm not a little girl any more. I can stick up for myself, and just you remember that!'

She gasped as his hand grabbed her knee more fiercely and painfully than before.

'You'd be surprised at what I'm capable of, sweetheart. There's more to yer old stepdaddy than meets the eye. And you want more money, don't you? You're always wanting my money.'

'Let me out of the car!'

He opened his mouth and a cackle came out, like the sound dead men are supposed to make before they die.

She wished that Mervyn Herbert were already dead. Better men than him were dead. But that was it. Mervyn was too mean to die, too nasty to end up in consecrated ground.

His hands were back on the wheel. She thought of opening the door and jumping out, but they were travelling too fast. Her tights were new. Her knees would be scratched.

Perhaps out of habit, or some vestige of memory, the old fear returned.

'Please, Mervyn. I'll do anything, anything . . .'

He grinned, his creased face a yellow gargoyle in the flashing glow of the street lights.

'Yes,' he said, pausing to slick his tongue over his lips, 'of course you will.'

The man who'd been following cursed. The stupid cow had got into a car, and not just any car – *his* bloody car! Bloody Mervyn Herbert's.

The night was black and empty. Everyone was disappearing fast.

Fortunately he managed to flag down what must have been the only available taxi left in Bath.

'Follow that car!'

The driver, a young Asian with white teeth and wearing a white shirt and tie with a black leather jacket, beamed with disbelief. 'You're joking!'

Fingers thick as sausages grabbed his collar. 'No! I ain't!'

The driver stabbed on the gas too fiercely; the car skidded on the water-covered tarmac, careering from side to side as he fought to regain control. Sweat glistened on the driver's forehead and he trembled as he followed the light-coloured Ford. It was now three cars ahead.

His passenger was impatient. 'Overtake! Overtake!'

Scared out of his wits, the taxi driver shook his head

emphatically. 'I cannot! I cannot! It is far too narrow here! There are many parked cars!'

His passenger tried to grab the wheel. A car travelling in the other direction blew its horn as they swerved into the centre of the road.

'Please,' the driver shouted, his hands clammy on the wheel. 'We cannot overtake. It is dangerous!'

Muttering an oath under his breath, the passenger slumped back in his seat. Ahead of them two cars went through a green traffic light. The next went through amber. The taxi stopped as the traffic light turned red.

The driver eyed his passenger from the comparative safety of the rear-view mirror. 'Where to now?' he asked, unable to control the trembling in his voice.

'Ferny Down Guest House. That's where they *should* be heading. It's on the Bristol Road. Do you know it?'

'Yes. Yes. I do.' His voice trembled. His eyes flickered nervously between the traffic light and the rear-view mirror. Late-night passengers troubled him, this one more than most.

The lights changed. The taxi moved forward across the river and right towards the Lower Bristol Road.

Robert Howard Davies, lately of Horfield Prison, Bristol, made himself comfortable. He knew the taxi driver's eyes were studying him, no doubt wondering whether he'd get his fare or not.

That depends, thought Robert, disgruntled because he'd got so close to reacquainting himself with his daughter. Still, no harm in going to see the wife; and God help Mervyn Herbert if he wasn't there when he arrived. There'd be some explaining to do, and he wasn't in the market for accepting excuses. Never had been; never would be.

Five

One day, one whole twenty-four-hour period, had passed and Elmer Maxted was still missing.

'Casper says you need to go down there and liaise,' said Neville over the phone.

'I was thinking the same thing. Whether I want to or not, I have to tell the police all I know.'

There was silence. Neville had placed his hand over the phone. Casper was giving orders.

He came back. 'Casper says you are to try and keep the lid on things.'

'At the same time as assisting them with their enquiries?'

Again, silence.

'That's right,' said Neville on behalf of Casper.

'I can't make it for an hour or so. My receptionist is out sick.'

Again the delayed response.

'We'll send help.'

'Thanks. I appreciate it. How come Casper's indisposed?'

The response was swift, the tone one of shocked surprise.

'Casper *never* answers the phone whilst soaking in the bath.'

Although it was Sunday morning, sauntering along to Manvers Street Police Station wasn't a problem as long as the promised help turned up. On the contrary, it was a welcome break.

Checking guests out flew by. One hour later she was brushing her hair, straightening her white cotton shirt and checking the seams in her stockings. Yes! Stockings. She always wore a skirt on Sunday. The stockings added to feelings of almost lost femininity.

Today had turned out exciting again. Nothing and no one could upset her mood – with the exception of her mother.

'I'm going on a cruise this summer.' She leaned closer. 'I'm going with a man friend. His name's Christopher Jordan, and he's a really charming man.'

Her mother scurried along behind her like an especially tenacious Jack Russell. 'Men are such good company. You should get yourself one.'

Honey swung left behind the reception desk.

Undeterred, her mother leaned on the counter top. 'I think I was telling you about my dentist. He's got a friend with a very nice little business . . .'

'I thought he might have,' said Honey with impatient reticence. She stabbed at the 'escape' key on the computer. That's what she wanted to do: escape the reception desk and escape her mother. But Susan, their regular receptionist, had phoned in sick. Honey had been expecting it. Lovesick! – that's what she was. A handsome young man from Hungary, working at another hotel close by, had moved into the bedsit below Susan. International participation was bound to happen – and did. This meant that if their days off didn't coincide, they fell sick. Today was the young man's night off – but not Susan's. Hence, she was sick, which meant Honey was dealing with Reception and was trapped. Mother had pounced.

With blonde coiffure, bedecked with expensive jewellery and wearing a silk trouser suit, her mother leaned on the reception desk. Her apricot lipstick matched her outfit.

Honey took shallow breaths in an effort to cope with the cloud of expensive perfume that fell over her.

'I've arranged for you to meet him in the Roman Bar of the Francis this evening at seven.'

'I can't go.'

'Why not?'

'I'm working.'

'Lunch time then. I'll rearrange it for twelve noon.'

'Mother!'

'Don't shout!'

'I didn't shout; I merely protested.'

A husband and wife from Sydney, Australia, chose that moment to check in, complete with three suitcases.

Honey took her time checking them in and giving them their keys, fliers and special offers on local attractions. The plan was that her mother would grow impatient and disappear. She didn't.

'Look, Mother . . .'

Jeremiah Poughton, Casper's very close friend, chose that moment to come breezing through the double doors. His fingers brushed over the brass handles as though he were checking for smudges.

'Casper sent me. I understand you're a trifle short-staffed, my darling. So here I am – lately of the hotel trade, but I do remember which buttons to press.'

'So what are you doing nowadays?' said Honey, purposely turning her back on her mother.

'I've got a stall in the Guildhall Market. It's called Herbs, Spice and All Things Nice.'

'There now!' Honey looked suitably impressed.

Unfortunately, so did her mother. Gloria clapped her hands. 'There! You can go on your date and enjoy yourself.'

'No. This is for this morning only. I shall go to the police station. Tonight I work.'

Honey sent the ergonomically designed – and very uncomfortable receptionist's chair – sliding on its wheels as she got to her feet.

'He's sent the details to the police by messenger,' Jeremiah went on, swinging his long limbs into the chair and sliding it back into place.

'If that's the case, I can't understand why he hasn't gone along himself.'

'He's not one for men in uniforms,' Jeremiah said, as though he'd read her thoughts. 'Reminds him of the bad old days. Now,' he said, leaning threateningly at the computer screen, 'no need to explain the system to me,' he said, already entering the Australians into their appropriate box on screen. 'Once you've used one, you've used them all.'

Honey grabbed her overlarge bag and slung it over her shoulder.

Her mother followed her to the door. 'Why are you going to the police station?'

Determined that everything should run smoothly in her absence, Honey ignored the question and addressed Jeremiah. 'There's a party for lunch coming in at twelve.'

Receiving no reply from her daughter, Gloria aimed her question at Jeremiah. 'Why is she going to the police station?'

Jeremiah was still taking in the orders Honey was throwing at him.

Exasperated, Gloria Cross slammed her hand down on the desk. 'Why is my daughter going to the police station? What has she done?'

Those guests sitting in the comfortable settees around the Reception area, waiting for taxis, teas or their check-out bill, fell silent. Curious eyes turned in her direction.

Honey played to the crowd. 'They're accusing me of planning to bury my mother under the patio. I told them it wasn't true, of course, and that I'd much prefer to drown you in malmsey, but they didn't believe me. Said they didn't think anyone would ruin good alcohol unless they were batty!'

'You're batty!' said her mother, looking thoroughly annoyed.

The guests grinned, chuckled and exchanged knowing looks. Obviously they too had mothers – and mad moments of sheer exasperation.

Honey threw a swift thank you to Jeremiah, who merely nodded and proceeded to tidy up the whole online booking system and the paperwork around him. He also threw a disapproving look at the flower arrangement. Like Neville, he was very good at arranging flowers. Hers were not to his taste.

Getting to the door had been easy enough compared to getting out of it. Her mother wasn't giving up *that* easily.

'Right. So you're off to the police station on official hotel business. That shouldn't take long. From there you can make your way to the church.'

'Mother! I don't do church.'

Too late. She was already tapping out a number on her cell phone, a determined jut to her chin and a 'no nonsense' look in her eyes. 'Right. Father Trevor is expecting you.

'I'm not a Catholic.'

'Well I think you should be.'

'My father wasn't.'

Her mother crossed herself. Becoming a Catholic had come late in life – once all the divorces were behind her.

'The service finishes at twelve. No need to hurry back. That nice poof in Reception will take care of things until you get back.'

'Mother!' What was the point? Honey shook her head. Her mother didn't know how to spell 'politically correct', let alone apply it. She was one of the old school and not up to speed on courteous terminology. Words used in her youth were still the ones she used now.

As she approached North Parade, heading for Manvers Street, she began questioning Casper's generosity in sending over someone to help out. Casper could be very nice when he wanted to be. At other times he could be downright ruthless.

On her way there she plucked out her phone and tapped into the address book. Casper answered almost immediately.

'Thanks for sending Jeremiah over.'

'Oh! Is that where he is?'

Honey frowned. 'You didn't send him?'

'I asked him to pop over and assist you. He wasn't keen and murmured something about me using him as a stopgap. I told him to go to hell. His interpretation is a little surprising, I must say.'

'But appreciated.'

'No doubt.'

It was a busy Sunday morning at the cop shop. The chalky smell of dried-out paint and well-worn carpet came out to meet her. So too did a tinge of Jeyes fluid each time the cloakroom doors opened in the foyer.

Once the desk sergeant had booked her in, she was told

to sit down and wait. Stressing that she was here by request and on behalf of the hoteliers of the city, and had little time to spare, failed to impress him. So she sat and studied the people waiting for attention. They were a mixed bag and therefore interesting:

Irate ex-motorists, relieved of their vehicle by some mindless drone who had fancied his chances at Grand Prix wheelies down over Brassknocker Hill. Grand Pricks were more like it, the cars mangled by now and dumped in some roadside ditch.

A crusty, complete with tangled dreadlocks, fetid smell and a scrawny dog, was demanding the return of his untaxed, uninsured and unroadworthy vehicle.

An American tourist wearing a tartan cap and matching Bermudas waited whilst the desk sergeant took down his particulars.

'What I can't understand is how they knew we were tourists,' he drawled.

Judging by their age, marriage had still been in fashion when they were young. The woman Honey took to be his wife slumped in the chair next to Honey.

Rolling her eyes, she whispered, 'I told him not to make himself conspicuous. But would he listen? I'm not changing my style for anybody, he tells me.' The woman shook her head dolefully. 'Style it ain't, I told him.'

Honey smiled. 'Beauty is in the reflection in the mirror. We see gravity taking its toll, and they see Steve McQueen. It's a man thing.'

'You got it!'

A door marked 'private' opened suddenly and a man wearing a black T-shirt and stone-washed jeans appeared. Plain clothes, passably attractive and looking for her.

His eyes swept over the waiting room.

Her eyes looked back.

He was of average height. Judging by the casual clothes and the stubble on his chin, he was attempting the rough-diamond look. Looking hard added gravitas when you were less than six feet in height. The fact that he had hands like shovels made it work.

A policewoman lurked in the shadows behind him as though she were watching his back. She gazed over his shoulder. Honey met the look. The woman's gaze hardened. Honey recognized green-glazed jealousy.

A pair of sharp blue eyes scythed over the mêleé and homed in on her. 'Hannah Driver?'

'That's me.'

A waiting room full of curious eyes watched her cross the floor. It was kind of like being on stage. But this was all real. All the senses kicked in. She was close enough to smell what remained of his aftershave. Three days or so since he'd shaved, but the pong was still there.

'I'm Detective Sergeant Steve Doherty.' He looked her up and down. 'So you're Bath's answer to Miss Marple.'

Sarcastic!

'Not quite. I don't knit or do crosswords, and neither do I frequent vicarage tea parties.'

Liaising wasn't in his blood. Contempt flashed in his eyes. He didn't want her here. His surliness travelled to his tone of voice. 'Well that's a disappointment. But there – amateur snoops come in all shapes and sizes.'

'So do cops. I thought you'd be taller.' She stood straighter in her three-inch heels even though they were pinching her toes.

For a split second his gaze fell to her 36Cs. He smirked. She guessed what was coming.

'Being of average height has its advantages.'

Spot on! If looks could have killed, she would have sliced his head off, but he didn't give her time.

'Through here.' He jerked his thumb in the direction of the shadow in uniform and the corridor behind him.

The interview room was exactly as she'd expected: plain walls, desk, requisite number of chairs and, of course, the tape recorder. Someone had lately run riot with a sweet-smelling aerosol – alpine flowers, by the whiff of it.

Doherty flicked the 'on' switch on the tape recorder. The usual words were said, the date and location. Next came the personal details. 'This is Detective Sergeant Doherty. Interviewee is one Miss Hannah Driver—'

'Mrs.'

Doherty flashed her an impatient look. '*Mrs* Hannah Driver. Also present is Detective Constable Sian Williams. Right,' he said, sitting back in his chair, 'tell me your involvement.'

'I prefer to be called Honey.'

'As in Honey Bee?'

She treated the comment with her own brand of contempt. She ignored him. 'Well,' she began, feeling like a suspect in some cheap television detective series, 'I have been appointed by Bath Hotels' Association to liaise with the police regarding any crime connected with tourism . . .'

'Yeah! I understand that,' said Doherty, the fingers of his right hand fiddling with the pen protruding from his left breast pocket.

Her first impression of him lingered. What he said next confirmed it. 'That kind of stuff out there' – he jerked his head, indicating the waiting room beyond the wall – 'muggings, theft and diddling the exchange rate: anything that upsets the tourist industry. Must keep ourselves a squeaky-clean image, mustn't we? – or the Yanks won't be visiting these hallowed shores.'

She sprang to her feet. 'Don't be so bloody condescending!'

He sprang to his feet. 'This is a cop shop not a bloody tea shop!'

They were like bookends, glaring at each other across the table.

Honey slammed her hands down, rattling the cups and sending a pen rolling.

The tape recorder rattled. 'Pleased to meet you too. Now look, I've got a chef that's threatening to slice out the butcher's entrails over the standard of the steaks, and a mother who's likely to get herself made into pies if she keeps trying to fix me up with dog-eared divorcees and bog-standard bachelors. Can we get this over so we can *both* get back to our work?'

Doherty blinked once and shifted in his seat. She sensed a subtle change.

'Sit down!' He sounded serious, *Yet you're not so serious*, she decided. All the same, she sat down.

Doherty sat sideways in his chair, eyeing her out of the corner of his eyes.

She copied his stance. If he noticed her mockery, he gave no sign of it.

'This bloke disappearing – I don't like the sound of it. I don't like it at all.'

It wasn't what she'd expected him to say. Suddenly the world had turned into a more exciting place. She leaned forward, her eyes in danger of popping out of her head. 'You think he's been murdered?'

He leaned forward too, lower arms resting on desk, hands clasped just inches from hers. 'I don't have a clue. Even private dicks go on mystery trips.'

Honey frowned. 'So what's happened? What is it you don't like?'

Doherty grimaced. 'I've been appointed as your official contact within the police force – Chief Constable's orders. I'll do my duty, but I'm not happy about it. I thought you should know that.'

Feeling incredibly deflated, Honey sat back in her chair.

The sound of a stifled snigger came from Detective Constable Sian Williams.

Doherty scowled. 'Shut that!'

The policewoman's pink lips wobbled a bit before coming under control.

Something was not quite right. Honey narrowed her eyes and threw Doherty a piercing look. He looked surprised, either because he hadn't expected such a response or because he liked the look anyway.

'So why the hell have you got that thing on?'

She screwed up her face and felt her wrinkles deepening as she pointed at the tape recorder.

He shrugged. 'It doesn't work. I just turn it on for the hell of it. Didn't unnerve you, did I?' One side of his mouth lurched upwards into a lop-sided grin.

'You're taking the mick!'

Honey got to her feet. 'Well stuff you, Doherty! You may

have time for fun and games, but I do not! I have a business to run and it depends on tourism, which, I might add, pays your wages!'

Up until now she'd seen mostly arrogance in his features. Now the blue eyes twinkled and the grin changed into an apologetic smile. He held up his hands in surrender. 'Look, I'm sorry.'

'You're not taking this seriously.'

He nodded at the policewoman, indicating she make for the door. It closed behind her.

Doherty noted Honey's brown eyes, the dark hair nicely contrasting with a crisp white blouse, a buff-coloured waistcoat and smart skirt. She was wearing stockings – he was sure of it – not tights. Stockings clung more closely to the skin. He considered himself a connoisseur of such things. Hannah Driver was not at all what he'd expected. She looked posh totty, but underneath that cool exterior he sensed something hotter.

Honey folded her arms in a way that shielded her bosom. 'I should never have taken this job,' she muttered.

Doherty looked surprised. 'You didn't want to develop a long-lasting relationship with a crime-fighting member of your local constabulary?'

She cocked an eyebrow. 'Don't flatter yourself.'

'I wasn't exactly spoilt for choice either!'

She didn't go into details of why she'd accepted the role. What would the likes of an unshaved, hard-nosed copper know about business?

Suddenly he sounded apologetic. 'Can we start again?'

She thought about telling him to get lost, but the shrewder side of her nature stopped her. Casper had promised her more fiscal reward. Filling her rooms to capacity and every table in the restaurant ordering three courses plus the best-vintage wine was not beyond the realms of possibility.

She sat back down. 'So! What about this Elmer Weinstock/Maxted or whatever?'

Doherty laid his hands flat on the desk and studied his fingernails.

'So! He was a private detective,' he said thoughtfully. 'Was he here on a job? Have you checked?'

'Yes. We have checked, and no, he was not here on a job. He was on vacation according to his office: "tracing his family tree", so I was told.'

Honey frowned. So why use an alias?

Doherty gave his own answer to the unspoken question in a voice that was a fair impersonation of Humphrey Bogart. 'These private dicks have a sense of the dramatic. They've been watching too many cop shows on TV.'

Honey eyed him accusingly. 'You're not going to investigate, are you?'

'No. Shall I tell you why?'

'You don't have to, but I guess you will anyway.'

'I think he's met up with a dishy broad and he's gone off to taste a last sip of the sweet honey of life. So what if he doesn't make his flight?' He leaned back in his chair, hands clasped behind his head and a dreamy look in his eyes. 'Yep. That's my theory. A taste of honey – that's what he's found.'

'Very poetic, but I think you're wrong.'

He spread his hands and winked. 'That's it, sugar.'

Blue eyes and dark hair: it shouldn't be allowed. A sneaking liking for him developed there and then. Her lips were sliding into a smile without a by-your-leave. She managed to wipe it off before it reached full bloom.

'I'm not going to encourage you.'

She got to her feet.

'So what are you going to do, sugar?'

She paused by the door, rested her hand on her hip and winked. 'I think I'll pay another visit to the house of a thousand ashtrays.'

He grinned. 'Cora Herbert.'

'You bet.'

'You're wasting your time.'

Honey held her head to one side. 'You didn't want to work with me and you still don't, do you?'

His expression clouded. 'It's nothing personal.'

'No,' she said, 'and it won't ever get that way.'

Sian came back after Honey had left, her stockings making a rustling sound as she slid one leg over the other. She folded her arms across her uniformed chest and grinned at him.

'You enjoyed that more than you thought you would.'

He stretched his arms above his head and flexed his muscles. 'Take that grin off your face.'

'She's an attractive woman.'

He spun to face her and pointed an accusing finger. 'Not another word, Williams. I still think this hotel nonsense is all a bloody waste of time.'

She cocked one eyebrow. 'But she makes it more palatable?'

Doherty smirked and a lock of dark hair fell on to his forehead.

Sian Williams went weak at the knees. Most women, her included, couldn't help falling for his rakish charm.

His smile was enough to leave her panting for more and she was always that. Last night his voice had poured into her ear like thick, dark treacle. She'd scored, but knew from Doherty's reputation that she wasn't the only one.

Steve Doherty was smiling to himself and whatever thoughts he was thinking were strictly private. When he spoke, she knew he wasn't really speaking to her. He was advising his inner self, telling it just what to expect next. 'Leave it with me. A little of the old Doherty charm and she'll forget all about being Miss bloody Marple. She'll be putty in my hands. I guarantee it.'

Six

Cora Herbert insisted that Honey take Elmer Maxted's stuff away.

'I can't have it blocking up my storage facility,' Cora said indignantly, an unlit cigarette jiggling at the corner of her mouth.

Honey grimaced at the memory of the dusty, dirty cupboard beneath the stairs. Describing it as a storage facility was stretching credibility. There was no real reason why she couldn't oblige. She had a small room behind Reception for guests' luggage and two more bags wouldn't make any difference.

Once they were in situ, she couldn't resist taking another peek. After checking there was no one hanging around in Reception, she closed the door behind her. Although she'd checked through things whilst shut in under Cora Herbert's stairs, she'd done it quickly. Now she had time to take things a little more slowly. Who knew what she might find?

She took out his passport, flight tickets and official documents and took them into her office and her private safe. On studying the flight ticket, she found the return date was only two days hence. There was a mystery here. Two days until he flew home? He should be making plans to go right now, checking railway and bus schedules or making arrangements to drop off a hire car – if he'd ever had one.

And there was something else. If Elmer was tracing his forebears, why no birth, marriage or death certificates, or even a half-completed family tree? She couldn't suppress the shiver that ran down her back. Nor could she throw off her first instinct: that Elmer Maxted was dead – murdered. But how and by whom? And why?

The hospitality industry consisted of sixteen-hour days, seven days a week. Public holidays, such as Christmas, Easter and the height of summer, were its busiest times. Even during the normal times, she rose at dawn and didn't fall into bed until the early hours of the next day. Tiredness led to short tempers. Had Cora or Mervyn snapped and done something stupid? She thought about it. Cora? No. The woman wasn't Mrs Cordiality of the Year, but the only murdering that went on in their guest house was probably burning the sausages at breakfast time.

The door to the office was well oiled, so she didn't hear Lindsey come in.

'Mother! What are you doing?'

Honey nearly jumped out of her skin. 'Are you trying to give me a heart attack?'

Lindsey was wearing her gym kit, her navy-and-white bag slung over her shoulder. She grinned. 'Not unless you've left me a fortune in your will. I might chance it then.'

'I suggest you speak to your grandmother on that score.'

Gloria Cross had had three husbands. All of them had been millionaires, including her own father. He'd shoved off back to Connecticut with a trophy wife. Undeterred, her mother had sued for settlement, got it, got a new millionaire and drunk a toast to her former husband's memory when he'd died in bed on his honeymoon.

'A fitting end to a man who loved women,' said her mother. That night she'd drunk two bottles of Krug and eaten a whole lemon meringue pie – her favourite. It still was.

Lindsey looked over her mother's shoulder. She smelled fresh as though she'd just showered. 'What are you doing?'

Honey sighed and began tucking the passports, papers and flight tickets back into the plastic zip-up and then into the safe. Just before finally turning the key she paused, her eyes again falling on the date.

'There's a disparity between the booking he made at Ferny Down Guest House and his return flight from London Heathrow. Where did he intend going between those two dates?'

Lindsey shrugged. 'Perhaps he was going to stay on at Chez Greasy Spoon a few more days.'

Honey thought about it, then shook her head. 'To book in for a week at a bed-and-breakfast is unusual in itself. Most tourists aren't that specific – certainly not in an establishment like Ferny Down. It caters for the lower end of the market.'

'We're not being snobby here, are we?'

'Realistic!'

Lindsey nodded. 'Sure.' She was as aware as her mother that certain tourists staying in certain establishments had definite travel plans. Depending on budget, one or two days sufficed in each place they visited. 'But there are always exceptions.'

Honey waved the airline ticket. 'He was flying home two days from now. That doesn't leave long for travelling anywhere – a day at most. The last day would have been set aside for travelling to the airport.'

Lindsey, who Honey sometimes forgot was only eighteen, agreed. 'Most people travel up to London the day before.'

Honey fluttered the tickets against her mouth as she thought things through. She raised her eyes and met Lindsey's equally dark ones. 'That means he would have left for the airport tomorrow.'

'And what else?'

Honey slid her eyes sidelong. 'He was researching his family tree, and yet there are no birth, death or marriage certificates in his luggage. I find that strange.'

Lindsey sighed and looked at her watch. 'He's been murdered.'

'Do you think so?' Honey's eyes stretched and a mix of fear and excitement tingled in her ample bosom. The possibility had entered her mind, but surely there was no hard evidence. Had Lindsey spotted something she hadn't?

Her daughter's response swiftly deflated any chance of enlightenment. Lindsey grinned. 'It's my off-the-cuff opinion – purely because I've got no time to consider anything else.' She glanced at her watch again. 'Oops! Must get changed. I've a bar to open.'

'Where do you get your energy?'

Lindsey kissed her mother's cheek. 'I inherited it from mother along with her good looks.'

'Really?'

Honey studied the muted reflection in a glass-fronted cabinet.

Lindsey wrapped a loving arm around her shoulder. 'See,' she said, her head resting against that of her mother. 'We're more like sisters than mother and daughter. So tell me, did you meet any good looking policemen?'

Honey opened her mouth to deny the fact. Doherty popped into her mind.

Lindsey had insight. In Honey's opinion, it wasn't right in a girl of her age.

'Mother, you're blushing.'

'No, no, no, no, no. It's my age.'

Looking amused, Lindsey stood by the door, a glint in her eye and her brown legs smooth and shiny. 'You may be my mother, but you're also a woman. I think it's time you lived for yourself not for me. Have a slice of romance, Mother. You deserve it.'

Honey gasped. When Geoff died in a boating accident, Honey had promised herself that she would put Lindsey first in everything. For that reason she'd shied off permanent relationships. She'd seen the problems it could cause. She'd never voiced that promise so it came as something of a surprise that Lindsey was aware of her sacrifice. And now?

Like a thickly iced cream slice, Doherty came to mind again. She smiled to herself. Naughty, but nice.

Lindsey winked. 'That good, huh?'

Once she was alone, Honey dragged her thoughts back to the missing tourist. Cupping her chin in her hand she stared out at the blank wall beyond the small window. If they had murdered him, where would they bury him?

She shook the thoughts from her head, zipped up the bags and shifted them into a far corner. *He's just gone walk-about*. Perhaps he'd met some old relative whilst tracing his family tree and was making up for lost time.

As she shut the door behind her and prepared to check

in a nice couple from Ontario, another thought crossed her mind. Would a man seriously researching his family tree leave the paperwork behind? Perhaps that might explain there being none in his luggage. But if that were the case, why leave his passport etc.? She shook her head. Her mind was in overdrive.

The Canadians she was booking in waited patiently until she'd come back down to earth.

'We have a room booked in the name of Whittaker,' said the nice middle-aged man.

Plastering a smile on to her face, she entered their names on the system, checked their passports and handed them their room keys, menu cards and a map of the city.

'There's plenty of information in the folder in your room,' she added, 'but don't hesitate to ask if there's anything else you require.'

They thanked her before moving off, Daniel – porter, handyman and a native of Croatia – helping them with their luggage.

Her phone rang. She recognized the voice. Doherty. Blue eyes, dark stubble. 'Hi there! I was wondering—'

'So was I. If Mr or Mrs Herbert had murdered Elmer Weinstock, Maxted, or whatever his name is, where would they bury him?'

'That wasn't what I was going to ask you.' He sounded disappointed.

Honey carried on as though she hadn't heard him. She had, but since taking on this mission she was getting curiouser and curiouser; just like Alice in Wonderland. And she wasn't sure how she should respond just yet – not until she got used to the idea.

'I suppose if you were looking for a body, you'd dig the garden up first, wouldn't you?'

Steve Doherty prided himself on being a bit of a ladies' man. No woman could fail to fall for his suave looks, his cheeky charm. So why wasn't she listening to him? He was about to tell her to forget it, when an idea occurred to him: humour her; make her think this really was going to be a serious case.

He cleared his throat. 'I've had second thoughts about this case and a few possible theories. Can we meet for dinner and talk about it – you know, away from interruptions?'

'You do think he was murdered!'

Doherty felt himself drowning in her rapture. More, please! A lot more. It wouldn't be in his interests to contradict her, so he didn't. He smiled in that secretive way he'd practised in front of the mirror – the sort of smile Bogart used to use. Left-hand corner of mouth lifted, right-hand corner turned downwards. 'Let's just say I have a hunch.'

Honey was all ears. This was just what she wanted to hear. Getting involved in murder beat washing dishes hands down. 'The Zodiac?'

Steve patted himself on the back. What a clever dick he was! 'Great. What time?'

'Some time after midnight, say about 12.30?'

Steve covered the phone with his hand as he swore. Wanting to have her to himself had backfired. The Zodiac was a restaurant beneath North Parade. Its entrance was on one side of the street. A set of narrow steps led down to a barrel-roofed cellar that swept out beneath the road. At the other end a glass-covered archway looked out over North Parade Gardens. Laid out in the eighteenth century, the gardens were below the level of the road. A lovely spot, the green lawns plastered with tourists by day, sitting on the benches, rubbing their bare feet and swearing not to go on any more ghost walks, Austen Walks, and tours of the Roman Baths.

The Zodiac didn't open until nine o'clock at night, and didn't shut until three in the morning. Hence the city's hoteliers and publicans, their only free time being between midnight and dawn, frequented it. *Like vampires*, thought Steve Doherty, *they only come out at night.*

Steve visualized his duty roster. On duty until ten tonight, and on again at six tomorrow . . .

'OK,' he said, 'I'll be there.' He pulled his face out of shape as a thought occurred to him. Sian Williams would be on duty with him tonight and a bird in the hand.

Honey made things easy for him. 'But not tonight. Not this week, in fact. How about Friday week?'

His whole body relaxed. That was when the roster changed. At least he'd get a lie-in the following morning. And Sian Williams would be on a different shift. Best to keep women divided. It kept them interested.

'Suits me fine.'

There was no one hanging around in Reception except for Mrs Spear pushing the vacuum cleaner. She was singing along to whatever she was listening to on a personal stereo.

Honey gave her a wave. She didn't notice.

A totally frameless conservatory, an extravagance she'd never regretted, led off the Reception area. Through its unsullied glass she could see the Abbey, the mansard roofs, the tall chimneys framing the green hills circling the city like giant arms. This was the view that tourists came to see; so why had Elmer Maxted stayed at a cheap guest house frequented by those on a very tight budget? His luggage was expensive and although private detectives were portrayed as dirt-poor in TV programmes, it wasn't necessarily true.

Her thoughts were interrupted. 'Honey! Honey, darling!'

She recognized the voice of Mary Jane Jefferies, who'd been a regular visitor to the Green River for years.

Wearing a pink kaftan over equally pink trousers, the tall woman floated towards her waving a copy of the Bath City bus timetable. 'I have a problem,' she said, taking hold of Honey's shoulder and steering her into the sitting room. 'Or rather, I think you have a problem,' she said, her voice dropping to not much more than a whisper. 'Take a seat.'

Honey found herself obeying instantly. That's how it was with Mary Jane. The sort of conversation they were about to have would come as no surprise. Mary Jane was a doctor of parapsychology, a ghost goddess, as she'd explained to Honey when they'd first met.

Honey had been dumbstruck. Yes, she knew the place was old and it creaked and groaned through the night, but then, didn't all old buildings do that? And yes, it was old, but not old when compared with Stonehenge or the Roman Baths. The outside was imposing but promised comfort; the large, oblong windows glowed amber with inner light at night and by day sparkled in sunlight. The décor was fresh and fitting for the age of the house. Honey had no trouble sleeping between its aching walls. What was two hundred years in the great scheme of things?

It was old by American standards, Mary Jane explained, and left it at that. Sometimes, perhaps because Honey was a relative newcomer to the hotel in comparison with Mary Jane, it seemed that the tall, lanky woman actually owned the place.

As Mary Jane chattered on, a retired university professor from Connecticut strolled past the window, her mother walking beside him.

Hopefully they'll elope together.

The sound of her mother's voice drifted through the window. 'Families used to stick together in the past and marriage was for life . . .'

And this coming from a thrice married woman. Honey almost choked.

'About this problem,' Mary Jane was saying.

'More than one problem, I think,' Honey murmured, a jaundiced eye following her mother and the professor until they were safely out of sight.

Her mother loved meeting hotel guests and did her bit to help out. She regarded herself as the official social secretary of the Green River Hotel, a bit like those she'd met on cruise ships.

At least it kept her out of the kitchen. Gloria Cross had learned first-hand that Smudger was likely to reach for the meat cleaver if she interfered in his domain. Honey had backed him up. Good chefs were hard to come by; interfering mothers were two a penny.

Mary Jane broke into her thoughts. 'I told her she was mistaken. He doesn't come from that side of the house. He's always come out of number five and walked along the landing. Mrs Goulding is trying to say that he's coming out of the closet and that he chases her around the room. Well!

It's nonsense. All wishful thinking and a figment of her imagination.'

Honey stared at the tall, gaunt woman sitting beside her as she tried to get the drift of this. 'A man is chasing her around the room?'

'Sir Cedric! She reckons he's coming out of her closet, when both you and I know very well that he lives – or rather – materializes from the closet in room twelve.'

'I see. Our resident ghost!'

It sounded wacky, but Honey had got used to it. Mary Jane was in her seventies and claimed she knew all there was to know about the afterlife and the spirits residing there. That's why she kept coming back to the Green River, which, according to her, was much favoured by the spirits of the departed. She particularly liked the eighteenth-century gentleman who resided in the closet in room twelve – the room Mary Jane always booked in advance. Sir Cedric was her particular favourite.

She listened patiently. 'Have you seen Sir Cedric lately?'

Mary Jane looked hurt. 'Well, no. But that doesn't mean he's deserted me. After all, I am his great-great-great-great-grandniece.'

And there's the rub, thought Honey. Not for the world did she wish to upset her old friend, but surely no one actually *owned* a ghost, even if they were related. But it was pointless trying to tell her that. Mary Jane had long ago made it plain that there were rules for those who had passed over. By the sound of it, she'd written the book.

'Don't worry,' she said, patting Mary Jane's liver-spotted hand. 'I'm sure she's just imagining things. And, as you point out yourself, Sir Cedric wouldn't desert you in order to take up with a perfect stranger.'

Mary Jane's crumpled face unfolded. 'No! Of course not. There's the family honour at stake! I told her that, but she dared question whether Sir Cedric really was one of my ancestors. Damn cheek! I told her straight that I'd traced the family tree myself.'

Honey's ears pricked up at the mention of tracing family trees. 'Mary Jane,' she began, '– isn't it true that a person needs birth certificates and all that stuff if they're tracing their family tree?'

'Best to have that, though if you've got gaps in your knowledge, there's always specialists willing to give you a hand.'

'There are?'

'Of course. A little information – some bits of family gossip and hearsay can go a long way.'

'Where's the best place to start tracing a family tree if you happen to be an American?'

Mary Jane's twinkly blue eyes twinkled a bit more. 'It varies. But I can tell you where I started. Are you going to do yours?'

Honey shook her head as the sound of her mother's voice and footsteps pattered out in Reception. 'I'd rather not know.'

Mary Jane appeared unaware of the distraction. Her eyes had a glassy look as though the other world she believed in had superimposed itself on the real one.

'Parish registers are good. So is the local registrar of births, marriages and deaths. First thing I would do is speak to the relatives.'

Honey dragged her worried eyes away from the sounds in Reception. 'Could you do that for me? I could give you some basic information. The name's Maxted.' She frowned. 'It doesn't sound very Bathonian or even North Somerset.' She shrugged. 'But it's all I have. What I'd really like to know is if an American named Elmer Maxted has contacted anyone about tracing his family in the last few weeks.'

Mary Jane nodded, her face bright with enthusiasm. 'I'll get on to it right away. Now,' she said, fumbling for a pen in her purse, 'in your case, the best thing I can do is to interview your mother . . .' Mary Jane had not believed that it wasn't for her.

'No. You misunderstand. I told you: it's not for me.'

She saw the surprise, even disappointment, on Mary Jane's face.

'Oh!'

Honey dropped her voice to a whisper and leaned close. 'This Mr Elmer Weinstock I mentioned, alias Maxted, has gone missing. He was researching his family tree.'

Mary Jane was unfortunate enough to have slightly protruding eyes; now they were full-blown protruding. 'You don't say!'

'Do you think you could help?'

Mary Jane's response was diametrically opposed to the Philip Marlowe low-key approach. She looked like a fizzing firecracker about to explode.

'Yesss,' she hissed, the word elongated because she was trying so hard to suppress the exhilaration that coloured her facc and lent sparkle to her eyes. 'I know just what he would do. First, he would speak to Bob the Job.'

She saw Honey's puzzled look.

Mary Jane explained. 'He's the first port of call in this city if you're looking to trace your pedigree.'

Eyes flickering towards Reception and her mother's advancing footsteps, Honey gave a casual nod. 'I have to go now, but I'd appreciate you making enquiries.'

Mary Jane was scribbling Elmer's name on the back of the bus timetable. 'If he's a serious player, Bob will know all about the guy.'

'I'm sure my daughter would love to hear about your research of the Pilgrims' Trail.'

As her mother's voice came closer, Honey began her dash for the French doors.

'*Well, I really don't think I've got the time just now . . .*' A male voice. The professor was stalling – thank God!

'Leave this with me,' Mary Jane was saying as Honey backed out through the doors and into the garden.

The pages of magazines on a table near the door fluttered on the incoming draught. Mary Jane got up and shut it. She said something Honey couldn't hear. She guessed from the movement and shape of her mouth that she was telling her to have a nice day.

'I will,' she called back, waved and ran.

Somewhere in the city was a taxicab that had ferried Elmer Maxted around the city before he'd disappeared. Cora had told of a black Ford with the name 'Busy Bee Taxi Cab Company' emblazoned in red on its side. That, she decided, was as good a place as any to start.

Seven

Devotees of Jane Austen and all things Regency thronged through Bath's elegant crescents and leafy squares. Some narrowed their eyes in an effort to blank out the traffic and pretend that Mr Darcy was striding the pavement, resplendent in tails and tight trousers.

Keener on cameras rather than books, the Japanese snapped pictures of each other leaning on lampposts or posing outside MacDonalds. The Australians made for a decent brew in a reasonably priced café. The Americans did the tours at lightning speed, determined to get as much value as possible from their transatlantic flight.

This morning those looking over the parapet towards Pulteney Bridge were very subdued. Something had happened that attracted everyone's curiosity, something that certainly wasn't on the tourist trail.

Uniformed police were filtering people around the blue-and-white 'incident' tape fluttering around the steps leading from the road and down on to the towpath.

The river thundered over the weir throwing up clouds of foam and filling the air with spray.

Steve Doherty narrowed his eyes at the span of Pulteney Bridge, its stone piecrust gold. The rain had cleared. Licked by the early morning sun, the crescents, parades and avenues of Bath tiered upwards like steaming slabs of honey to the crisp blue of the sky. What a spot! – all blue and gold on postcards sent home to Mom in Illinois or Auntie Meg in Alice Springs.

He was down on the towpath examining the body. Above him the curious watched in hushed silence until an incident tent hid the bloated body.

Flanders, the Scene of Crime Officer, a man with pale eyes and even paler skin, gave him the low-down.

'Been dead a while. Look at him. Reminds you of a—'

'Stilton cheese,' Doherty interrupted, knowing he was going to comment about the effect of blood congealing in the veins. 'I know, I know.'

Flanders' pallid features took on a dejected look. He so loved flaunting his knowledge, especially if it meant he could make someone sick with the details. It was easier to make young constables sick, more difficult with seasoned detectives.

Doherty had burst his bubble on the first count, but he wouldn't on the second – Flanders was pretty sure of that.

The man had been found fully clothed with a sack covering his head. Flanders carefully removed the sack. The side of the man's head was caved in. 'Blunt instrument,' he said flatly, as though he'd seen thousands in his life. He had and had long ago given up counting.

He picked up a transparent evidence bag. 'See this piece of wood?'

Steve Doherty narrowed his eyes. The piece of wood was old and weathered.

'Part of a door,' said Flanders, warming to his subject. 'It had a number on it. See? He pointed to the faint indentation on the wood. 'A nine or perhaps a six: it was lodged beneath his armpit.'

Doherty's attention strayed to a group of office girls, leggy, lovely things and young enough to be his daughters.

'Give you a full report later!' the old codger puffed once he'd reached the top of the towpath steps and was only a few steps and a few more puffs from his dark-green Citroën. Nearby a traffic warden checked her watch, pursed her lips and clenched her jaw. This morning her routine and her tally were sharply curtailed and she looked pig sick about it.

Doherty smiled at the office girls before barking out orders to the assembled team. 'Come on lads. We've got work to do. Let's be having you. I want it swept with a toothbrush if need be. No skimping and no moans about bad backs and cups of tea.'

One of the forensic boys chose that moment to lean over the wall and spray the towpath with a shower of whatever he'd had for breakfast that morning. The office girls groaned and began to disperse.

Flanders kept on about the piece of wood.

Doherty refused to be impressed. 'So what? The river's high. There's always flotsam and jetsam floating about.'

'Do you want me to throw it back in?'

Flanders was being sarcastic. Doherty had no time for that and it showed in his attitude.

'The second word's "off"!'

Flanders bowed to his job, his white plastic siren suit crackling as he carried out the last rites as far as a cop is concerned: going through the deceased's pockets. No money on him, no watch, just a white mark where it used to be. 'A dead-cert mugging.' His probing fingers hesitated. 'Hello, hello! What have we here?'

Flanders held up the Amex credit card so he could more easily read the name. 'Elmer John Maxted.'

'You don't say!'

'I do.'

Doherty watched with narrowed eyes as it was slid into yet another transparent evidence bag. Turning away, he took out his phone and scrolled down the numbers until he got to hers.

She answered after the fourth ring. It sounded as though she were in a hurry.

'Hannah – Mrs Driver? This is Detective Sergeant Doherty.'

'I'll ring you back.'

He frowned at the phone. It wasn't the response he'd been banking on. He'd been about to eat humble pie. Blow her. He'd tell her in his own good time.

Eight

A row of taxicabs waited, on the rank alongside Bath Abbey. A few of them were of the old-fashioned London black-cab variety, like a row of black beetles queuing for a meal. The others were smart and shiny saloons. Only Busy Bee Cabs proclaimed their trade in red lettering along the sides.

After making enquiries, she was directed to a man named Ivor Webber, a stocky Welshman of West Indian descent.

'He's the one who got the fat fares last week,' someone told her.

Ivor was sitting in the driving seat of his cab sipping at an elderberry crush and reading what looked like a copy of *Mein Kampf*.

'Sorry to interrupt you,' she said, bending down close enough to see that he really *was* reading Hitler's one and only attempt to woo the world with the written word.

Ivor flipped his sunglasses back on to his forehead. 'Where to, lovely?' he said. He closed his book and placed it on the seat beside him.

Honey jerked her chin in its direction. 'A surprising title.'

His teeth flashed in a healthy white smile. 'Well there you are, lovely – I'm a surprising man. I like to form my own opinions, you see. It attests more reasonably to my intellectual growth. Now where can I take you?'

'Nowhere.' She leaned on the door. 'Just a question. Do you remember an American you picked up from Ferny Down Guest House?'

His amiability was undiminished. He threw back his head and slapped the steering wheel. 'You mean good old Elmer. Wish I had a few more like him in a week: a most generous tipper. There's not many of them nowadays what with the exchange rate and all that.'

Honey smiled and nodded, sensing she was off to a good start. 'Must have been some journeys. Where did you take him?'

'Here and there.'

Ivor Webber had a happy face. She fancied the smile was a permanent fixture.

'Pretty far, so I hear.'

He nodded. 'I did.'

Honey brought out her notebook and pen. 'So where, exactly?'

His smile melted. 'You the fuzz, lovely?'

'Now what makes you think that?'

The wariness of a man who hasn't always been upright and law abiding came to his eyes. 'Instinct, lovely, just instinct.'

She decided to come clean. 'Look. He's gone missing and his relatives are wondering where he's got to.'

OK, so it wasn't one hundred per cent clean, but a little white lie about worried relatives wouldn't hurt, surely?

Ivor showed the whites of his eyes. 'Is that right, lovely? Well I never. I took him to a few places – bit of sightseeing – usual stuff like Bradford-on-Avon, St Catherine's Valley, Lacock – you know – that place they use on a lot of historical dramas on television and film and suchlike.'

Honey nodded appreciatively. This was going *so* well! 'You sound as though you like history,' she said.

'I do, but not that fancy-pants and heaving-bosom stuff. I prefer World War Two myself. See?' He held up the offending tome. 'Not so much the military and political side, though that, of course, is interesting: I like to investigate how it started, you see – just in case. You know what they say about history, don't you?'

Honey didn't bother to tell him she knew very well; he was going to tell her anyway.

'History repeats itself,' he said with the air of a man who's spent his time analysing world politics whilst awaiting a fare.

Her phone rang again. She thanked him before turning away to take the call. This time it was her mother.

Her voice was thin – not exactly wavering and weak; more wavering and worked on.

'I fell down the stairs, dear.'

Honey raised her eyes to heaven – or at least as far as the pigeons squatting around the fancy bits on the Abbey roof. It was the way her mother said 'dear' that raised her hackles – and falling down the stairs had nothing to do with it.

'Mother, you've done this before.'

'It's my age, dear. One gets very tottery as one gets older. I need you here.'

Honey gritted her teeth. 'That wasn't what I meant.'

'Oh dear! I feel quite faint.'

Yet again her mother had played the guilt card. Her instinct told her that she'd probably only tripped down one stair and that if she phoned Lindsey she'd get the truth. Her sense of duty made her head for home, but she had an inkling her mother had an ulterior motive for getting her there.

Nine

It was gone midday and Lindsey was on Reception when she got back. She looked extremely businesslike, a pen in one hand and a pile of invoices in the other. Her eyes slid sidelong in the direction of the lounge.

'Grandma's in there. She's got a man with her.'

Honey hunched her shoulders questioningly.

Lindsey mimicked the same action. 'I've no idea who he is.'

Forearmed but wary, she followed the smell of fresh coffee.

Her mother was semi-prone on a settee, bandaged ankle resting on a stool.

Someone was sitting on a chair opposite her. They looked to be in close conversation.

Her mother saw her and looked up. 'So! You came back to see how I am.'

'You look good.'

'My ankle doesn't.'

'I suppose it could be better.'

'You bet it could!'

Normally she avoided the men her mother chose for her. On this occasion the set of his shoulders and the casual demeanour attracted her attention. She forced herself not to give in and faced directly forward.

Her mother didn't leave things there. 'Hannah? This is John Rees.'

'Mother, I can't stop . . .'

Her first inclination had been to throw a killer look at her mother and a contemptuous one at the man she'd found for her. Instead she found her brittleness melting away in the warmth of his smile.

'Hello.'

'Hello.'

'He's just opened a bookshop in Rifleman's Way. He's from Kansas.'

John took her hand and shook it firmly. 'Originally from Kansas. I live in San Diego nowadays. Or rather, I did. Now I live here – in Bath. Best little city in the world.'

His voice was like silk. His hair was light brown shot with just a little white at the temples.

'Well that's . . .'

She was about to say how nice that was, but the first notes of Beethoven's Fifth were throbbing against her chest.

'My phone,' she said, inwardly groaning as she plucked it from her bag. Making sincerely meant excuses she backed towards the door.

She recognized the rough-diamond copper's voice. 'I thought you'd like to know; we've found Elmer Maxted.'

'Great!'

Her eyes strayed back to John. He was tall and lean and had a merry look in his eyes – not at all the dusty professor or accountant sort her mother kept digging up. For once this might be fun. And she had time now, didn't she? The case of the missing tourist was all but over, wasn't it?

It wasn't. Doherty told her how it was. 'He's dead: murdered. I need to talk to you.'

Drat! Honey placed her hand over the phone. Her smile flew like a bird to gorgeous John. 'I'm sorry. I have to take this call, but if you'd like to leave your details, perhaps we can get in touch. Unless you'd like to wait.' She bit her lip. Business and pleasure were colliding here. Normally business would take precedence, but John had a certain look about him.

'Honey? Are you still there?' The sound of Steve Doherty's voice seeped through her fingers.

Reluctantly, she bent her lips back to the mouthpiece. 'Sorry, I just had something to arrange.'

'Can you meet me at this place he was staying? What was it again?'

'Ferny Down Guest House on the Lower Bristol Road.'

'That's it. I'll see you there.'

'Sorry,' she mouthed to the delectable John Rees. She wriggled her fingers in a wave at her mother.

'What about my ankle?' her mother called after her.

'Ask Chef for a bag of frozen peas.'

She tried to phone Casper to see if he'd heard the news. He was out of the office and never, ever used a cell phone. She asked Neville where she could find him.

'Not a clue.' Neville sounded snappy. They rowed infrequently. It had to be about something important. She made the mistake of asking him what was the matter.

'He wanted harvest-beige in Reception and I wanted blush pink.'

'Heavens! Who won?'

'He did.'

'So where is he?'

'I don't know.'

'Oh, come on. Casper tells you everything. You're his bosom buddy.'

She sensed the stiffening on the other end of the phone. 'Not all the time! Sometimes he's in a world of his own. No consideration. None at all!'

Casper was aloof, superior, elegant, efficient and homosexual; she'd never known before that he could be secretive.

'Tell him—'

Neville interrupted. 'I suggest you tell him yourself!' The connection was terminated with an angry click.

So Casper had secrets. The fact surprised her. She wondered what his response would be once he knew that their missing American had turned up dead.

Her mother had got to her feet. 'Are you staying for lunch, dear?' No mention of spraining her ankle or feeling faint.

Honey looked over her shoulder into the lounge at John Rees. He was finishing his coffee. She was sorely tempted, but Doherty and a dead body awaited her. She shook her head. 'I can't.' She threw a smile in John's direction. 'Duty calls. Another time, perhaps?'

'Sure. I'll make a note of your number.'

For the second time that day she was in two minds about a situation. Lunch with a charming guy or suffer the dead ash in Ferny Down Guest House, courtesy of Cora Herbert. Curiosity overwhelmed temptation. She couldn't resist. Murder was taking precedence over pleasure.

On passing through Reception she remembered Jeremiah Poughton. Lindsey traced his number and asked him if he knew where she could find Casper. He told her.

Ten

Casper St John Gervais appreciated balance and having things in perfect order. He also found it mesmerizing just how quickly one minute flowed into another. That's why he collected clocks. Clocks were one of the reasons he visited Simon Tye. Simon was as at home with the underworld of a small city as he had been with that of a large one. In London he'd upset the wrong people – which is why he'd headed west and opened a clock shop.

Tye's Timepieces was tucked away in a bow-fronted shop down a set of damp green steps. Only crumpled pavements and a mass of wandering tourists separated it from the sticky aspect of Sally Lunn's Teashop.

Casper paused before pushing the door open. Already his heart was beating faster. What would he find inside? Simon Tye, of course. But what gems of mechanical chronology would he have there to tempt him?

'Get a grip,' he muttered against his impeccably knotted tie. He smoothed his hair back from his forehead in an effort to calm his nerves. Once properly under control, he pushed at the door.

An old-fashioned door bell clanged overhead. Mechanical whirrs, taps, ticks, scrapings and dull thuds filled the air. So did the pungent cloy of bees' wax and linseed oil. No matter how hard he attempted to maintain his self-control, something similar to passion clutched at his heart.

Brass, mahogany, oak, maple, and marble decorated with French ormolu, the clocks surrounded him, their ticks and their chimes as sweet as words of love to his keen ear and knowledgeable mind. Instinctively, he knew there was something special for him here.

It was set on a chest of drawers with a serpentine front and hanging brass handles, as fragile as fine string. Simon always did have a way of showing things off to best advantage. 'Presentation is what matters, guv,' he always said. He was right. The honeyed glint of the satinwood emphasized the ice-cold perfection of white porcelain. It was brilliant: four feet wide and three feet high Dresden figures grouped around a china faced clock figured with brass.

He ran his fingers over the beautifully defined muscles of the crisply carved shepherd. 'Divine,' he breathed.

'You wan' it?'

Like a grinning satyr, Simon Tye's face appeared over the top of the clock, one bony elbow close to the porcelain shepherdess who leaned nonchalantly against the round barrel of the clock face.

Casper stepped closer, his eyes taking in every intricate detail: the shepherd, a lamb flung around his shoulders: the shepherdess, a crook in her dainty hand, her skirts piled like a pumpkin between her narrow waist and her graceful little ankles. Sheep and lambs gambolled before them and graceful naiads held the clock above them on porcelain ribbons.

It was gorgeous and there were myriad questions he'd like to ask about it, but more so he calculated the price. 'It's very nice, but not the best I've seen.' He was lying and could see from the shopkeeper's face that he knew it. Never mind. He would brazen it out.

Simon grinned as though he were looking through him and knew the truth. He looked almost part of the clock itself, yet a lot less beautiful: wide mouth, almond-shaped eyes and a straggly mass of blue grey hair that hid a hunk of reddened gristle and gaping hole – all that remained of his left ear. That's what came of grassing up blokes in the East End of London. No wonder he'd headed west and opened up a clock shop.

'I knew you'd want it the minute you saw it, Mr St John, sir.'

Casper licked the dryness from his lips. Damn the man! He tried to ignore the smile that was spreading across

Simon's face like melting cheese. To hell with it! Unable to resist, he reached out and trailed his fingers over the gleaming glaze. A thrill shot through his body. He breathed deeply before he asked the first question.

'Dresden?'

'Dead right!' Simon's smile was unaltered. Someone else's discomfort, especially someone as ostensibly wealthy as Casper, was incredibly enjoyable. 'Made for the Paris Exhibition years and years ago. Brilliant, ain't it!?'

Casper squirmed inside but hells bells, he certainly wasn't going to take it all without giving some out.

'Did you get it legally, Mr Tye?'

Simon looked hurt. 'Mr. Tye is it? Are you tryin' to throw me off balance, get the better of me an' 'ave it away for nix? It was a legitimate purchase. Cross my 'eart.' He made the usual sign on his narrow chest in the place where his heart might have been.

Casper took advantage. 'So?' He lifted his eyebrows questioningly.

'To tell you the truth I bought it off a lady who brought it 'ere in her car. Said the 'ouse was cluttered with stuff and she needed the room. Took a song for it, she did – though, I shouldn't be telling you that.' His eyes narrowed.

Casper shook his head and tutted reproachfully. 'What sort of person would want to get rid of a lovely thing like that?'

'A woman who don't like too much dusting, I s'pose, though mind you, she didn't look the type that got 'er 'ands dirty too often.'

'No taste,' said Casper, his eyes fixed on the clock.

'No shame,' echoed Simon.

'How much?' he asked, the words spitting from his mouth as though he had no control over his tongue at all.

Triumph shone in Simon's watery-grey eyes and slunk in shiny wetness along his wide, flaccid lips.

'I could get seven at auction.'

'Hundred?' said Casper hopefully.

'Leave it out – thousand!' Simon retorted feigning insult.

'Exorbitant!'

Simon's eyes were pinpricks in narrow slits. 'No it ain't, and you know it ain't.'

Casper laid a well-manicured hand across his chest. His heart was racing like an express train. It was now or never. He braced himself to forego the temptation. He even made a half-turn towards the door.

Alluringly, the clock began to chime its siren song, the note lucid – heavily seductive to a clock collector's ear.

He stared at it, aware that Simon was watching him like a hungry hawk, his fingers thoughtfully tapping at his bottom lip, scratching at his chin. But his eyes stayed fixed on Casper's face. His self-control wobbled like a jelly and finally toppled. 'I'll give you five.'

'Well . . .' said Simon thoughtfully. His eyes were hooded. He was looking downwards so Casper couldn't see how delighted he was. 'Let's say five thousand five hundred shall we?'

Not to be outwitted, Casper fixed his gaze on Simon and set his jaw in a firm, determined line. 'Let's say five thousand two hundred.'

Simon chuckled and shook his head. For a moment Casper was almost panicked into raising his offer. He forced himself to hold out, though his mouth was as dry as the bottom of a bird cage.

'It's a deal!' Simon spat on his palm and reached out.

'Fine,' said Casper, declining to shake hands. 'I'll get it collected,' he said before the brass bell jangled and the door chamfered shut.

Wonderful day, he thought to himself, smiling at the world that eddied and flowed around him. A coachload of German tourists was taking photographs of the flowers, the edifice of the Guildhall, the entrance to the Roman Baths. He beamed at them as they methodically set up their shots, checked their lighting and posed their portraits. This year would be a very good year for the city and for La Reine Rouge.

The day was a good one and remained so – until he sauntered into his favourite restaurant.

The Saville Roe, which served all manner of seafood,

nestled beside an alley of polished cobbles just behind the Theatre Royal. Panelled walls alleviated by the use of white damask tablecloths and silver-plated cruets gave it a rich, gothic-style ambience. The clientele were well-heeled and on a lunch time businessmen outnumbered tourists. He was shown to his usual table in the far corner. A menu card and wine list as white as the table linen was brought within a minute of him sitting down.

Just as he was deciding between a goat's cheese and salmon concoction and slices of sea bass flambéed in pear juice, the waiter brought him a cordless telephone. 'For you, sir,' said the handsome Italian as he handed him the phone.

It was quite usual to receive calls at his favourite haunts from those that knew him and also knew of his distaste for cell phones. For a brief moment he eyed the proffered receiver with something close to disdain. He was also slightly miffed that his habits had become so – well – habitual that people knew where he could be contacted.

Never mind, he told himself as he accepted the call; *you've had a good day. It's June and the sun is shining, business is good and you've had a stroke of good luck.* Then Honey spoke and told him about Elmer Maxted. Suddenly the June sky dulled to November.

Eleven

It became obvious to Honey from his attitude that it wasn't Doherty's idea that she should accompany him to Ferny Down Guest House.

'I don't see the point,' he told her bluntly.

Honey hid her grimace in a yawn. Dealing with the public had well prepared her for characters like him. Identification was instant – grumblers, groaners and disgruntled Doctor Jekyll types who began their complaints with, 'I'm not one to complain, but . . .' And they became grumblers, but in the next instant were nice as sugary sorbet. Like them, there were two sides to Steve Doherty: his social side wanted to do more than embrace her; his professional side wanted her out of his way.

He'd adopted a glum look, an unmistakable grimness around his mouth as the disgruntled grumbler took over.

She stated what she thought was the matter. 'You were told I had to come along.'

He shoved his hands in his pockets. 'The Chief Constable thinks he might get more media coverage with you on board. He likes having his picture in the press.' He said it through gritted teeth.

Honey couldn't help grinning. 'Never mind,' she said, patting his hand; a cold hand. What was the saying? Cold hands, warm heart? Nice. 'You've been ordered. I've been ordered – well, more or less. So let's leave it at that and get on with it, shall we?'

He grunted something. She couldn't tell what.

'I'll take that as an affirmative.'

There was nothing for it but to settle comfortably into her seat and eye the passing scene.

Doherty sat silently beside her.

'The flowers look lovely this year. I like pink and mauve together, don't you?'

He took his eyes off the road long enough to glance at her. 'Mrs Driver, this is hardly the time to be noticing flowers.'

Maintaining her smile and her bright disposition, she tilted her head sideways so that a sweep of hair blanketed her right shoulder.

'It's a question of keeping things in proportion. Flowers are like music: they soothe the nerves. That's what I'm here to do. Think of me as a flower.'

'What?'

Yes! A response! Emphasizing the point, the car swerved towards the centre reservation, earning a blaring horn and a two-fingered salute from white-van man.

Showing no sign that she'd noticed, Honey carried on. 'You're like a stone – steadfast, as you ask Mrs Herbert a lot of questions. I'm the flower that calms her nerves.'

Doherty shook his head in disbelief. He also sniffed the air. French perfume. Honey smelled good and looked good. She was wearing a pink-checked jacket, cream skirt and candy striped shoes. Good enough to eat.

'So!' Honey went on, 'you're going to arrest Mrs Herbert?'

'I didn't say that.'

'But you're not discounting it.'

'That depends on the evidence and her answers to my questions.' Doherty's square chin turned squarer.

She sensed his confusion, personal and professional colliding behind the resolute exterior. 'I doubt that she did it, though she is a criminal – of sorts. She should be locked up just for her choice of clothes and make-up. Now that's criminal!'

'Yeah, yeah, yeah,' said Doherty as he turned off the engine. 'Right. Now there's a few questions I've got for you, flower.'

Honey pointed at her chest. This was a direction she hadn't counted on. What did she know?

'Yes,' said Doherty, who had noticed her sideways glance, 'you. You said that her old man was manhandling a chest freezer out of the back gate when you first visited.'

She nodded. 'That's right. The council truck was waiting outside to take it to the recycling plant for degassing before it's crushed.'

He stroked his chin thoughtfully. 'Is that so? Are you sure about that?'

'It's an environmental thing they have to do.'

'I wonder whether they've crushed it yet.'

She sensed where this was leading and shrugged. 'I don't know.'

'I'll get it checked.'

He made the call before they got out of the car.

The flowers in the hanging baskets were wilting slightly. Honey wondered whether Mervyn had been the one who used to look after them. Not necessarily of course. It could be Cora but she was down in the dumps so maybe had forgotten. Not surprising.

His expression was deadly serious as he rang the doorbell. Comprehension regarding Honey's innuendos blinked into his eyes when Cora Herbert answered the door.

Her black-rimmed eyes landed on Honey. 'What? You again!'

'It's me,' Honey said, trusting her smile would override the hint of hostility in Cora's voice. She needn't have worried: Cora's attention swerved to Steve Doherty. A deep intake of breath ballooned her bosoms.

Her sense of style hadn't altered one iota. She was wearing a cropped black top and chequered skirt with a ragged fringe around the hem. Her eyes were heavily outlined. A gold droplet dangled from her pierced belly button. Her flesh was white like dimpled bread dough. The gold droplet heaved in and out as though it were gasping for air.

If Doherty had been the cream and she'd been the cat, he would have been all gobbled up by now.

She was straight to it. 'And you are . . . ?'

Doherty took a side-step. Partially shielded by Honey, he flashed his identity card. 'Detective Sergeant Doherty. I need to speak to everyone who was in this house on the day he left.'

Cora gushed the information. 'Me, me husband and me daughter.'

Doherty's chin shot forward when he nodded, his jaw almost resting on her shoulder. The stubble rippled as his mouth moved.

Honey watched it ripple. Funnily enough, it was exactly the same length as two days previously. It occurred to her that he trimmed it to just the right length in an effort to make exactly the right impression.

'Just the three of you live here.'

'And guests, when we've got any. Mind you, I can always find room for a nice-looking bloke like you.'

A nerve ticked beneath Doherty's right eye, but, fair dos, he kept his nerve.

'Fine, then I need to speak to you, your daughter and your husband.'

Thick with mascara, Cora's eyelashes flickered like the wings of tiny bats. 'Our Loretta's up in her room. Merv isn't here. In fact, you could say that I'm all by meself.'

Honey recalled Cora telling her where he usually enjoyed his quality time.

'Perhaps if you could tell me which pub . . .'

Her interference was not welcome. Cora glared and her tone turned like a frozen fish. 'He's not gone to the pub. He's gone away. He's allowed to go away, isn't he? God knows but we work hard enough, put up with enough . . .' Aware that her attempts at flirtation had flopped, the belly she'd attempted to hold in relaxed into its natural pudding shape. 'For goodness' sake,' she muttered, 'it's only a tourist gone on a mystery tour! That's my opinion, anyway.'

Steve Doherty's face set like quick-drying cement. 'Mrs Herbert, today a body was pulled from Pulteney Weir. We believe it to be the body of your former guest, a Mr Elmer Weinstock, also known as Maxted. We would like you – or your husband – to make a formal identification.'

The wind knocked out of her sails, Cora Herbert looked taken aback. The botoxed bottom lip hung puffy and quivering. Her eyes stretched to prominence in the podgy, pallid face.

Still wary of Cora's intentions, Doherty let Honey take the lead.

'Right,' she said. 'Can we come in and discuss what you know?'

Cora nodded and retreated into the green-and-white hall.

Honey recalled the fug in the conservatory and prepared to take small, shallow breaths. To her relief, they were shown into the guests' lounge instead. A 'no smoking' sign was prominently displayed on the mantelpiece. The room had a pleasanter smell than the conservatory by virtue of a can of air freshener: lilies of the valley, by the whiff of it.

Cora Herbert didn't offer them tea or invite them to sit down, but they did anyway. Cora perched on the arm of a chair immediately opposite them – like a vulture deciding whether to fly off or stay and pluck their eyes out.

Steve Doherty got out his notebook and a smart looking pen. 'Right!'

Honey eyed him sidelong. Murder had made him a serious man. All the same, he appeared to make himself comfortable. Honey sensed he was far from that. She noticed he was making a list on the pad and ticking the items off – far too slowly for her liking. Overwhelming urges to know *everything* and *at once* took hold of her. She found herself counting the seconds he was taking to ask the first relevant question.

It was obvious that he was terrified of Cora Herbert. But for goodness' sake, he was a policeman. Weren't they brave, fearless and bold? *Start! Go on. Start!*

He didn't. So she did. 'Can you tell me who was here the last time you saw the man you knew as Mister Weinstock?'

Policemen were usually forceful – or at least they were on television. Steve Doherty looked almost relieved that she'd taken the lead.

As is the way of some women of a certain age, Cora did not welcome female dominance. Her reply was aimed directly at Doherty as her hands smoothed her skirt following the contours of her thighs. 'First there's Mervyn, of course, then my daughter, Loretta.'

'How old is she?'

'Seventeen.' Her smile was weak, but her simpering spilled out, unhindered by recent events. 'I had her very young you see . . .'

The door to the lounge creaked open. The truth bounced into the room. 'I'm nearly eighteen and my ma isn't as young as she makes out!' The rectification came from the over-made-up girl poking her head around the door. Her blonde hair was streaked with three shades of copper. Her earrings were big enough to swing on and she wore six rings on her right hand alone.

Doherty nodded a greeting and turned back to Cora. 'Right . . .'

Waffler, thought Honey, and retook the advantage, directing her question at Loretta.

'The man you knew as Mr Weinstock is dead. Did you have anything to do with him whilst he was staying here? – you know, general stuff like saying hi in the morning and how's the weather?'

She could feel Doherty's resentment burning into the side of her head. She ignored him.

Loretta's earrings made a tinkling noise as she folded her arms beneath her pert breasts. Definitely six rings on three fingers of each hand and one on each thumb; none on her index fingers.

She was wearing a red sweater with a keyhole design over her cleavage that left nothing to the imagination. Like her mother, her belly button was pierced.

Like Mother, like daughter.

Loretta shook her head. 'I didn't have much to do with him meself. He chatted to Mervyn a lot. They used to booze a bit in the den.'

Cora smiled at Doherty. 'I don't think this nice policeman has got any more questions for you, Loretta.' She turned back to the girl, her expression hardening just a teeny, weeny bit. 'I'll be along shortly to make yer lunch, love.'

Honey saw the contempt in Loretta's eyes. Teenagers

sometimes looked at their parents like that and took a while to grow out of it. All the same, she sensed discontent, even an air of secrecy.

'Come in, Loretta. Perhaps there's something you might remember that could help us.'

'Yes. That's right,' said Doherty. He was doing his best not to sound aggrieved.

For her part, Honey was trying not to stare at Loretta's skirt. If it had been much shorter, she would have seen her dinner. *If my Lindsey wore a skirt like that . . .* But Lindsey wouldn't, even though she had dancer's legs that seemed to reach all the way up to her shoulders.

Doherty was asking Loretta when she had last seen her father.

'He's not my father.'

'My first marriage,' Cora explained with a weak grin to them and a warning look to her daughter.

Loretta shrugged. 'The other night when I heard him talking to Mr Weinstock was the last time I saw him – or, more like, heard him.'

There was something in the careless way she shrugged that set the alarm bells ringing – at least for Honey. She glanced sidelong at Doherty. Did he have teenage children?

No. He did not. He hadn't seen that telling slide of the eyeballs that was meant to show casual indifference but in fact meant something entirely different. He was asking her questions. Honey knew beyond doubt that, whatever Loretta said, she'd be lying.

'You overheard what was said?'

'Yes. They were in the kitchen. Mr Weinstock had asked Mervyn for ice.' A wicked grin crossed her face. 'Mervyn hated having to get crushed ice. Not that it was any big deal, wrapping cubes in a tea towel and bashing them to smithereens. Is it true he's dead?'

Doherty nodded. 'The man you knew as Mr Weinstock is dead, yes.'

Loretta's eyes lit up. 'Bludgeoned to death? Could it have been done with a rolling pin? Old Merv was a dab hand with that rolling pin. That's what he used to crush the ice.'

'You little bitch!' Cora sprang to her feet. Fingers like claws reached for her daughter's throat.

Honey got in between them. 'Now calm down.' She frowned at Doherty. 'So how was he killed?'

'We're not sure yet,' said Doherty. 'Once we have the details of the post mortem, I can—'

Honey was losing patience. 'Can we get to the point, please?' Both the policeman and the teenager looked surprised. A cloud of perfume emanated from the trendy teenager when Honey addressed Loretta. 'What were they talking about?'

A thunder-faced Cora butted in again, her lips quivering slightly. 'She's just told you. Mervyn was crushing some ice. That's all.'

'No! You said they were talking,' said Honey, fixing her gaze on Loretta and refusing to take notice of the sour looks Doherty was throwing her way. 'Now to my mind that means after the ice was crushed. Is it possible that the man you knew as Mr Weinstock had his own bottle of whisky? Quite a few Americans buy their own to save on bar prices. Could he have asked Mervyn to sit down and have a drink with him?'

Loretta hesitated before she answered and began fiddling with a wispy strand of hair caught around her earring. 'Yes. They were. I could tell they'd had a drop by their voices. It echoes a bit in the den anyway.'

Honey pounced on this extra bit of information. 'The den? What den? I thought they were in the kitchen.'

Loretta studied her fingernails in a nonchalant, cocky kind of way. The polish looked black, or at least dark purple. 'They were in the kitchen first getting the ice, and then they went into the den. Mervyn was showing him his watch collection.'

Honey's ears pricked up even more. She could feel Doherty's eyes on her, but didn't look his way. Things were beginning to get interesting. Casper had enrolled her for this job and collected clocks. Mervyn collected watches. Now what sort of coincidence was that?

Twelve

Mervyn opened his eyes but saw nothing. Everything was dark and his head ached. The dryness on his tongue was like iron filings and for some daft reason he could smell something that reminded him of Christmas.

With each breath the sack covering his head was sucked up into his nostrils. Whatever dust it contained was drawn up into his nasal passages. What with that and the gag around his mouth, it was difficult to breathe. A sense of panic overwhelmed him. He was going to die – not comfortably, perhaps not even quickly, but slowly suffocating, struggling for even the slightest morsel of air.

No! No!

He tried to remember exactly what had happened, but all he could think of was Loretta. Everything began and finished with her. Even in this his worse nightmare, the thought of her nubile body assuaged his fear. Eventually his fear won the battle.

What was he doing here!

Mentally, he retraced his movements. Somehow he couldn't move forward from Cora's first husband giving him a beating. All he'd done was to give Loretta a lift home. He'd tried to explain that it was raining, but to no avail. The blows still fell hard and fast. That was when he'd made the decision to leave. If that moron was walking free and easy, then he was off – for good! First get some money together . . .

Something about that gelled in his brain. Money! Some time after that he'd arranged to meet someone, but for the life of him he couldn't remember the guy's name or why he'd arranged to meet him.

His clothes were chill and damp against his skin. He knew he'd sweated a lot. Now he was cold, terribly cold. One shiver came fast upon another. If he hadn't been gagged his teeth would have chattered. He tried moving his arms, flexing his fingers, squirming against the ropes that bound his wrists.

Suddenly he became aware that someone was there. The footsteps were muffled because of the sack over his head. He tried to lift his head, to roll away.

He never saw the hand that killed him. He saw only the wasted years of his life flashing before his eyes before even the memories drained away along with the blood and bits of brain.

The cellars were deep, one tier upon another. A thin scum of orange silt covered the cracked concrete and dented cobbles, a result of those times when the river was swollen, the lower levels flooded.

It was like that now, slippery and smelling of river mud and untreated effluent. Coke cans and plastic shopping bags bobbed around just below the ledge that dipped into the river. This was the very lowest cellar and slowly, with the passing of the years, the river was claiming it as its own.

The body had softened and was faintly marbled by virtue of resident bacteria. He'd covered the head with a small sack so he didn't have to look at the staring eyes. The sacks were readily available. He used them frequently for other things, less gruesome things.

The rest of the body was wrapped in a length of polythene that crackled when he lifted it up. The man wasn't light but not too heavy either. Carefully so as not to slip, he carried Mervyn Herbert down the last flight of steps. There was a good flow on the river, a welcome effect of the earlier rains. On the opposite bank he could see ranks of sodium street lights winding through the darkness. Spots of reflected amber light danced on the racing river.

On his side there were no lights – only the black, square shadows thrown by the circling colonnade above. The night was his, as dark as his mind.

Gently, still holding on to his precious piece of polythene, which had once covered a mattress, he let the body slide into the water. It bobbed about a bit, clung to the bank as if unwilling to leave him.

Beneath his breath he cursed the strong flow and with the help of a torch searched behind him for something to poke the body away from the bank and into the main stream. What had once been a door lay cobwebbed and rotting against the wall. Just as he'd done before, he tore a piece of rotten plank from it, green paint clinging in odd patches over its rough surface.

With the fingers of one hand, he gripped the crumbling door lintel overhead. In the other he held the wood. Still holding on to the flaking masonry, he reached out and poked at the body until it was safely carried by the current. Then, carelessly, no longer interested in the bloated flotsam he had consigned to the water, he flung the piece of wood after it.

Unafraid and uncaring, he watched it ebb into the black night and black water. What was it to him? What was anyone to him except with one notable exception, one person who he loved more than himself?

The rush of water and a slight bumping sound made him look back again. The body had returned, the river current pinning it against the bank.

There was no option but to drag it back on to the slime-covered flagstones. It had to be got rid of, but where?

He sat down and thought about blame and throwing the police off the scent. Blame and guilt. He knew a lot about them and about restitution, making things up to those you loved.

An idea came to him. Suspicion fell initially on close acquaintances in a murder case. So, if the body was found in the right place . . . ?

Thirteen

One thirty. Smudger the chef was complaining about the butcher again.

'I swear to you, it's rubbish. Trust me. Let me tell him that if he don't up his standards, I'm for chopping out his liver!'

Honey rolled her eyes. How was a woman to cope?

Her mother was rabbiting on about a very upright and uptight type she wanted her to meet. 'You must meet him, Hannah, darling. I'm sure you'll get on like a house on fire.'

'Mother, I can arrange my own dates.'

Her mother shrugged. 'Doesn't seem that way to me.' Digging her painted nails into Honey's shoulders, she flipped her round and faced her.

'Tell me the truth, the whole truth and nothing but the truth. Do you have a man friend?'

'Yes.'

'Yes?' Her mother sounded incredulous. She clapped her hands and looked extraordinarily happy. 'You do? Who is he?'

'Just a guy.'

'That's his name?'

'Jeremy.'

Her mother frowned. 'I don't know him, do I?'

'Right. You don't know him.'

First, deal with the chef.

'Smudger? You will not threaten the man. If he fails to deliver decent meat, then he doesn't get his bread. Savvy?'

He grinned cheekily. His sandy-coloured hair curled out

from beneath his tall, chef's hat. 'Great! I can't wait to see his face when I tell him to stick it.'

'No!' Honey wagged a finger at him. 'That isn't what I said. Just insist that he keeps his standards up, or else . . .'

'I chop him!' A gleaming meat cleaver waved with gleeful anticipation.

'No! I don't pay him – that's what. Smudger, hurting comes in many forms. A light bank account hurts more than a wound!'

Smudger looked disappointed, but accepted her judgement.

'And for my next trick,' she muttered to herself.

'Right. Mother.' She wheeled her mother away from Smudger's realm and into the conservatory.

'Doesn't the garden look lovely,' she said – a calming measure in anyone's book. They marched the width of the conservatory until they were nose deep to the glass.

Her mother glared. 'You haven't got a boyfriend, have you? You were lying.'

'Yes.'

'Well, I've got one for you.'

'I don't want one.'

The conservatory looked out over an enclosed garden. The trees had grown high and wide, obliterating the view of other buildings. If you lay flat in the grass and stared directly upwards, you could almost forget you were in the heart of the city.

Her mother looked puzzled, her lips parted as though there was something she wanted to say, but she wasn't quite sure how to phrase it.

Faced for once with the minimum of response, Honey decided to make the going – just as she had with her counterpart in the police force. 'So you met him at the dentist.'

'Yes. He's a widower.'

The vision of the gorgeous guy she'd seen standing beside her mother at the beginning of the week flashed into her mind. Somehow she hadn't envisaged him as being a widower.

Giving herself time to digest this, Honey banged on the

window at Mary Jane and waved. Mary Jane was practising her t'ai chi and managed to include a slow wave amongst her movements.

Accompanied by her mother's listing of reasons why she should meet this man, Honey continued to watch Mary Jane's sinuous arms rolling and wafting outwards, one leg slowly raised, one little twist of her spine.

'OK, he's a bit of a steady Eddie, but I'm sure he's the right man for you.'

This last sentence sank in. 'I'm really surprised. He didn't strike me that way,' said Honey.

'But you haven't met him yet.'

The vision shattered. 'What?'

Her mother smoothed her corn-coloured tunic as she settled gracefully into a chair. Once she was sitting, she looked pensive, the fingers of her right hand curving over her chin. A slight frown creased the professionally plucked eyebrows. 'You haven't met him, dear.'

Honey frowned. Was she missing something here? 'But he was here the other day. You said he was a bookseller. His name was John Rees.'

Her mother looked nervous for a moment, but it wasn't long before her natural brazenness took over. 'Not him. I meant Edgar Paget. He's my dentist. And a very good one,' she added, as though that in some way recommended him as a potential suitor.

A creeping chill ran down Honey's back. Escape time had come. 'Mother, I don't think I can take to a guy who makes a living from peering into people's mouths.'

'He's not just *any* dentist! Private patients only.'

Honey turned her back on Mary Jane, who had just entered into the final movements of her daily routine. Folding her arms across her chest, she eyed her mother with a mixture of disbelief and total confusion. Was this woman really her mother? And what was she trying to do?– get her to notch up the same number of marriages as she'd gone through?

But first things first: 'So this bookseller. What was he here for?'

'To organize a book fair. He wanted to make a booking. I just got talking to him. He seemed very pleasant.'

Honey's jaw dropped. 'A booking.'

Her mother nodded. 'Yes, dear.'

'So why didn't you pass him to Reception?'

'Because he asked to see you.'

Honey sighed. 'I'll have to phone him.'

Her mother looked taken aback. She frowned. So far her efforts to fix her daughter up with a suitable man had proved fruitless. But she didn't give up easily.

'So what about my dentist – Mr Paget?'

'No!'

Her mother rarely frowned. *It causes wrinkles, dear.* Her indignation showed in the way her heart-shaped face became elongated as her chin dropped. The wrinkles came anyway and would have looked good on a bloodhound.

'Well that's a change of attitude, I must say.'

Honey's thoughts were elsewhere, but there was room for the gorgeous guy who'd called in earlier in the week.

Mary Jane caught her just as she was rushing from the conservatory and into Reception.

'I'll speak to you later,' Honey called over her shoulder.

'There's no need to panic. He said he'd call back,' said her mother, yet again scurrying along beside her.

Honey refused to listen, rummaging among the bits of paper in a basket marked 'file'. Everything that didn't have a home – which included the calling cards of salesmen selling disposables – went into the 'file'.

'Have we had a booking for a book fair?' she asked Deehta, who came in to cover on Tuesdays and Thursdays.

'No.' Deehta shook her dark head vehemently. When it came to efficiency, Deehta was top of the pops. Honey had no recourse but to believe her.

There was no sign of a business card marked 'bookshop'.

'Never mind,' Honey said, once she was satisfied that her filing tray was its usual, uninteresting self.

Mary Jane, who let nothing interrupt her t'ai chi session, called out to her. 'We need to talk,' she said in a hushed rush of a voice, as though secrecy and speed were paramount.

Needing solace after her brush with chef and mother, Honey's first inclination was to say that she was too busy. But Mary Jane's animated features caused her to change her mind.

'I know where he went,' said Mary Jane, '– that guy who went missing; I know who he was asking about and where he went.'

Honey took hold of Mary Jane's bony elbow, hauled her into her private office and shut the door. 'Tell me!'

'He enquired about a family called Charlborough.'

Honey frowned. 'Do you mean *the* Charlborough family?'

Mary Jane's face wizened into a question mark. 'Do I?'

'They live at Charlborough Grange out at Limpley Stoke.'

Mary Jane's face brightened. 'That's the place. That's where he went.'

It added up. Ivor must have taken Elmer to the church at Limpley Stoke, though he hadn't mentioned it.

'And Elmer was related to the Charlboroughs?'

Mary Jane shook her head. 'Oh, he couldn't say. He wasn't specific, according to Bob.'

'Am I right in thinking our missing tourist would have learned a lot from a parish register?'

'He sure would,' said Mary Jane. 'That's one thing you can say about the church: they certainly kept tight tabs on everybody.'

Fourteen

The alarm woke her just after eleven p.m. A quick shower, fresh make-up and hair dried; a search through her clothes: jeans, a black T-shirt and pearl earrings. Casual but classy, she thought after a brief glance in the mirror.

On the way to meet Detective Sergeant Doherty, she passed the taxi stand, looked for Ivor's car but couldn't see him. If she had she would have asked more about Elmer's visit to Limpley Stoke. Mary Jane was emphatic about her subject, but it wouldn't have hurt to confirm it.

The night air was still and cool. The lights of the city obliterated the blackness of the river, which was running high and fast and didn't look its normal friendly self. Possibly there'd been heavy rain upstream.

Doherty awaited her. He'd mumbled something about sharing information. Well that should be taken with a pinch of salt! Never mind the professional liaison – a personal liaison would be much more to his liking.

As she descended the steps down to the Zodiac Club, she considered whether she should tell him what Mary Jane had told her about Elmer having been in touch with a man named Bob the Job. Crazy name, but there: people hoping to find fame or notoriety in their background were a bit crazy – devastated when they realized their ancestry contained nothing more than generation after generation of farm labourers, housemaids and itinerant drunkards.

Right! She was going out to meet a policeman. Should she tell him where she'd *thought* Elmer had gone, or should she check this oddly named guy Bob the Job? Better still, she'd get Ivor to confirm it. Until then she would also keep it to herself.

The Zodiac was a private club. When she rang the bell, a small slot opened. A pair of eyes looked out and a muffled voice asked for her name and whether she was a member.

'It's me.'

The eyes opened wide in recognition and the door opened. 'Good evening, madam!'

'Good evening, Clint. I think that's the first time you've ever called me madam.' She looked him up and down. 'Nice suit.'

As he smoothed the front of the black evening suit, Clint, her part-time washer-up, grinned from ear to ear. Despite the spider's web etched into his skull and the gold earring, Clint looked very presentable – and slightly menacing; in fact, ideal for the job.

'I got it at Oxfam. Not bad, is it?'

'No. Not bad at all. Should last you a while as long as you don't go washing up in it.'

His grin stretched across his face. 'I won't be doing that. Serving in me mate's shop is my daytime job, washing up is early evening, and this is my night-time job.'

'So when do you sleep?'

He grinned. 'When I can. Got to have a social life, ain't I?'

'You certainly do.'

And all for cash, thought a bemused Honey. It occurred to her that he could be making more money than she was, and enjoying a better social life.

'Look,' she said. 'I'm expecting a guest. His name's Steve . . .'

'Doherty. Yeah.' His grin collapsed into a stiff grimace. 'The dude's already here.'

There was no point asking him how come he knew a member of the local constabulary. She could guess, but Clint was Clint and his business was his own.

Threading her way through the smoke brought to mind old black-and-white movies: clubs where shady characters clustered in dingy alcoves. The ceiling was barrel-vaulted and the walls bare stone. Downlighters picked out swirls of blue smoke drifting from the sizzling steaks being grilled in the restaurant. Apart from them the lighting was minimal, if not downright scarce.

Steve was propped up in the corner of the bar. A space had opened up around him; news of his professional standing had no doubt travelled. Isolation didn't seem to worry him. His eyes were everywhere but stalled once they landed on her.

'Drink?' he asked, shifting his stance and digging his hand into the pocket of his black leather jacket.

She ordered a vodka and tonic. 'With ice and lemon,' she added.

He took the money from his pocket. No wallet, she noticed. A cautious man. She wondered where he kept his credit cards.

'Are you hungry?' he asked her suddenly.

She shook her head whilst eyeing the clientele, noting who was there playing after hours. Hotel and pub managers, plus those who owned, ran and worked bloody hard in their own hotels.

They studied each other, a meeting of eyes, a furtive appraisal of each other's attributes.

For his part Steve admired her clear skin, a handsome rather than pretty face. Her hair was dark, her eyes blue and her legs went up to her shoulders – or at least, that was the way they seemed.

'Cheers!' They clinked glasses.

Honey glimpsed the glint of a gold bracelet on his right wrist. His hair was too densely coloured for a man of his age. Doherty wasn't taking middle age lying down. She wondered whether he realized that he had something in common with Cora Herbert. Doubtful. Though they'd never admit it, men were vainer than women.

'So,' she said after taking a generous sip of vodka and tonic. 'Have you informed the relatives?'

'He doesn't have any. Apparently there was a sister, but she died just a few months ago.'

'So he went travelling to get away?'

Doherty shrugged. 'I suppose so. Who knows? They reckoned he was well into doing research. Tracing ancestors was the latest thing. Before that it was haemophilia.'

'The bleeding disease.'

'That's the one.'

She finished her drink over the small talk. He insisted on buying her another one.

Do I deserve another?

You bet! Weekends were hard in the hospitality trade: The world and his wife came away on weekend breaks, and the locals were out for wining and dining. Add that to the huge influx of tourists at this time of year, and you've got a punishing schedule.

'OK.'

It came to her suddenly that they were in competition with each other. He wanted all the glory in cracking this, and so did she. She hadn't thought she had before, not when the job had first been foisted on her. But now? Something was stirring. Unfortunately for *good ole Steve*, it wasn't passion that had coloured her decision to meet him, but curiosity, a driving need to find out exactly what was going on. That was the reason, she told herself, but still her eyes kept sliding sidelong. Steve Doherty was only average height but had a good body, strong rather than stocky.

She shook the thoughts from her head.

'Bubbles,' she explained on seeing Steve's quizzical expression. 'Are there any clues?'

'Minor things. A piece of wood jammed into the side of the deceased. The river's full of debris following heavy rain. But it was interesting. There was an indentation on it where a number used to be. Could have been a nine. Could have been a six.'

'Depending on whether you're Australian.' She smiled as she said it.

Doherty had a blond moment. He didn't have a clue – or perhaps just no sense of humour.

She took it slowly. 'Upside down. A six if you're upright and living in the northern hemisphere, and a nine if you're upside down, i.e. Australian.'

'Very funny.' He gave a weak laugh.

No sense of humour, she decided but then, on reflection, it wasn't a very good joke.

Doherty went straight into the facts. 'He had a sack over his head. Not a big sack. A small one. It had a smell. Not a nasty smell. A nice smell.' He said it as though only he knew its significance.

Honey nodded appreciatively as though she somehow knew the significance of such a thing. But why should she? A sack was a sack was a sack. And the smell? Hemp, surely?

She noticed how quickly he had spoken, giving away information that perhaps he shouldn't: anything to maintain her interest. He fell to silence. She sensed him looking at her. Decided it was her turn to speak.

'And he wasn't in the freezer?'

He shook his head. 'No. We checked. It was still there waiting to be degassed and whatever. It was empty.'

Just as she'd guessed, it wasn't long before he got on to personal things. 'So! I take it you're divorced.' He had a hopeful look in his eyes when he said it.'

She shook her head. 'No. He died in a sailing accident.'

'I'm sorry.'

I'm sorry. That's what everyone said. But she wasn't. Racing and delivering sailing yachts had taken precedence over her and Lindsey. The more impassioned he'd got with his sport, the less they'd seen of him. It didn't help that most of the crew he hired had been female.

'*They bond well and do all that I ask of them.*'

You bet they did!

The usual questions followed. 'Any children?'

'One. Lindsey. She's eighteen.'

'Get on! You don't look old enough.'

'Very kind, but I've heard it before.'

His tone softened. 'I meant it. Does she look like you?'

'No. She looks like her father.'

She knew he was making small talk and that he didn't really want to know what Lindsey looked like at all.

He nodded sagely, as though she had said something very profound.

She asked him about himself. He told her he was divorced – something she'd already guessed – and that he'd moved to Bath from London. 'To make a new start,' he added. 'Got fed up with the pressure of work in the Met.'

He told her he rented a flat in Lansdown Crescent, but was looking to buy when he could find something affordable.

She knew where he was coming from. Bath was expensive. Georgian houses of elegant proportions, and horrendously expensive to maintain, had long ago been divided into flats, their elegance undiminished, their interiors furnished in a suitable style with expensive antiques; nothing in a really good location came cheap.

She let him make the headway until she finally judged the time was right to make her excuses. Carefully avoiding a puddle of wetness, she gathered her navy-blue satchel from off the bar.

'I'm cooking breakfast in the morning.' It wasn't strictly true. Smudger never did breakfast if he could possibly avoid it. Dumpy Doris, a woman of dumpling roundness with arms a Sumo wrestler would have been proud of, cooked up a cardiologist's nightmare: fried sausages, fried eggs and fried bacon. It was sometimes joked about that even the cornflakes would be fried if Dumpy Doris had her way. Good help on a weekend was hard to come by.

He offered to walk her home.

'No,' she replied as Clint, his eyeballs bouncing between Doherty and her, opened the door.

'It's no trouble.'

'It's no distance.'

Doherty threw a backward glance at Clint before the door slammed shut. 'I know him.'

'Everyone knows Clint,' she said. She hid the ensuing grin as she began her ascent up the steps to the road. She didn't want to know what Clint did when he wasn't working; she didn't want to know what offences Doherty might have charged him with. She might never employ him again. Best let sleeping dogs lie. When they got to a certain age, automatic dishwashers were notoriously unreliable. Clint was not.

'Are you sure you'll be all right?' he said once they were up on pavement level.

'Fine.' She nodded vehemently. 'It's not far.'

'No,' he said, taking her arm. 'I insist.'

'Will you frogmarch me if I refuse?'

'Possibly. You know us cops: brutal, insistent – but cute.'

'Shouldn't you add conceited?'

'I can't see why.'

Bath didn't have the night smell of the big city – the stewed traffic fumes, dank river and heat rising like dust from concrete buildings. Set like Rome in a sweeping valley surrounded by tree-topped hills, its lawns and well-kept flower beds lent a springlike freshness to the air. The mellow walls of ancient buildings glowed in the borrowed gleam of well-placed lighting. Even at this hour the streets had a safe feeling about them, as though the ghosts of the past stood sentinel over those treading its cosy alleys and broad thoroughfares. Late-night revellers wending their merry way home raised a hand, called and waved goodnight.

Pulteney Street flew straight as a dart from the centre of the city to the Warminster Road. The Green River was close to the very end, tucked away down a cul-de-sac.

Doherty sniffed the air. "I love this place. There's something immortal about it. It looks beautiful even at this hour. It's sacrilege that we're talking murder.'

She agreed with him, but it occurred to her that he hadn't mentioned much about the murder tonight, though goodness, she was grateful for the details he had given.

'Almost there,' she added, her footsteps slowing. She stopped and faced him. 'Look. You don't need to come any further.' She smiled as she said it. No, she did not want him to see her to the door. The windows would be black, the minimum of light falling from the Reception area; everyone would – or should – be in bed. Not necessarily so. Like a lot of seniors, her mother was a light sleeper and had opted to stay overnight. Questions would be asked. She'd prefer them not to be.

She turned swiftly away before he had a chance to kiss her. She wasn't ready for it. Not yet. 'Goodnight.'

'Goodnight.'

He sounded disappointed, perhaps even hurt. She glanced

back to ensure he had indeed strolled off towards Lansdown Crescent and his bachelor pad. His form, his shadow and the sound of his footsteps faded into the night.

Walking on tiptoe was never going to be easy. The flagstones skirting the cul-de-sac were uneven and badly worn from centuries of use. Her steps slowed the closer she got to the hotel. At last, once she was sure he was gone, she stopped and turned round.

The night breeze was cool as water against her face when she looked for him. He was gone. Counting to ten, she waited, then slowly, still with her heels held barely off the ground, she retraced her steps. She heard a car and presumed he'd got a taxi. Certain she was right, she increased her speed, then paused as her fingers felt something in her pocket. Why was she bothering to walk to the taxi rank? Ivor Webber had given her his number.

Taking out the card, she held it to catch the gleam of a street light, took her phone from her pocket and dialled the number.

Ivor answered.

'How's the book going?' she asked.

'Too busy for reading at present, lovely. What can I do to help you?'

It was obvious by his response that he didn't recognize her voice.

'It's the hotel lady that was asking questions about Elmer Maxted. I suppose you've heard the news.'

'Yeah.' He sounded horrified. 'Poor bloke. Who would have thought it, eh?'

She counted off all the bits of information she'd come across. Was Bob the Job for real or was he as imagined as the ghost Mary Jane insisted came out of the closet? Was her information likely to be pure fabrication?

Here goes, she thought to herself.

'When you drove him around, did you ever take him to Limpley Stoke?'

'Sure. He wanted to visit the church. Took his time, of course. Wanted to meet the vicar, you see. Had things he wanted to ask, so he said.'

She breathed a sigh of relief. Her confidence returned. 'What sort of things?'

Ivor paused before his words began again in that very Welsh, sing-song way. 'Well, I can't say for sure, mind you, but it was something to do with family.'

'His family?'

'Yes.'

'And he stayed there quite a while?'

'Three days in a row.'

'Three days!'

She couldn't help sounding surprised. Why would anyone – even the most ardent sightseer or family historian, want to spend three days peering into old and very dusty archives? Surely he couldn't have spent all that time in the company of the vicar? Just in case she was wrong, she asked Ivor.

'He saw the vicar on the first day. I saw them talking. But not after that. He just went into the church and walked around the gravestones and all that. Took some time, that did. I waited until he came out and we went sightseeing. Not that he seemed that interested in the sightseeing. He was quiet when he came back. Doing a lot of thinking, you see. Finding out about your ancestors can be a bit daunting, you know.'

After thanking Ivor for his help she put her phone away and turned for home. So Mary Jane's friend was right. There was no mention that he'd actually visited Charlborough Grange and introduced himself to the family. According to Ivor, he'd gone no further than the church and its grounds. Would searching through the archives take three consecutive days?

That, she decided, was a question that had to be answered.

The hotel was in darkness. Loud snoring drifted out from the settee in the room just behind reception. The night porter was – almost – on duty.

She took off her shoes.

'No point trying to creep in, Mother.'

Lindsey's head bobbed up from where she was lying full stretch on a brown leather chesterfield.

Honey jumped. 'I wish you'd stop doing that.'

'Scaring you or waiting up for you?'

'Both.'

Honey eased herself on to the settee beside her daughter. 'Are you spying on me?'

'Yes. You're such a virgin when it comes to men.'

'Excuse me?'

'And don't remind me that I'm your daughter. I mean you haven't indulged for a while. That's why I've got to look out for you.'

'Lindsey, I've only been out for a drink.'

Lindsey reached over and made a lengthening motion from the tip of her mother's nose.

'OK, my nose is growing like Pinocchio's.'

Lindsey huddled forward, her face, even in the gloom, glowed with interest.

'So! Tell me what he's like.'

'Who?'

'The policeman. And don't try and look so innocent. Grandma was dusting in the dining room and overheard your conversation. She put two and two together.'

'There's nothing to it.'

Lindsey gave her that 'who do you think you're kidding' kind of look.

Honey held her head to one side and looked at her daughter. 'Are you always going to be looking out for me?'

Lindsey nodded.

'I thought so.'

Fifteen

She wasn't thinking of sacks; in fact she wasn't even thinking of the murder when she took a shortcut through the Guildhall. For the first time since becoming an amateur sleuth, the tension had left her shoulders. She was approaching her mission in a more relaxed manner. Her mind was open to possibilities. In fact it was like a great white board on which the problem was detailed in green felt-tip and all the connecting factors were entered around it.

The Guildhall market was a magical place where stalls dealing in antiques jostled with those selling a wide variety of cheese, garlic sausage and dried flower arrangements. She sniffed the air, enjoying the mix of fragrances and the way it cleared her head and her mind. Suddenly it was there – the unmistakable tang of oriental spices. She looked round in the hope that she might find the source of the smell, perhaps a suspect. Stupid, really. Was there likely to be a sign saying: 'Get your small sacks here: ideal for placing over the head of your victims'?

When she saw where the smell was coming from and the stallholder, she smiled. Jeremiah Poughton: the very same as who had taken over her Reception area on orders from Casper. She could tell by the look on his face that he wasn't missing the hospitality trade one little bit.

Cloves, cinnamon, bay leaves, turmeric and a host of other scents filled her head and cleared the excesses of the night before. There was a clichéd exoticism about them: a hint of the east, Persian markets, the Alhambra and overindulgence of the senses. It was all for sale under the sign printed in garish red letters on an apple-green background which screamed: 'HERBS AND SPICE AND ALL THINGS NICE'.

Jeremiah's stall; he waved before beaming a smile at a woman customer. She was giving him aggro.

'What's that one?' The woman's voice had all the enchantment of iron filings.

'Turmeric, honey.' Jeremiah settled one hand on his slim hips. They were tightly clad in tan suede trousers. He wore a matching waistcoat festooned with embroidered flowers all down the front over a peasant-style shirt.

'And that?' The woman poked her finger at another small sack and sniffed.

'Paprika, dahling.' He nodded a greeting to Honey. 'Looking for something exotic to spice up our life, are we?'

The woman did not appear to notice that he was talking to someone else. She pointed a podgy finger.

'Pretty colour. Got much taste?'

'Lots, honey.'

The woman frowned and shook her head. 'I'm not sure. I normally only buy such things when uncontaminated by human hand. Preferably in plastic bags and on a supermarket shelf. Are your hands very clean?' asked the woman, her small eyes narrowing in her pudding face.

Jeremiah threw her an indignant look. 'If you want something in plastic, go trot along to the supermarket.'

Jeremiah was committed to all things green, and free trade and free love and everything else that didn't come prepackaged and with a hefty price. His tone was dead-end and don't pass Go.

The woman took on a shocked expression, wrapped her sheepskin coat more tightly around her body, then shuffled off to the next stall.

Jeremiah recovered quickly. 'Win some, you lose some. Oh, well. There's great demand for what I sell.'

As stalls went Jeremiah Poughton didn't have a bad one. It was a well-stuffed pitch – wooden shelves at the back filled with sacks of vibrant-coloured powders, beans, nuts and other items she didn't recognize. Bunches of herbs, thyme, parsley, fennel and sage hung in bunches overhead. Some stuffed in between looked questionable.

'Jeremy, can I ask you something?'

His eyelids fluttered nervously. 'Sure. But if it's a date, I'm not your type.'

She smiled. 'No, and I'm not yours.' She looked over his stall and upwards at the sign, face spiked with amusement. 'Nice little spot, Jeremiah. Herbs and Spice and All Things Nice.'

Suddenly Jeremiah was all smiles and floating hands. 'Spice adds a little colour to your cooking – you should try some.' The words came rat-a-tat-tat out of his mouth. 'It's mine and Ade's.' He nodded towards his partner, who was wearing a green T-shirt, matching silk scarf and trousers too tight for decency. *Like an unripe banana,* thought Honey.

He smiled briefly by virtue of the fact that he was bagging up half a pound of dried beans for a crusty with three rings in his nose and the usual uniform of ragged parka jacket, half shaved head and half-starved dog.

'I will. But not today.' Honey dug her thumbs into the waistband of her jeans.

'On the house.'

Honey grinned. 'Can I put this in my mother's curry?'

'What you do to your mother is your affair. It's a free sample – we give it to other customers too.'

She eyed him quizzically. 'Just how highly spiced is it?'

Honey took the brown paper bag and slid it into her bag.

'Go on,' he said. 'What do you want to ask me?'

She didn't question how he'd guessed she wanted to ask him a question. Never look a gift horse in the mouth.

'About these sacks . . .'

The necks of the sacks containing the spices were rolled over, revealing the brightly coloured contents. Honey fingered them thoughtfully.

'They're just sacks,' said Jeremiah with a nonchalant shrug. She noticed his eyes slide sidelong to his partner.

'One of them was found covering the head of the man they dragged from the weir the other day.'

Jeremiah jumped and grew taller. He wasn't smiling anymore. 'He was murdered?'

'He was.'

'How terrible! Poor man! Suffocated with spices and hit over the head with a blunt instrument.'

She wasn't sure either by his expression or tone of voice whether he was being facetious or strangely enraptured. She didn't know him well enough to judge but felt obliged to burst his bubble.

'You know I'm Crime Liaison Officer for the Hotels Association, don't you?'

She hadn't been given a formal title, but the handle seemed close enough.

He looked at her askance.

She took advantage of his off guard moment. 'He was killed three days ago. Saturday night sometime.'

'Dreadful.'

'Where were you last Saturday?'

His features froze for a moment. Then he laughed nervously. 'You're just joking. You can't really ask me questions. You're not a policeman, dahling.'

She raised one questioning eyebrow. 'A sack smelling of spices? You've got loads of them here.' She spread her hands, indicating tier upon tier of small, filled bags. 'A friend of mine who *is* a police detective would be interested in hearing that.'

'You wouldn't!'

She nodded. 'I would.'

He glanced nervously towards his partner, then back at Honey. His eyelashes fluttered. As he leaned closer, the smell of his perfume obliterated that of the spices. 'I was out two-timing my boyfriend,' he said softly. 'You won't say anything, will you?'

Honey fixed her eyes on Jeremiah's partner who was still serving. 'Who were you with?'

His tongue swept along his bottom lip. 'I really couldn't . . .'

'Perhaps I should ask your friend.' She made a sideways move. Jeremiah followed her like a mirror image.

'No! There's no need to.' He glanced over his shoulder.

Ade was now talking with the young man from the coffee stall.

'Andrew Charlborough – I was with him.' The name came out in a rush of breath.

Honey frowned. She wasn't often amazed at what people with status and money got up to in their spare time. She'd seen Andrew Charlborough at a number of auctions and he'd seemed the sort of citizen that was in bed by eleven with a good book and a long-lasting wife.

'You mean the antiques dealer?'

Jeremiah nodded. 'And before you jump to conclusions about the man, I was invited to give a quote for some plants he wanted. A bloke who works for him and sometimes delivers for us asked if I'd be interested. He introduced us, said he was interested in very big tropical plants.'

'So why wouldn't you want your partner to know?'

Jeremiah chewed at his lip. 'I kept the deal to myself. And the money. Of course.'

Honey's mind was already darting elsewhere. It kept coming back to her that Elmer's head had been covered with a small sack smelling of spices. 'So what happens to the sacks once they're empty?'

Jeremiah shrugged. 'Mostly I give them away. Or chuck them. Some people buy by the sack – the big customers that is.'

She eyed him speculatively.

He wasn't long interpreting her look.

'I have not got a killing bone in my body!'

She shook her head. You couldn't detect a murderer just by the looks of him. Just because he denied the fact didn't mean anything either. She'd hedge her bets.

'Can you provide me with a list of regular customers – the bigger buyers?'

Jeremiah shrugged his narrow shoulders. 'There's only a few. Shipping orders ain't our style. Half a pound here, a pound there. That's what I call big, honey.'

Honey kept her gaze fixed on Jeremiah's face. 'Please. It would be a great help.'

Recognizing he had to put himself out, Jeremiah sighed and nodded. 'I'll do what I can.'

Sixteen

The next morning, before doing anything else, she phoned Doherty.

'Any developments?'

'No.'

To say he was not forthcoming was putting it mildly. Well two could play at that game. 'OK. So I won't tell you what I know. See you.'

'Hang on there!'

She smiled. *I won't show you mine unless you show me yours*.

'We're tracing his movements. We've spoken to the taxi driver who ferried him around.'

'I guessed you would. I hear Elmer was interested in the Charlborough family. Do you know them?'

'I've heard of them. What's the connection?'

'I think they figure somewhere in his family tree. It's possible that's why Elmer went to the church. He was checking out the parish register.'

'Stop right there. That line of enquiry is a dead end. Elmer was taken there and back by the taxi driver. It's not a case that he went missing in the grounds or thereabouts. We found him in the river, which means he must have been killed somewhere in the city. Mrs Herbert did say he went sight-seeing there and on the night he disappeared, he went out quite late.'

He had a point.

'So there you are,' he crowed. 'That's the way it was. We have a witness who overheard Elmer arguing with Mervyn Herbert. She also gave us a very good description of his car.'

'So Mervyn Herbert is the chief suspect. You're still looking for him?'

'Ah! Yes.'

He asked her out. She said she'd take a rain check. It wasn't that she wasn't attracted to him; she was. It was nerves. Plain and simple.

As if there wasn't enough to do in running the hotel, her mother had stopped over and was hounding her about having carpet laid over a truly lovely stone floor. 'Look, Allied Carpets are doing a great deal . . .'

'Mother!'

She was in the middle of checking the new menus – Smudger liked to change them every three months – and having her mother breathing fire over her shoulder did nothing to help her concentration.

Lindsey saved her bacon.

'That nice bookseller is here to see you again,' she said as she flounced past, a litre of Gordon's gin in one hand and a bottle of Glenfiddich in the other.

Honey stopped what she was doing. 'Is he?'

'No,' she said, shaking her head. 'I couldn't.'

Lindsey's footsteps went into reverse. 'Two guys are better than one.'

'Lindsey!' She tried to look shocked.

Her daughter nudged her elbow. 'Even if you dump both, play around a bit first. It'll make you feel good about yourself.'

Honey's jaw dropped.

Lindsey made a clicking sound, gave her customary wink and resumed her trek to replenish the bar.

The menus were shoved into a folder until later.

'Lead me to him. Mother, this is the sort of man you should have found for me.'

Her mother frowned. 'A bookseller? Do you think I would introduce you to a bookseller? You know there's no money in selling books. It's a mug's game. Besides, he's American.'

Honey's mouth dropped. 'Dad was an American.'

Her mother made one of those sounds a senior citizen

makes when they've been caught out and is reluctant to face the consequences.

Mary Jane waylaid her on her way to greet John Rees. 'I need to make arrangements to hold a séance,' she said. 'Do you know of anyone whose loved ones have passed over who might be interested in attending?'

Honey turned round just in time to see her mother beating a fast pace across reception. 'Mother! Mary Jane would like a word with you.'

Her mother came to a giddy halt. It wasn't often she got trapped into doing something she didn't want to do. She was usually the trapper.

Mary Jane's lucid voice rang across Reception. 'Gloria, my dear . . .'

Honey exchanged a secretive smile with her daughter who had just emerged from the bar.

Lindsey shook her head. 'Granny won't be pleased.'

'Never mind. It'll keep her occupied for an hour. Now, where have you put my visitor?'

'Prince Charming awaits you in the lounge with a cup of coffee,' said Lindsey, then smiled as Honey unconsciously tidied her hair as she passed an ornate French mirror.

'I wonder, is he really Prince Charming or a frog in disguise?'

'You won't find out until you kiss him.'

Nothing was going to stand in the way of her plan to drive out to the church at Limpley Stoke once she'd phoned the vicar and made an appointment. John Rees had delayed her plans, but even a girl pushing forty has to have fun.

His hair was sandy, his face slim and warm hazel eyes danced with humour behind frameless spectacles. He removed them when she entered and stood to greet her. It was old-fashioned and oddly touching. She half-expected to look down and see that her sensible skirt had turned into a crinoline.

'Mr Rees. I'm so sorry I missed speaking to you when you last called. There was a misunderstanding. I thought your being here was my mother's doing.'

One side of his face seemed to rise in amusement, his

eyes twinkling as though he'd read her mother just like – well, a book.

Standing in front of him like this made her nervous. She rubbed her hands down over her hips and offered to pour another coffee.

'No. Thank you,' he said.

Making the effort to sound the professional hotelier, she tucked her skirt beneath her as they both sat back down. 'So! What can I do for you?'

'I want to hold a book fair.'

The Green River had a very handsome conference room overlooking the park at the rear. Conferences and wedding fairs brought in good revenue. Why not a book fair?

'I think we have exactly what you are looking for. Our conference room holds sixty people—'

'No,' he said. He raised his hand, his palm facing her like a halt sign. 'You misunderstand. I'm holding a book fair at the shop. I run themed evenings complete with wine and cheese and whatever – and sometimes the books are about wine and cheese. I pick a theme, you see, select the books covering that particular subject, and objects featured in those books. For instance, I've done a modern art theme. The books were on modern art – the wine and cheese were the same – but I asked local artists to lend me their paintings for the evening – price tags included.'

Honey wasn't quite sure where this was going, but hazarded a guess. 'You're going to use hotels as a theme? Haute cuisine, perhaps?'

The inclusion of the latter sent a shiver down her spine. What if the epicureans attending were mean with their praise and slated whatever dishes the Green River produced? Smudger didn't take criticism. He got huffy very easily and it was her that had to contend with his moods.

'I favour a Victorian theme for my next event and that, of course, will include the clothes of the era. Not the big crinolines and stuff like that – I don't have the room – but smaller things; gloves, mittens, hats . . .'

'Underwear?' said Honey as the Queen's voluminous undergarments, already displayed behind glass, came to mind.

'Exactly,' he said. 'I heard you were a collector, so if I could borrow a few things. Just enough to set the scene. And then I'll select the books to go with it.'

Honey nodded. The fact that she wasn't going to earn anything out of his fair wasn't important. But something else was.

'Am I invited?'

He smiled. 'Would you come?'

She smiled back. 'Of course I will.'

Seventeen

Casper St John Gervais enjoyed the good things in life. He took pride in running a superbly furnished and well-managed hotel. He adored cashmere sweaters, tailormade jackets and trousers, and nothing could compete with a pure cotton shirt made by a skilled Indian gentleman in Savile Row, London.

His exquisite taste extended to his surroundings. His hotel had graced inflight brochures, *Hidden Hotels of the World* magazine, and was frequented by the rich and famous, confident they would receive excellent service and absolute discretion.

He didn't live there himself. He lived in a beautiful house, one of the impressive thirty-three that made up The Circus, that ring of mathematically produced elegance from the fevered brain of John Wood.

As with many Georgian houses, the ceilings were high and the windows large. The Georgians had excelled in letting in as much light as possible in the days before Edison lit up and invented the electricity bill.

The paintwork was finished in traditional colours; the furniture was even more elegant than in his hotel. Gilded mirrors reflected the star bright quality of the chandeliers, prisms of light flashing outwards. Thick Turkish rugs hushed his footsteps. The only other sound, besides the beating of Casper's heart, was the incessant ticking of his clocks. He had more in his home than at his hotel.

He was sitting admiring his latest purchase when the front-door bell rang. Sighing, he put his single malt on to a silver coaster to avoid marking the small piecrust table near his chair, then unlocked and walked along the passage to the front door. He opened it to find Simon Tye standing there.

'Did you smell the cork out of the whisky bottle?' he said casually.

'If you're offering, I'm accepting,' said Simon and, without being asked, swept past him, striding through the hallway purposefully as though bad news had come with him.

Simon was oddly quiet as Casper poured.

'Enough?' he asked, raising the glass so Simon could inspect its contents.

Simon's eyes were fixed on the porcelain clock, his brows furrowed as if he could see some flaw in it that he had not seen before.

'Don't say the woman who sold you it wants it back,' said Casper as he handed him the drink.

'No,' said Simon. 'But her husband does.'

Casper raised his eyebrows quizzically.

'It appears she never had permission to sell it.' Simon clutched his glass with both hands and looked totally embarrassed. 'I'm sorry, mate, but Charlborough wants it back.'

Casper was all attention. 'Charlborough? Do you mean who I think you mean?'

Simon nodded. 'Yes, the same bloke who bid against you for the Chepstow long-case up at Marlborough in the summer.'

Casper took a slug of whisky. So did Simon.

'He reckons he's goin' to sue if he don't get it back.'

Casper caught the caginess in the sidelong expression Simon threw him.

'I told him I sold it to you.'

Casper groaned as he slouched back in his chair.

Simon nodded. 'Sorry, mate.' He began to dig in his pocket. 'There's your money.'

Casper eyed the bundle of fifties Simon placed on the table. They looked grubby and therefore beneath his fastidious ideas of cleanliness. He would get Neville to gather them up or use the pink washing-up gloves kept in the kitchen drawer.

'I'll take it now, if you like, though you'll have to help me.'

'I don't do lifting,' said Casper with a shrewish pout and gazed blankly into space. The thought of letting the clock go too quickly gave him great pain. Perhaps he could persuade Charlborough to let him keep it – offer him more, double what he'd paid Simon Tye. It was certainly worth a try.

Simon shook his head. 'No,' he said resolutely. 'It has to go back.'

Casper sighed and although there was still plenty in his glass, he set it dumbly down on the table.

'You can count on me to make arrangements.'

His second visitor that night helped the situation along.

'I've come to make my report,' she said, breezing in more joyfully than Simon Tye had done.

She told him what the taxi driver had told her.

'Couldn't you get in trouble for withholding information from the police?'

Honey shrugged. 'Sergeant Doherty has his own theories. He's adamant that the victim was murdered close to the river. I must admit, he does have a point.'

'He's trying to hit on you?'

'Something like that: anyway I thought I'd go along and ask the vicar what our American friend had found out about his family tree.'

She looked surprised when Casper stated he would go with her. He looked quite down about it.

'Two birds with one stone, my dear girl. We both have quests to perform.'

Eighteen

The Warminster Road winds up a hill out of Bath, passing substantial Victorian villas with far-reaching views over the meadows dipping down into the Avon valley. Like a blueprint from history, a canal and a railway line run alongside the river. Together they span the centuries. Further out the villas are replaced by modern detached houses, and further out still the sunlight twinkles through battalions of trees standing sentinel at the roadside.

The road to Trowbridge branches off to the left, under a railway arch and into the village of Limpley Stoke. Some way up the hill, in the older part of the village, the church nestles amongst houses of its own age, built in the years of the Stuart kings.

Casper insisted they first return the clock before she made her enquiries of the vicar. He'd phoned Charlborough and offered more money, but had been refused. His mood was sullen and it was a fairly silent drive.

It was no trouble for Honey to alter her prior appointment. As she drove, she rehearsed mentally the questions she thought relevant.

Casper was a picture of sullen resentment. He was brooding on the fact that he had to travel at all. That woman! That bloody Charlborough woman had upset his equanimity. He wished her ill. No, he thought changing his mind. He wished her dead.

Pamela Charlborough had come back from Spain under duress and she was dead pissy about it.

If her husband Andrew hadn't discovered she'd sold the clock, she would have been back out there now, lunching in one of the smaller but more select quayside restaurants in Puerto Buenos, rubbing shoulders with the owners of luxury yachts. As it was, her personal bank account was sadly lacking, so she was here in England and bored stiff.

'I needed that money. You're such a skinflint.' Her comment and request for more money had been ignored. 'You care more for that clock than you do for me.'

Annoyingly he'd agreed with her.

She paced the conservatory, which was an old and elegant structure erected by some Victorian antecedent of her husband Andrew. The man should have been named Midas but was more formally named Reginald. He'd spared no expense on this particular monstrosity. The place was filled with a wide variety of tropical plants from all over the world. It was lush, almost beautiful, but there was a wild carelessness about it. The plants were huge, thick-leaved affairs. Rather than the place being somewhere pleasant to sit surrounded by dotted palms, it was the chairs that were dotted and the foliage that was overabundant.

There were two views from the conservatory. To the rear were massive greenhouses full of even larger tropical plants. Huge leaves pressed against the glass as if trying to escape from the dank humidity that prevailed inside. She'd gone in there once. Once was enough.

From the other end of the conservatory she could look over the drive and the wide steps that led up on to the parapet to the front door. She sighed. The drive was empty and she was lonely. Oh for a bit of red-blooded company.

She took a red leather address book from her handbag, opened it and ran her finger down the letters of the alphabet, stopping at the letter 'P'. With one well-manicured fingertip, she flicked the book open at that page and smiled at the entry. She kept the book open, picked up her phone and dialled. It rang for a while then was answered. The sound of his voice made her go weak at the knees.

'Well hello,' she purred. 'And how is my favourite little pussycat? Due for some well-earned leave yet? Spain is still very warm, you know.'

The response on the other end of the line was negative.

Her smile stiffened. Expensive heels of exquisite shoes dug into the tiled floor and her smile faded.

'You haven't got time? For me you should make time.' She gritted her teeth and her lips felt stretched and dry. 'Don't worry about it, darling. After all, you're just a number on my list – just as I am on yours. One of my older numbers, of course. *Adios, amigo*!'

She snapped the phone shut then flung it as far as she could.

'Damn you!' It bounced off the back wall and disappeared into the greenery. The sound of car tyres crunching on gravel made her look towards the drive.

Nineteen

'I smell money,' said Honey.

Her eyes took in the fudge-coloured stone, the leaded windows set into stalwart mullions. Elizabethan?

'Old money,' corrected Casper, suddenly breaking his silence. 'Enough of it to allow Sir Andrew to do more or less what he wanted in life. Started off conservatively enough: Eton, Cambridge, followed by the army, followed by some acting and then the writing of his memoirs.'

'About his time wearing tights?' asked Honey with a grin.

'Don't be facetious!' He sighed. He ducked slightly so that his gaze could sweep unimpeded over the elegant façade. 'Apparently the place was in danger of falling down back in the nineteen-fifties. Annoyingly gorgeous now!'

Honey noticed that Casper kept his eyes averted from the clock draped like a beautiful woman on the back seat. Her car, of course. He'd made perfectly relevant excuses as to why they couldn't use his.

'Darling, mine's a two-seater. Isn't yours one of those people-carrier contraptions?'

She'd gritted her teeth. No. It wasn't, but a two-seater was no contest. Of course they'd have to use her car.

Casper slammed the car door as if banning the timepiece from his mind. Looking distinctly unhappy, he clumped up the mossy steps to the next level of gravel. Italian terra cotta pots lined each tread and terraces. Each contained a froth of straggling lobelia, nasturtiums and variegated ivy.

The front door opened as if by magic. Andrew Charlborough had white hair and strong features. The ruddiness of his complexion was typical of a man who'd served in the army, climbed mountains and tramped through the jungles of Borneo. Not too good on an actor, perhaps, but his bone structure was good.

He wore a powder-blue sweater and matching trousers. A crisp white shirt collar emphasized the colour of his complexion. He glanced swiftly at his wrist. The gold strap of a very expensive wristwatch glistened.

'You're late.'

He addressed Casper, turning away once the words had been snapped.

Unfazed, Casper replied. 'Do accept my apologies, old boy, but due to circumstances beyond our control.'

'The traffic was heavy,' added Honey, suddenly irritated by Casper's flowery words.

Charlborough barely glanced at her. Again he addressed Casper. 'Have you brought it with you?'

'Yes indeed, though the thought of returning such a wondrous object weighs heavy on my heart.'

It sounded like Shakespeare, but wasn't. Honey raised her eyes heavenwards. Casper was doing everything to impress.

Charlborough was unmoved. 'Bring it in here.' He turned away. Casper looked as though he was about to blow a gasket.

'I do not hump!' he said, both hands resting on his silver-topped walking stick.

Honey looked down at her shoes in an effort to hide her grin. Did Casper realize what he'd just said?

'My butler and his wife are off today,' said Charlborough, his expression unaltered. I'll see if the gardener and someone else can give a hand. Perhaps you'd like some coffee whilst I arrange things?'

Casper grabbed the chance to have a nose round – just as Honey had known he would. One more chance to ogle his beloved clock.

They stepped into a hall where the walls were lined with heavy oak panelling and the floor thick with the rich colours of ancient oriental rugs. There was a dark-green tapestry along one wall where a hunter sat on a pale horse, his dogs and retainers around him. A falcon perched on his wrist. Against the tapestry and set on a long Jacobean table with barley-twist legs was a display of eighteenth-century silver. It was an incredible collection, handed down, Honey guessed, rather than purchased. Above a stone mantelpiece sat a skeleton clock, its workings suitably protected beneath a dome of Victorian glass.

'Such exquisite items,' breathed Casper, his eyes shining with delight. 'Absolutely exquisite.'

All the clocks stated it was two thirty-five. Honey checked her watch. They were quite correct.

Casper gave it one last try. 'I came here to see if we could not come to some understanding. I'm willing to offer more than your wife was paid for the clock.'

Charlborough paused and eyed him as though he were considering the depth of Casper's pockets.

Pretty deep, thought Honey. *La Reine Rouge* must be worth in excess of four million, plus the house of course, one of the few in The Circus that had not been converted into luxury apartments. Even so, compared to Charlborough Grange it was peanuts.

'Haven't I seen you at Sothebys?' Andrew Charlborough directed his question at Casper.

Casper visibly grimaced. 'We've bid against each other on a number of occasions.'

'I'll ring for refreshments,' said Charlborough.

Honey asked if she could use the bathroom.

Charlborough indicated a corridor of panelled wood and more tapestries running off the main hall.

'Take that passage, turn right, then left at the end. It's on the right.'

She cursed the elderflower concoction her mother had foisted on her at lunch time.

'The ginseng will put a spring in your step,' her mother had told her.

It hadn't done, unless you counted having to move smartly in the direction of the nearest loo!

She heard Charlborough tell Casper that they would talk in the study.

After ogling and using the delft-tiled bathroom, it was time to play hunt the study. *It has to be off the reception hall*, she told herself and began trying a few doorknobs. Some were locked.

'Can I help you?'

She started. The thick carpets had smothered the sound of his footfall. He looked pleasant enough, was around thirty and carrying a tea tray.

She smiled. 'I'm looking for the study.'

'Follow me. Andrew asked me to bring you tea.'

She wondered at his familiarity, calling Sir Andrew by his first name. 'Are you a member of the family?'

'I've been here for some time,' he said, which didn't really answer anything. 'I suppose you could say I was. But I get paid for being here.'

His smile was disarming.

'In here.' He indicated a door.

She opened it.

The study was as impressive as the rest of the house. Rich spines of old books lined packed shelves; there was a white-marble fireplace of a later age than the house and an overmantel above it of later age still. The clock was of black marble, round and nestled on a mock carriage of ormolu and decorated each side with fat-bottomed puttees.

Bunches of carved grapes wound in fertile splendour up and around the huge mirror forming the backpiece of the mantelpiece. Honey mentally assessed its height at around eight feet and it was about the same across.

There were a few pictures on the wall – black-and-white snaps and one or two colour ones: family shots, a wife, a child. And, later, just a young man, the child grown up, perhaps? But no wife. No woman at all.

Sir Andrew did not acknowledge the young man who'd brought the tea.

'Would you like to pour?'

Honey realized he was directing the question at her. 'Um. Yes.'

For a brief moment his eyes met those of Sir Andrew. Then he was gone.

Honey did the honours. It occurred to her that the relationship between Sir Andrew and the young man was not servant–master.

'The young man says he's been here quite a long time.'

'Mark? Yes. I suppose he has. Now. Shall we get down to business?'

Charlborough went to where three decanters sat on a silver tray. He began to pour himself a drink. He didn't offer them one. Casper and Honey exchanged contemptuous looks. Tea for them, brandy for him.

They exchanged looks. *The class system is alive and kicking.*

'I admit to being disappointed,' said Casper as Andrew Charlborough seated himself behind a desk that was almost big enough to be a dinner table.

'I apologize,' said Charlborough. 'My wife had no business selling the clock.'

'But would you reconsider . . . ?

Casper's wheedling tone surprised her. She'd never known him wheedle to anyone.

There was an awkward silence during which she allowed her gaze to drift. She got up and paced the perimeter of the room.

'Had quite a career in the army, sir.' She nodded at another line of photographs that covered a good footage of panelling. They were black-and-white, unmistakably in foreign parts and full of smiling soldierly faces. Most of those pictured looked boyish. Charlborough, whom she just about recognized, looked more head-boyish and a touch superior.

'Indeed yes. Great days. Great boys.' Charlborough's jowls drooped with nostalgic sadness. He was on his second glass from the decanter. No further mention had been made of refreshments. And there would be none. The man was a self-centred moron.

'Do you know Jeremiah Poughton.' She adopted her sweetest voice. 'West Indian parents, born in Gloucester, now runs a spice stall in the Guildhall Market.'

'I've never heard of the man.'

'He deals in spices and plants. You invited him here to talk about plants, I think.'

He shrugged. 'Perhaps I did. I don't recall the name.'

You might recall what he looked like. He's very . . .' She paused for the right word. There was only one. '. . . colourful! – wears interesting clothes. A bit of a peacock, you could say.'

Charlborough remained as cool as his powder-blue sweater. 'Oh yes. The plants. I don't handle the domestic side of running this place. Anyway, what's that got to do with my clock?'

'Nothing really, except that the sacks . . .'

Uneasy with the line of questioning, Casper got to his feet. 'Look, I'm sorry about this; we really have taken up too much of your time, but if you should ever reconsider—'

'The clock is not for sale – at any price! And now . . .' The glass was slapped down.

Honey recognized the sign for goodbye. Sir Andrew had had enough.

He pressed a buzzer fixed to his desk. 'Mark will show you out.'

The young man who'd brought the tea quickly appeared. Honey wondered if he'd been listening at the door. He didn't look that sort. Still, you could never tell.

Casper pouted all the way down the steps to the car. As he walked, he swung his silver-topped walking cane.

'Watch out,' said Honey, ducking to one side. 'You look as though you're going to bash someone with it.'

'That man! Why couldn't he indulge his wife a little, let her sell the clock and spend the money at will? I could swear, I really could!'

He slumped in the front seat and slammed the door.

Honey got behind the driving wheel and turned the key. 'Don't do that, Casper. We're off to see the vicar next.'

Twenty

A downcast Casper opted to stay in the car.

'Walk it off,' Honey said to him.

He glowered.

She persisted. 'A bit of fresh air will do you good.'

'I don't want to be done good! I want that clock!'

'Children,' she breathed quietly and headed for the arched and ancient entrance to the parish church.

The interior was very dim by virtue of its narrow Saxon windows. The walls were whitewashed but looked ice-blue in the light diffusing through stained glass.

A woman arranging flowers told her where she could find the vicar. 'Through the chancel and down the steps to the crypt.' She pointed a skeletal finger tipped with bright-pink nail varnish. 'He's got an archive down there.'

Apart from her painted fingernails, the woman seemed a sensible sort. She wore a flowered dress and lace-up shoes. Her eyes darted about as swiftly as her nimble fingers. She looked Honey up and down in the same way as her mother.

'You could do with wearing something warmer. Cold as death it is down them steps – though only to be expected, I suppose. It's only a skip and a spit from the crypt.'

Charming. What better way to spend a warm summer day?

'Don't worry. I'm quite resilient.'

Stone steps led down into the chancel; cold air met her at the bottom and she shivered.

The Reverend Reece Mellors was bending over what could only be a parish register. It was huge, big enough to make a tabletop – a coffee table at least.

'Reverend Mellors?'

He looked up.

She beamed warmly. 'I'm Hannah Driver. I rang you.'

'Well, good afternoon!'

His voice ricocheted off the cold walls and coffins. His hand swallowed hers. She'd expected a pasty-faced vicar with horn-rimmed spectacles and a vague look in his eyes. Instead she was confronted with a tall man who had to stoop beneath the vaulted roof. Black was the best way to describe him: black hair, black eyes, black bushy eyebrows, and dressed in black. The blackness contrasted eerily with his pale complexion. Like Count Dracula, she thought, and found her gaze fixing on his mouth when he spoke. No sign of fangs.

'I spoke to you about an American tourist, a Mr Elmer Weinstock, though he may have used the name Maxted.'

The vicar's smile lifted his saturnine features. 'Ah yes. Interesting chap. Couldn't quite get out of the habit of using a pseudonym, I think. He told me both names and that he had his reasons. He also swore me to secrecy as to his real name. I had no problem with that. In my opinion I think he liked the excitement of having two names. I can't think of any other reason for him doing so.'

Well, this was something. Perhaps after all there was no secret to him using two names. It was just the habit of a detective's profession.

'Were you of any help?'

'Oh, I think so, although he had done quite a bit of groundwork himself.'

'I wouldn't have thought either of those names would be very common around Bath.'

'They're not. He wasn't tracing his own kin. He was tracing his wife's, and even then only by marriage. His wife's cousin married Sir Andrew Charlborough in this very church.'

'Is that so?' Now this was interesting.

'That is so.' His finger traced a relatively late entry in the parish register.

'She died about twenty years ago.'

Honey recalled the photographs: black-and-white of Charlborough and his lady and a child, then a later one of a young man, the child grown into manhood.

'And the son? Is his name and birth date listed?'

The Reverend Mellors slammed the book shut. 'Not in this one.' He reached for another hard-covered book. 'His baptism would be in here.'

She watched as he rustled through the pages.

'Ah! Here it is. Lance Charlborough was baptized eighteen years ago.'

Honey's thoughts returned to the photographs of the handsome young man. Some had been fairly recent. And his mother had died twenty years ago. She was just about to point this out, but Mellors beat her to it.

'Not his birth date, you understand,' said the vicar having noted the expression on her face. 'That would be in that book,' he said, patting the former epic tome he'd been perusing.

'Aren't baptisms or christenings usually done within a few weeks or months of birth?' she asked him.

He pursed his wide, sensuous mouth when he nodded. 'Usually. There must have been some reason – perhaps that they were abroad at the time. Sir Andrew did serve in the army, I believe.'

'Did Elmer have children?'

'No. I did ask him, you know, out of interest, as one does in the course of a conversation. He said something about his wife having had an inherited disease, so they'd chosen not to. Apparently she died some time ago. He's alone now.'

It was on her tongue to ask him to look up Lance Charlborough's birth date, when the woman who'd been arranging the flowers called down the stairs.

'There's a phone call for you vicar. I took it in the study.'

'I'll be right there.' He grinned ruefully. 'Sorry about this. I quite often put my phone on 'divert' so I can take it on my mobile, but Mrs Quentin puts her trust in God, not modern technology. She picks up the receiver within the first three rings.' He sighed. 'Oh well. Sorry about this.'

'Never mind.'

'I'll look it up for you and give you a call. Shouldn't take too long. Is that all right with you?'

'Of course.'

Mrs Quentin, the swift-moving flower arranger, escorted her down the aisle to the church door – a bit like a wedding in reverse.

'The vicar's a bit lax when it comes to security,' she said in rushed tones as though impatient to get back to her flowers. 'But I like to make sure that anyone who comes visiting is properly shown off the premises.'

Honey knew all right. Women like Mrs Quentin didn't need a computer-based diary when it came to recalling who had visited, where they'd come from and what their intentions were. The naturally nosy had a ten-megabite memory installed at birth.

Honey asked the obvious question. 'Do you recall an American who came checking out his family tree?'

Mrs Quentin nodded. 'Mr Maxted. He came here three days on the trot, poring over the old registers and asking questions. He snooped around a lot. I caught him behind the church. That was when I realized he wasn't just interested in his family tree,' she said, her voice falling into a disdainful hush. '*She* was there. I saw her out back on t'other side of the fence. Hussy, she is. Lady Charlborough indeed. No lady she! The first Lady Charlborough – now she was a lady. But that one . . .!'

A woman! Was Elmer having an affair?

'Did you happen to overhear what they were talking about?'

The red lips pouted with disdain. 'Certainly not! I am not in the habit of listening in on private conversations!'

Honey mumbled an apology.

'Besides, they were talking normally, not like that man who came along after him that day. Scruffy looking individual he was. Perhaps that's unfair. Not so much scruffy as pallid and bland. And loud. Twas no wonder they didn't come to blows. The American were none too happy with him I can tell you.'

The sun warmed the coldness of the crypt from her back, but a fresh chill ran down her spine. The description was familiar. Dare she ask?

So! This was Steve Doherty's witness. 'You didn't catch a name, did you?'

Mrs Quentin shook her head. 'No. But I saw his car.'

Honey contained her excitement. 'You don't happen to remember what make or colour of car?'

The powdered cheeks puckered into a knowing smile. 'I does indeed! One of them cars that keeps the lights on all day. And it was dark blue. And an estate. Let's see, it begins with a "V" . . .'

'A Volvo?'

'V for Volvo. That's the one!'

Honey resisted the urge to skip all the way back to her waiting car.

'Home,' muttered Casper, who was lying back in his seat, his hat pulled down over his eyes.

'Not yet,' said Honey, hardly able to control her excitement. I think our American might have been having an affair with Charlborough's wife.'

Casper peered out from beneath the brim as she swung the car away from the kerb. 'Steady on old girl.' Accelerator stabbed to the floor, they were off down the road heading back to Charlborough Hall.

'I declare I am totally wearied by all this detective work,' muttered Casper. 'I only asked you to liaise with the police, not run the case.'

'I never do things by halves, Casper.'

He waved a hand in surrender. 'Please yourself. But don't expect me to go back into his superior presence. He is not the type I would wish to include even on my 'B' list of acquaintances.'

Now that was a turn-up for the book!

'Never mind him. Now listen to this, Casper. According to the vicar, Elmer was Sir Andrew's brother-in-law by marriage, but not the present marriage – the first marriage.'

'You're suspecting familial skulduggery,' he said profoundly. 'Or might I suggest, that you hope it is.'

'Do I sound as though I do?'

'Yes. Like a bulldog. You have sunk your teeth into this bone and you're not letting it go.'

'One of the women who does the flowers in the church heard Elmer having an argument. Guess who with?'

'Go on. Tell me,' Casper said wearily, the brim c
bouncing on his nose.

'Mervyn Herbert!'

'Ah! We have our murderer.'

'We would if we knew where he was.'

Swinging the car down the drive, she targeted the gap between the stone pillars on either side of the entrance.

'He also met Pamela Charlborough at the church.'

'Just the church?' asked Casper in that sharp, sudden way of his.

'Just the church,' she replied grimly. 'Ivor said he was there for hours three days on the trot.'

'Pretty church,' said Casper. 'I took a walk all around it's perimeter.'

Honey remembered thinking the interior was a bit gloomy. 'It was dingy inside.'

'As I said, my dear, I walked around the perimeter. There's a very neat graveyard surrounded by ivy-covered walls and laurel hedges.'

'How very poetic.'

'There's also a stile and no more than two fields between it and Charlborough House.'

Honey gripped the wheel, her eyes shining with delight. 'So Ivor wouldn't have known if he'd visited Charlborough Grange or that he'd met Pamela Charlborough.'

'Should you not be calling her *Lady* Charlborough,' said Casper in passable resemblance to Noel Coward.

'From what I've heard she's far from that!'

'You're prejudiced. And don't think I am not aware of where your thought process travels. You are assuming she was having an affair with our American friend.'

'Right. If he wasn't having an affair, then why did he make her acquaintance?'

'The meeting could have been prearranged or it could have been by chance. Either way, there's still our missing Mr Herbert to consider. Mr Maxted is found murdered and Mr Herbert has disappeared. To use detective parlance, I think it's an open-and-shut case.'

Honey shook her head. 'I can't see that it's that simple.

If his wife's cousin was dead, what was the point?' A spine-chilling answer sprang into her mind. 'Unless he hadn't known she was dead. Unless he suspected . . .'

'Now you're talking pure fiction. You're making up the plot as you go along.'

She wasn't listening. Absorbed in what-ifs and whys, she shot past the main gate of Charlborough Grange. Casper cried out in alarm as she spun the car round on the spot.

'Sorry. I was miles away.'

Casper righted himself and readjusted his hat. 'So was I. If it wasn't for my seatbelt I would have flown through the windscreen.'

This time no one answered the front door.

Honey looked down to where she'd left the car parked on the gravel drive at the bottom of the steps. Casper looked comfortable enough, his arms folded over his chest, his hat pulled down over his eyes, but she knew he was brooding. He'd lost the clock and he was pig-sick about it.

The door stayed shut. The windows looked out sightless over the warm stone terraces simmering in the afternoon sun. The shadows of trees were growing longer across the lawns and the heads of flowers quivered with honey-seeking bees. The air was ripe with floral perfume and ripe green leaves, the smell of grass gently baking in the summer sun.

She made a snap decision and followed the path along the front of the house, through an arch and into a rose bower: a tunnel of blooms heavy with scent, yellow roses vying with white ran the full length.

Through a gate she found herself in a walled garden where fruit trees clambered over warm red brick. Such gardens had existed in medieval times; perhaps this one predated the present house, the house itself standing on the ruins of an older dwelling.

The workmanlike surroundings, the rubbish bins, a small cement mixer, a ride-on lawnmower waiting to be put away, led her to the tradesmen's entrance. The rear of the house was as silent and bereft of human contact as the front.

'Hello?' she called out.

The sound was lost in the warmth beating against the

red-brick walls, the sturdy metal objects standing sentinel at the side of the path.

She stood absolutely still, drinking in her surroundings. If you listened hard enough and were very observant, you could almost smell danger. She did just that, bringing all of her senses into play.

Nothing!

No surprised countenances appeared at the windows; no curious eyes watched as she found a back door, opened it and went in.

She found herself in a conservatory, where the greenery was as virulent as in the Amazon rainforest.

'Who the hell are you?'

Even before she turned round, Honey guessed she was in the presence of Lady Charlborough.

She was sitting in a wrought-iron chair, her finger poised over what appeared to be a diary or address book. A gold sovereign hung from a chain around her neck. She wore a gold belt, gold high-heeled sandals and earrings to match. Despite the contempt in Mrs Quentin's voice, she'd still expected a mature Chelsea rather than Essex girl. It was hard to keep the surprise from her voice.

'Are you Lady Charlborough?'

The woman, whose hair was Scandinavian blonde, had a tan only obtainable from somewhere like southern Spain. She was holding a glass in her free hand. The liquid in it was clear and sported a slice of lemon: gin rather than water.

Lady Charlborough looked her up and down with the utmost disdain. Plucked eyebrows rose, and dusky-rimmed eyes opened wide with a mix of street-acquired caution and upper-crust disdain.

'Yes. I'm Lady Pamela Charlborough. Who the hell are you?'

'Honey Driver.' Her hand shot forward. It wasn't taken.

Pamela Charlborough threw the book to one side and raised her eyebrows. 'Is that supposed to mean something?'

'I suppose not. I really wanted to ask you about your brother. You know he's dead, don't you?' It was the first thing to come into her head. *Pretend you thought he was her brother. Take it easy before hitting her with the big one.*

'No he is not.' She said it with supreme confidence.

Honey reached a conclusion. 'You don't have a brother.'

'That's right. I don't.'

'Ah! And I suppose you're not the first Lady Charlborough?' Something else she knew already, but it was best not to let on that she'd been prying.

The expertly made-up face stiffened. 'No! I am not. I'm the second wife,' smiled Lady Charlborough. 'The trophy wife you might say.'

'Oh!' The words 'chipped and tarnished trophy' came immediately to mind.

Lady Pamela slugged back the dregs of the cut-glass tumbler, took out the lemon and ate that as well.

'So what the hell do you want?' No hint of friendliness. Lady Pamela wasn't the sort to make friends with the lower orders – not female friends, anyway.

But Honey shot it to her. 'An American tourist was fished out of the river the other day. I was under the impression he visited you here. His name was Elmer Maxted, though he did sometimes call himself Weinstock.'

Lady Charlborough tapped her pen on the chair arm and glanced impatiently at it and her address book. 'I don't think he's listed.'

'So do you often go hob-nobbing over the church wall at the bottom of your land? Or were you just passing by?'

The pink lips twisted into a snarl. 'Old Mother Quentin. Nosy cow! Time she was pushing up the daisies in that bloody church instead of putting them in pots!'

'Were you having an affair with Elmer?'

Lady Pamela's jaw dropped. 'How dare you! Who the hell do you think you are!'

'Let's just say an interested party affiliated to the police. I can't help the questions being asked. The police would ask the same. Maybe it's better if you told me the truth rather than them.'

'But you're not the police!'

Honey didn't flinch. OK, it was all bluff, but bluff might baffle brains – that's if Pamela Charlborough had any.

For a brief moment the flesh beneath the expertly made-up face squirmed as though Lady Pamela's skin had got too tight to cope with. Telling the truth and saving face were fighting it out.

She snapped it out. 'I saw this bloke on the other side of the wall and we passed the time of day. Anything wrong in that?'

'There's no such thing as coincidence.' Honey bristled. 'I wouldn't have given it a second thought except that Elmer Maxted married a cousin of Sir Andrew's first wife. Now that's what I call too strong a coincidence!'

Lady Pamela raised her tanned, honed body from the chair. Her botoxed lips curled back, displaying perfect teeth. Honey estimated they had cost the same as a luxury car.

'That's the way out,' she said. 'Now get out before I call the police!'

'You can if you like, bearing in mind that I've already told you that I happen to be working with the police.'

'Don't care! Clear off! Go on! Clear bloody off!'

Honey paused. 'OK, Mrs Charlborough. I'm off.'

'*Lady* Charlborough, if you don't mind!'

Honey didn't hold back the sneer.

'Are you kidding? As long as you've got two nostrils in your nose, you'll never make a lady!'

The sound of smashing glass sounded as she closed the door.

'Temper, temper,' she muttered to herself.

She tapped in Steve Doherty's number on her phone, determined to tell him all she knew.

No signal. Drat. The wall of the house was preventing her finding a signal. Surely in these spacious gardens there should be somewhere there was one.

She retraced the path she'd taken. There was a kitchen to one side, an empty place with deep white sinks and the sort of atmosphere left over from the Victorian age when servants provided the cogs in the wheel and outnumbered the family they served.

Turning away from the kitchen and the house, she made her way down the path and out of the walled garden. On the other side of an arched door turned silver by centuries of English weather, she found herself in a vegetable garden. A path led back round to the front terraces and she would have tried phoning again, but the greenhouses caught her eye.

They were huge but dominated by one in particular much bigger than the others. The greenery pressed thick and dark against the glass or plastic material that held it. *Like plants from* The Day of the Triffids, she thought, *about to pull up their roots and escape*.

Like the house, the place seemed deserted. Pots of fresh earth waiting for new bulbs or seeds for next spring sat on tables just inside the door of the first two. There were seed trays, specimen pots, cardboard boxes of plants, packets of seeds and bulbs pulled from the earth and nestling in brown-paper bags tied up with string. The smell of turned earth mingled with the stink of a compost heap. Freshly mildewed cabbage leaves lay like a floppy hat on top of the rotting pile.

Wrinkling her nose, she stepped past it and headed for the second greenhouse, then the third – the most interesting.

Sandbags were heaped around the door. She remembered they used to pile them around bomb shelters and gun posts in the Second World War. They were meant to protect a place from bomb blast. A first-aid box was nailed to a post next to a jeep covered with a camouflage net: all terribly military.

The wall of sandbags hid a Perspex door. It had a handle, and handles were meant to be used. Like Alice she pushed it open and entered Wonderland – of a sort.

Moist air hit her face like a damp blanket, taking her breath away. The smell of vegetation growing thickly and roof-high was so strong, the humidity too thick to breathe – exactly like a jungle. The effect was so real that she stopped and listened, half-expecting the chattering of monkeys or the screech of parakeets. Mind bogglingly real!

'Me Jane. Where's Tarzan?' She whispered it under her

breath, took a few more steps and looked up. Thankfully there was no sign of beefcake wearing nothing more than a pillowcase around his loins. The humidity seemed to solidify as the door slid silently shut behind her.

The narrow path between the huge greenery petered out just a few feet from the door. If she was to go on, she would have to part the thick foliage Great White Hunter-style; a machete would have been useful. No, she decided, stepping back. It was too dark in there. Too real.

It suddenly occurred to her that Charlborough might keep wild animals in here. The Marquis of Bath kept a whole menagerie at Longleat; lions, tigers and leopards prowled the grounds. Who knew what you could keep in a small jungle!

'Now's the time to panic.' She uttered the words in the weeniest whisper, and even that seemed too intrusive in this strange jungle hidden on an English estate.

Was it hidden? If so, why?

Backtracking was on autopilot. She could have turned round. Going forwards was always quicker than going backwards. But she didn't have eyes in the back of her head and she *needed* to see what was behind her. Just in case . . .

'Halt!'

Her breath stopped! Her heart stopped! Her feet certainly did. It was as though she'd backed into a barn door – one made of oak – big, hard and locked! It took a big scoop of courage to make her turn round.

Facing this human barrier was worse than not doing so. Chiselled features, chiselled body, as though welded from sheets of steel and thus having no rounded corners. Being eye to eye with his pecs was disconcerting. Raising her eyes failed to improve matters.

'You are trespassing.' His voice was higher than she'd expected, like a voice is when the larynx has suffered a severe blow. The two didn't go well together. If her legs hadn't been shaking, she might have laughed. Instead she played the trump card, the acceptable excuse.

'I'm working with the police with regard to the disappearance of an American tourist.' She chanced a grin and a casual shake. 'Just thought he might have wandered in here – you know how these Americans can be.'

She hoped he didn't detect the last trace of the accent she'd inherited from her father years ago.

'What's happening here?'

A draught of fresh air heralded the arrival of Sir Andrew. For a moment he took in the situation. Alarm flashed in his eyes then was gone. His smile was controlled.

'I thought you'd gone, Mrs Driver.'

Her heart stopped racing. A suitable excuse leapt from her tongue. 'Mr St John Gervais wished to take one last look at your clock. He's pretty upset about losing it. I said I would ask your permission. No one came to the door when I knocked, so I came around here. I thought I saw someone here.' She threw a tight smile in the direction of metal man. 'And I did.'

'Trevor is my gardener.' He turned to the man. 'That will be all, Trevor. Mrs Driver is just leaving.'

Sir Andrew took a firm grip on her arm. It wasn't quite frogmarching, but not far off. She took a last look over her shoulder at Trevor – the gardener? Did jungles need gardeners?

The question was suddenly of no consequence. She'd been aware that Trevor was carrying something, but hadn't stirred up enough courage to identify what it was. Now she saw him toss a small sack on to a pile of other sacks. It rolled off and something rolled out.

Trevor cussed.

Honey gasped. Eyes stared up at her from a severed head.

Her legs wobbled. Her head swam. She needed air – fresh air. Right now!

Twenty-One

Andrew Charlborough couldn't help chuckling at the woman's reaction to one of the many props they used in their war games.

Longleat had its wild beasts and extensive grounds in which to keep them. Most of the estate surrounding Charlborough Grange had been sold off years ago. War games, complete with a pretend jungle and bodies, provided a decent income, besides which, he enjoyed them. It took him back to other times and other places. He'd explained all this to Hannah Driver. He'd seen her recover, seen her blush and then seen her off the premises.

Amateur sleuths were the least of his worries. His features hardened as he watched the car pull away. Once it had gone, he went back along the corridor to the study. From his pocket he took a neatly folded cotton handkerchief, the initials 'LTC' embroidered in dark red at its corner. Gently he wiped the handkerchief over Lance's photograph before straightening it. He fingered its frame.

'God, Lance, I do miss you,' he said his voice trembling with emotion.

Suddenly he became aware that he was no longer alone.

'You're an obsessive! Do you know that?'

Pamela's strident voice pierced through his sorrow and his skull. She sashayed towards him, hips rolling, blonde hair clipped tightly around her pronounced cheekbones.

His face reddened. 'Get out of here!'

She blew fiercely on the cigarette she was smoking. 'It's your own fault he stays away from here, you know. You're too overbearing. The boy wants to lead his own life. And why shouldn't he? What's it to you, darling? Eh? If you really, really think about it, what's it to you?'

Her husband's eyes followed her as she walked around the room purposely tapping the corner of each framed photograph so it no longer hung straight. 'You don't answer!' she said with a light laugh. 'I've heard how you talk to him, insisting that he toe the line, or else . . . and the dear boy . . . he so loves his father . . . *his father!*' She laughed like a gurgling drain.

If eyes could be knives, he would have stabbed her twice.

She came closer and purposely blew smoke into his face then rested her hand on his chest. 'What if he knew the truth? I wonder how much he would love you then? Because I know, you know. I met Mary's brother-in-law. He told me what you did. Now,' she said, a red-painted fingernail tapping the matching colour on her lips; 'perhaps I should tell the police about this before I tell Lance. Or should I phone that woman and tell her?' Her expression hardened. 'What's it worth not to tell either of them, Andrew? Eh? Fifty thousand? One hundred thousand?' She shook her head. 'Chickenfeed. And this chicken deserves more than that, I think.'

Andrew clenched his jaw as he gazed down into his wife's face. 'Marriage to you has been torture, Pamela.'

Her eyes opened wide with feigned surprise. 'What else did you expect? I didn't marry you because I loved you. It was all for money – for your beautiful, beautiful money! What else! And when we divorce, I'll take half of it with me.'

'Over my dead body you will!'

'Your dead body! Wonderful. Could you possibly arrange your death and I'll forego a divorce. After all, I would much rather be a seriously rich widow, darling, than a moderately rich divorcee.' She patted his chest. 'How's your heart, darling?' She laughed. 'Silly me. You don't have one. At least, not as far as your wife is concerned. You only love your son . . . if he was your son.'

'Pamela, have pity . . .'

She stopped and pouted. 'Pity has a price, darling. Think

about it.' She was still laughing when she left the room. Her husband stared after her, sweat pouring down his brow as thoughts of what he'd like to do to her roared through his mind.

Mark Conway looked up at the ceiling. The room held only this bed, a chair and a low table. The rest of the house was divided up into flats. This was where they always met, where he would sate his physical desires and where she would tell him of her contempt for her husband, his employer. He would listen – just listen and not make any comment.

Her fingers continued to trace circles over his chest. Her voice was low and huskily enticing. He knew the sex had been good for her. She'd told him so. Now she was saying other things – things that filled him with dread.

'I wish he was dead. How easy would it be to kill him? You could kill him, Mark. Just think . . .' Her lips were full, but cold upon his. Strange he hadn't noticed that before. 'If he were dead, we could spend all day in bed. All day. Every day. How easy would it be to kill him, do you think?'

'Easy,' he said, because he knew it was the truth. 'Very easy. But then, why should I? He's very good to me. He's always been very good to me.'

Her tongue flicked at his ear. 'Because, my darling, if he was dead you'd have me.'

'And you would have all his money.'

'That's right. Just me.'

'What about Lance?'

'What about Lance? No doubt he'd get something, but nowhere near what he's been used to. I'd get the lion's share.'

'You sound very sure of that.'

She smiled like a cat as her hand slid down over his loins and did delicious things between his thighs.

He moaned as though never before had he experienced such ecstasy.

'Because I know something that you don't. I know that all Andrew's money could easily become mine.'

Twenty-Two

First she dropped Casper off. He'd thrown his head back and laughed when she'd told him about the plastic head and the war games in the greenhouse.

'My dear, never have I seen you so pale.'

'Not a word to a soul,' she said, shaking a finger before his aquiline nose.

Placing his right hand across his chest and adopting a suitably serious expression, he made a promise. 'In the interests of our continuing harmony,' he added.

She was surprised to see that Doherty was waiting for her when she got back to the hotel. *And not a word to him*, she said to herself.

Plastering a smile on to her face, she trotted into the small lounge just off the main residents' lounge. This room she kept for business appointments.

A tray of coffee, brown sugar and cream sat in front of him. She could tell by the look on his face that this was not entirely a social visit.

'I would have preferred a whisky,' he said, jerking his chin in the direction of the untouched tea.

'You could have asked for one.'

'I did. Your mother turned me down.'

'Oh! I'll get you one.'

'Never mind.' He rose to go. 'I haven't time to hang around.'

'Really,' she said flippantly. 'Who's been murdered?'

Wrong comment! His expression told her that she'd hit the nail on the head.

'Who?' she asked, ashamed she'd sounded so offhand.

'I told the Chief Constable I didn't have time for all this, but he insisted I inform you.'

His bluntness stung. And just when she was getting into this job.

She was just as blunt back. 'So inform me.'

'Mervyn Herbert.'

'In the river?'

Doherty shook his head. 'No. In his own garden under the rockery. There'd been a gas leak and the gas company dug up the garden. And before you ask: his head was bashed in and he had a sack over his head. A spice sack – same as before.'

'Poor man.'

She'd only met the man in passing and hadn't much warmed to him. But still, he was another human being and had met a pretty dreadful fate.

'Do you think Mrs Herbert did it?'

'An obvious conclusion, but the lab boys tell us otherwise. We don't think he was murdered there, but Mrs Herbert is in a bit of a state. And there is that first husband to think about.'

'Oh yes. Loretta's father.' She'd been thinking of smoked-salmon salad all the way back from Limpley Stoke. No time. She grabbed a handful of peanuts from a dish on the bar. 'I suppose I'd better go along and see her.'

Doherty got to his feet. 'Until we've done a thorough investigation, we have to treat her as a suspect.'

'Even though the murder was done elsewhere?'

He shrugged. 'In the house, in the garage, or even outside in the alley: who knows?'

'I take it you've already questioned her?'

'The doctor wouldn't let me. Said she was in deep shock.'

'There,' she said, swinging her bag over her shoulder. 'All the more reason for taking me with you. It might help calm the poor woman. Even if she is your prime suspect.'

'I didn't say she was my *prime* suspect.'

'As an accessory with her first husband? – Loretta's father?'

They were out on the street. He frowned. 'Are you by any chance a mind-reader?'

'Only as far as men are concerned.'

'You needn't come. You don't have to.'

'And you don't want me to.'

'I don't see the point. I never have.'

'Thanks a bunch.'

He grunted an unintelligible sound, like an ape, and ambled off to his car.

Well just wait until I tell you what I know, she thought as she got in beside him. I'll surprise you. I'll make you *want* me to be with you on this.

On the drive there, she told him about her visit to the vicar, but not about her snooping in the greenhouse. She'd never live it down. 'Elmer's wife's cousin was Sir Andrew's first wife. I think he went calling at the Grange. Pamela Charlborough met Elmer when he was wandering around the churchyard.'

'Is that right?'

'So says Mrs Quentin. I asked Lady Charlborough, but she's not the warmest heart I've ever met.'

Honey looked out of the window. The early-morning rain had disappeared. A rainbow twinkled above the viaduct taking the railway line to London via Green Park. The air smelled fresh and new.

Doherty appeared to be thinking. 'And do you think he was having an affair with Lady Pamela?'

'Of course not! If he visited Charlborough Grange at all, or if he talked over the church wall to Lady Pamela, it would be something to do with his family. He was keen on what he was doing. Perhaps he found an old family skeleton and got bumped off for it.'

Doherty shook his head. 'Too melodramatic. OK, so he'd planned an activity holiday – if you can call it that. Believe me, the root of the problem is at Ferny Down Guest House. Mervyn Herbert was a sleazebag – too fond of his step-daughter, from what I can gather. I want to know where her father is. He's got something to do with this.'

Honey chewed at her lip rather than say outright that she thought he was talking out of the top of his head.

Doherty noticed. 'Are you worried or hungry?'

'I didn't have breakfast.' Pathetic excuse.

Doherty tutted. 'The most important meal of the day!'

'I skipped lunch too.' Honey's head turned sharply. 'Did my mother ask you whether you were married?'

'No. She asked me whether I prefer carpet or wooden floors.'

Honey groaned. 'That figures.'

He looked intrigued and turned his eyes from the road. 'What?'

'Look where you're going.'

A blue double-glazing van veered away into the nearside lane. The driver shouted something about getting a driving licence. Doherty's driving attracted rude comments like confetti at a wedding.

Their destination was reached too quickly. Feeling as though her heart was somewhere behind her belly button, Honey held back, waiting for Doherty to get out of his car and ring the door bell.

Two uniformed policemen were standing guard outside. She nodded a brief acknowledgement. They nodded back and eyed Doherty as he got out of the car.

'I see he's eating humble pie,' said one.

'Had to,' the other responded. 'That's if he ever wanted to handle a murder case again.'

'What sort of humble pie?' she asked.

They exchanged a snigger. She had an inkling of what their answer would be. '*This* humble pie,' she said, tapping her collarbone.

Doherty was there, so they didn't reply.

Smarting though determined to see this through, she stood patiently whilst he rang the bell. What had she let herself in for?

She'd never been present at the scene of a crime. Hopefully the body had already been taken to the morgue. One fright per day was more than enough.

'That doorbell's been well polished,' she said.

Doherty looked at her.

'People clean things like there's no tomorrow when they're nervous or in shock.'

Wasn't that one of her mother's observations? She winced.

The older she got the more she realized that one generation took on the baggage – and mundane sayings – of the one before.

Loretta answered the door. Her clothes were basically as before: no sign of a black armband, even, and she had colour in her cheeks. The numerous rings she wore glinted as she shut the front door.

'Ma's out back,' she said brusquely. 'Straight down there.'

A solitaire diamond flashed on her index finger as she pointed in that direction. Nice, thought Honey, who couldn't remember noticing that one before.

'Nice ring. Is it new?'

Loretta blushed. 'A present. From a mate.'

A male mate, Honey decided, and intimate. Only intimacy brought that bright a red to a girl's cheeks.

Cora Herbert was sitting in her favourite spot in the conservatory. A mug of tea and an ashtray sat on the table in front of her. Beyond the door men in jumpsuits methodically moved earth from one part of the garden to another.

The thick black lashes left traces of mascara on her damp cheeks. A pall of cigarette smoke rose and circled in the air. The cigarette trembled as she flicked the length of ash into the tray. She looked grim, tired, her eyes outlined in a red that almost matched her lipstick. Black roots ran like a basalt valley through her hair parting. The rest was dry, blonde and in need of a wash.

Honey's throat was like sandpaper. 'I'm so sorry, Mrs Herbert.'

Both she and Doherty took a seat. Tea wasn't offered. The room was stuffy and filled with smoke. The door was shut, the smoke seeking escape through a fanlight set in the plastic roof.

Cora nodded an acknowledgement.

Doherty went over the details again. 'When did you last see your husband, Mrs Herbert?'

Honey was instantly reminded of a famous painting – the one where Oliver Cromwell's men are asking a young boy the whereabouts of his father, Charles the First.

'I've already told you that,' Cora snapped.

All resemblance to a royal painting flew out of the window. Cora was, to put it mildly, rough around the edges. Cora looked like Cromwell.

'Tell me again,' Doherty said slowly.

Listening to his line of questioning decided her. She nudged his arm. 'Can I have a word in private?'

Doherty pursed his lips. Yet again this was a different Steve from the one who let loose in a local bar. This was his profession. He'd trained for it, started at the bottom and worked his way up. Whereas she . . .

His hostility was mild, but definitely existed. He looked as though he were about to refuse. Whatever made him change his mind could be down to the old adage that two heads are better than one. Or did he really think he was in with a good chance of going to bed with her? Either way, they made their excuses and went out into the garden, shutting the door behind them.

Not that Cora seemed to care – smoking, staring at the floor, flicking ash and barking orders at Loretta. She didn't seem actually upset, just anxious, as though she wanted this to be over, and the quicker the better.

Skirting the heap of dug-up earth, they made their way to the far end of the garden, where a plastic garden gnome peered through a canopy of rhubarb leaves.

Honey folded her arms. 'What's this all about?'

Doherty adopted a blank look. 'I don't know what you mean.'

'Liar!'

He shrugged and spread his hands. 'What?'

Honey eyed him accusingly. 'OK. Don't explain. Let me guess. Your last case was a shambles and so when the Hotels' Association asked for a police officer within the force to work with them on their idea, you were ordered to volunteer. And then . . .' He opened his mouth to protest. 'And then,' Honey went on, determined to have her say, 'when Elmer Maxted's body was found, you determined to hold on to the case. You saw it as a means to repair your reputation. That's why I'm here, isn't it? You don't like it, but I'm tolerated.'

He began to laugh, bending from the waist, lower arm across his belly. 'Wh–a–t?'

Honey was unmoved. 'And now we have the laughing policeman!'

The look in his eyes contradicted what the rest of his body was doing. The eyes certainly had it, and that was what she would judge him by.

'Don't ever go on the stage.' She headed back for the conservatory, satisfied that the air between them was at last clear.

All the same, she was feeling uneasy. The whole scenario had changed. This wasn't just about a misplaced tourist. It wasn't even about the likelihood that Elmer had been mugged and murdered purely by chance. Such things rarely happened in Bath. For the most part the city was peopled by the cultured, the civilized and the upwardly mobile. On the face of it this second murder had nothing to do with tourism. This was outside her experience and made her nervous.

'Anyway,' said Doherty from behind her as they headed back, 'Mrs Herbert has to be the prime suspect. Who else would plant their husband in their own garden?'

Although tempted to slam the door on him, Honey left it open. Irritating as he was, Cora's cigarette smoke was worse.

Cora was sitting in exactly the same position as when they'd left her. Goodness knows how many cigarettes she'd consumed in their absence. She was on a chain-smoking marathon. Her eyes were watery and had a vague look. Despite the make-up, her complexion was greasy and white.

'I didn't do it,' she said before anyone had asked her.

'So how did he get there?' asked Doherty.

Cora's eyes popped like marbles. 'How the hell should I know?'

Loretta lurked in the background, leaning against the wall, arms folded, her expression as dark as her mother's flaking mascara.

Doherty was sounding serious. 'I'm afraid you're going to have to come into the station for further questioning.'

Honey could find no words of sympathy and nothing helpful to say like, 'It's surely a mistake; I shouldn't worry if I were you.' The evidence was damning. Like Doherty had said, who else would plant their husband in the garden?

'I'll walk back,' Honey said, once they were outside and Mrs Cora Herbert had been helped into the back seat of a police car.

Doherty shrugged. 'Please yourself.' He turned to Loretta. The girl's face was expressionless, as though she were still digesting what was going on.

'What about you?'

Loretta's bright eyes narrowed and her red lips twisted into a contemptuous snarl. 'I don't travel with pigs. I'll be down to see her.' She stood on tiptoe and shouted at her mother. 'I'll be down to see you, Ma! You can count on it!'

Honey caught the sob in her voice. 'Will you be all right?'

'I'll get down there later. Mum would want me to take care of things.' She jerked her head back at the 'No Vacancy' sign. 'We're expecting paying guests. Have to look after them, don't I?'

'You're a good daughter. It must be upsetting. I think you're very brave.'

Loretta shrugged again, causing the straps of her top to slide down over her thin shoulders. 'Not really. I know she didn't do it. There's no evidence.' The statement was made confidently. She was standing with her arms still folded protectively across her chest, her head held high. Was that a smile Honey could see wavering around her lips?

Her smile vanished when she saw the enquiring look on Honey's face. 'Don't look at me like that!'

'I'm sorry.'

It wouldn't do to leave on a negative note. She forced a smile. Her eyes dropped back to the flashing diamond. At least it looked like a diamond. 'That's a pretty ring,' she said, trusting her instant change of subject didn't sound too contrived.

The comment lifted Loretta's heavily made up face. 'Nice, ain't it?' She flashed the ring. 'My dad gave me it,' she said in a strange and dreamy kind of way.

'That's nice. Are you close to your dad?'

'Yep!'

'But not to Mervyn.'

Loretta's expression darkened into a deep scowl. 'A prime-time creep!'

Honey imagined the effect Loretta's skimpy attire might have had on Mervyn Herbert. 'Did he bother you?' It sounded ineffectual, stupid to her own ears, so Loretta's response did not surprise her.

'No,' she said, shaking her head, a sarcastic smile twitching around her mouth. 'He didn't *bother* me! He *raped* me!'

Twenty-Three

Honey murmured and stretched her tired body. The sound of surf brushing over a golden beach changed suddenly.

Funny, she thought languorously, *the sea sounds just like my telephone at home . . .*

Drat! Just when a gorgeous hunk was handing her a long, cool drink, the dream was broken. Swearing under her breath, she switched on the light and reached for her watch. Twelve thirty-two. The phone was still purring.

Drawing her other hand from beneath the thick layer of sheet, blankets and satin eiderdown, she eased herself up against the pillows and reached for it.

'Hope you weren't doing anything special.'

Doherty! The inference was obvious.

'Just sleeping.' Well, actually, she'd been dreaming of him, but – drat! – she had no intention of further inflating his ego.

'At this time of night?'

'Stephen! I do sometimes go to bed before midnight!'

'Do you?' He sounded genuinely surprised. The truth was she was tired out after serving a party of history buffs holding their annual bash. History was sometimes viewed as dry; the historians ensured their throats were always wet. Dreaming of him had provided a little light relief.

'Look, Stephen, running a hotel and being a sleuth—'

'A super-sleuth.'

'—Thank you – is quite burdensome. Anyway, what do you want?' There was a pause. 'I've had a heavy day – you know, Mrs Herbert and all that.'

Honey pulled herself up into a more comfortable sitting position. She'd rung the station earlier to enquire what was going on. Cora was still being questioned.

'So?' She frowned at the thought of poor Cora ending up in a cell on a bed that wasn't her own.

'There've been developments.'

It was a case of 'pigs might fly' to hope that Mervyn Herbert had been a random killing. And did Doherty know that Mervyn had raped his stepdaughter? Did her mother know, for that matter? She thought about mentioning it, but decided otherwise. Perish the thought, but how would she have felt if it had been *her* daughter? Sickened! Angry! Downright vengeful! The likelihood of Cora having killed her husband wasn't that far-fetched.

That didn't excuse Doherty ringing her at this hour. Let him make the running. Let him tell her what the 'professional' detectives were up to.

'Well? Are you going to tell me?'

'Yes,' he answered in such a robust fashion that she assumed he was slightly tipsy. 'But only if you agree to meet me at the Zodiac.'

She groaned as though he was the last person she wanted to see. Not true, but necessary with a man like him. Anyone could see he was vain. Worse still, he knew the effect he had on women.

'I don't know . . .'

'The night's still young. And so are we.'

'I don't feel young.'

'Let's live whilst we can.'

She thought about it. Two dead bodies in less than six weeks. Life was certainly getting precarious. Could she? Should she?

She looked anxiously at the clock. Not yet one o'clock. She swung her legs out of bed. 'Give me twenty minutes – no, thirty. It's a pretty fair walk.'

'No need to walk. I'm parked outside.'

A sweater, jeans and loafers, plus a quick brushing of hair and she was ready.

As he drove, she blinked at the impatient city where visitors still wandered, taking in the atmosphere, and late-night revellers and theatre-goers headed for nightclubs or a taxi home.

Doherty was driving extremely steadily. No van drivers were honking horns at him. Not that many van drivers made deliveries at one in the morning.

'How much have you had to drink?'

'Two small ones.'

A borderline case in drink driving? She wasn't sure, but she wasn't chancing it. 'Can we go for a walk,' she said suddenly. 'I don't really feel like a drink.'

He gave in without a fight. 'OK.'

They headed for Pulteney Bridge, parked the car and got out. Not a word passed between them. Honey was comfortable with that. She presumed he was musing over the day's events, but also enjoying making her wait for what he had to say. They stopped at the water's edge, and looked towards the bridge and the river.

Doherty leaned on the parapet. He fixed his gaze on the lights reflected in the river.

'Mrs Herbert's out of the picture. Pathology confirmed a time of death when she was out at bingo.'

'So what next?'

'We're looking for Mrs Herbert's first husband.'

'Because of Loretta?'

He looked at her in blank ignorance.

Her stomach churned. He'd not heard about the rape and now she'd mentioned it . . . She waited before committing herself.

Doherty looked curious but carried on. 'He's not long out of prison. There's nothing between him and the ex-wife, but he's very protective about his daughter.'

A breeze blowing off the river whipped her hair across her face. It was too late. He'd twigged there was something she'd left unsaid.

Leaning forward, his hands resting on the parapet, he looked up into her face. 'You know something I don't. I can see it in your eyes.'

'You can't see my eyes.'

'Do I have to beat it out of you? I can play good cop, bad cop, if called upon.'

She sighed. 'Can I call upon you to buy me a coffee instead?'

'Yeah. Sure.' His gaze wandered to the other side of the river. 'Look. At its edges the current runs faster. I reckon Elmer came down on the current on this side of the river. If the current on the river is just as strong upstream as it is here, then the body could have been put in anywhere along that stretch. But that piece of wood came down with it. He stood thoughtfully for a moment.

'And Mervyn Herbert?'

He shook his head. 'Another sack over his head and traces of coriander. That's a spice, isn't it?'

She told him it was and thought of Jeremiah. The sacks had to have come from him. Before she had chance to mention it, Doherty stepped in.

'We questioned a spice stall in the market about their sacks.'

'But not the stall owners. They wouldn't have a motive.'

'Not at this moment they don't, but who knows? Something may crop up.'

Honey thought of Jeremiah and Ade. No. There was no possible motive. She rubbed at her forehead as she tried to work out where this was going. Being dragged out of bed for midnight walks didn't happen very often. Midnight walks were something lovesick teenagers did when they couldn't afford anything else after a lively night out.

'Are you insinuating that Loretta's father murdered Elmer and Mervyn?'

'I think so. The spice links them. And Davies has a record.'

'So do a lot of people.'

'Do you?' He looked faintly surprised.

'Not a criminal one. I just carry a lot of baggage – you know: failed marriage, widowed, raising a kid, mad mother . . .'

'I wouldn't say you were mad.'

'I meant *my* mother.'

'No need to snap.'

'Sorry.' She rubbed at her frowning forehead again.

'Right. Now what is it you know that I don't?' He sounded insistent. She wondered if he would drag her down to the station for questioning if she didn't spill the beans. Possibly.

'Blow the coffee. Loretta Davies was raped by her stepfather.'

Doherty raised his eyebrows and his jaw dropped. 'Christ!'

Honey looked at him in amazement. 'Mrs Herbert didn't tell you that?'

He looked suitably dumbstruck.

Honey might have crowed out loud if the situation hadn't been so grim.

'She might not have known.'

'It happens.'

'So why Loretta's father?'

'You've just given me the best motive in the world: revenge. And who could blame the man?'

'Mervyn deserving what he got won't keep Loretta's father from prison.'

Doherty grunted. 'At least he's used to it.'

Late-night revellers chose that moment to come skipping along the promenade like six-year-olds. Every so often they leapt up at the flower baskets hanging from the lamp posts, hitting them with their hands and sending them swinging.

He waited until they'd gone by before explaining. 'Mrs Herbert told us at first that Mervyn had gone to the pub, the Green Park Tavern – a favourite of mine, so it happens.'

Honey nodded. The Green Park Tavern was a fair walk from the guest house towards the viaduct and the train station. 'She told me that,' said Honey. 'He did it quite regularly, apparently.'

'When did she tell you?'

'On the first occasion I went there when Mr Weinstock, as he was then, went missing. Mervyn shot off at the same time. I presumed he was avoiding me – you know: just another busybody to blight his days. Obviously that wasn't quite the case.'

Suddenly the scene that day came back in full clarity. 'Oh my God!'

'God's not here. Just me. What's the problem?'

'You remember I told you he was helping some men from the council take out a large chest freezer. It was being dumped. I never saw him after that.'

Doherty flicked open his phone, punched the short-cut button and immediately introduced himself and what he wanted.

'Check the file. Where's Davies working?'

There was a pause as the lowly police officer on the other end obeyed and checked the particulars.

Something was said that she couldn't hear.

Doherty didn't look too pleased. 'That's all it says? The council? Didn't anyone think to check which department?'

Obviously not. He slammed his phone shut.

'Chimps. The lot of them. Qualified by a bit of paper and they're all bloody chimps!'

'Never mind. You already know that there's nothing in the freezer now.'

'Absolutely.'

Doherty's arm brushed around her back. She took it as a signal to resume their walk. He was surprisingly serious as he talked, his eyes now fixed on the ground in front of them. If he was being 'fresh', as her mother used to say, he showed no sign of it apart from the encircling arm. He was into his subject, recounting what had happened – as related by Mrs Herbert.

'Sometimes, when he'd had enough of Bath and tourists, or when her former husband was threatening to bash his head in, Mervyn used to jump on a train.'

'Where to?'

'Anywhere. Two days or so and he returned. But not this time. Then Davies turned up and was more than pleased that he wasn't coming back. Offered to move back in. Loretta was all for it. Cora didn't seem too offhand about it. They could have worked in collusion.'

'What makes you think that?'

'He's scarpered! That's a sign of guilt. Probably in Mervyn's Volvo estate. We haven't found that either.'

'The moment the body came to light.'

'That's it. And now what you've just told me about Mr Herbert raping his stepdaughter . . .' Doherty only barely refrained from punching the air with his fist. 'It's him! It has to be him!'

Twenty-Four

'Good evening.'

Honey smiled as she greeted diners arriving for dinner in the restaurant of the Green River Hotel. Most were guests, but Smudger had a reasonable reputation, so there was always a smattering of locals wanting to sample his seafood thermidor or his heaven-sent white chocolate mousse with orange liqueur.

Mrs Welsh, a regular, was in with her husband. She had a habit of asking if the chef had 'something for her pussy'. She owned three cats and always asked for a 'kitty bag' after her meal. However, the request never failed to bring a blush to Smudger's freckled face.

Mary Jane had two weeks before she went home. She came floating in wearing strawberry-pink chiffon, her long feet encased in Roman-style gold sandals the straps of which finished in a knot halfway up her shins. A septuagenarian, Mary Jane intended growing old outrageously.

A look of contentment suffused her gaunt features and her eyes glittered with a far-seeing look – totally suiting a woman who claimed to number ghosts among her friends. The incumbent of her regular room had left and she'd immediately changed rooms. Once again it was left to her and Sir Cedric.

Room five was spooky; there was no other way to describe it. Honey disliked the high wooden ceiling and the silly closets that were lacking in depth and had no room to hang clothes. She planned to renovate during the off season. Sensing her plans would not be welcome so far, she had not mentioned this to Mary Jane.

'Sorry I'm a little late coming down,' said Mary Jane in

a lazy Californian drawl. Close up her eyes shone with unworldly brightness.

Honey guessed what was coming.

'I have been conversing in the most intimate terms with dearest darling Sir Cedric,' she said, her eyelashes fluttering, and her long fingers resting on her ribcage. Her voice dropped to a whisper. 'He has confided some really scandalous family secrets.'

Honey feigned awestruck interest and adopted the same hushed voice. 'Is that so?' At the same time she guided the elderly and very tall lady to her usual table, where the long legs and torso folded obediently into a chair.

'Indeed. He had three wives, you know!'

She tittered as old ladies are prone to do – though, it had to be said, Mary Jane did not quite fit the comfortable old-lady image.

Honey handed her the menu. 'He didn't chop off their heads, did he – you know, like Henry the Eighth?'

'Oh, no,' came the adamant reply. Her expression was deadly serious. 'It was very naughty, and I've been sworn to secrecy.'

'Then I won't pressurize you,' said Honey, smiling.

'But I must tell you,' said Mary Jane, her sinuous fingers locking over Honey's arm. 'I'm going on one of these fabulous ghost walks this evening. It visits some of the places Sir Cedric has told me about. Would you like to come along?' she asked, eyes of periwinkle-blue youthfully bright in her wrinkled face.

Honey eyed the steadily filling restaurant. 'I don't know whether I've got time for that.'

Mary Jane looked crestfallen. 'I quite understand, my dear. Now let me see,' she said, rummaging in her solidly square bag, 'I have a bus timetable here somewhere . . .'

Honey couldn't be mean. 'No need for the bus. I can't come on the walk, but I could spare ten minutes to give you a lift.'

'Oh good.' The voluminous bag was snapped shut. 'Your mother said you would.'

Honey maintained her smile through gritted teeth. It galled

her to find out she'd already been volunteered before she'd had chance to offer.

She might have stayed prickly if her eyes hadn't lit on John Rees. He was wearing a smart but casual cream linen shirt with shoulder tabs. It gave him a soft-military kind of look.

'How are ya?' he said, getting to his feet and shaking her hand.

She wanted to say, 'All the better for meeting you,' but she didn't.

'I'm very well. And you?'

She held the professional smile. He might be here just to sample the food and not to see her. And anyway, once she came back down to earth, her gaze strayed to his partner.

The woman was slim – not just in a *thin* way, but glossy, as though a copy of *Vogue* had fallen open and the model had stepped out fully fleshed.

She was sipping water and her eyes were downcast. The latter were perfectly made up: dark smudges in all the right places, lashes as thick as furry caterpillars.

'Miriam,' he said by way of introduction, 'this is Honey Driver, who owns this fantastic place.'

Miriam nodded, murmured good evening, but didn't look up. Honey resisted clenching her jaw. After all, what did it matter if she'd been fantasizing about their assignation at his bookshop. The stuff he'd wanted to adorn his walls beside the artwork and books had already been collected. OK, so although it was by invitation only, it was still basically a public event. Anyone could go in and buy tickets, but at the back of her mind . . . well . . . she could dream.

'I'm looking forward to the open evening,' she gushed, keeping her smile trained on gorgeous John. My God, she sounded like a teenager.

'So am I.'

There was something about his manner that was different. He smiled, but his features were stiff. She guessed he was coping with tension and Miriam, his glossy, bronzed companion with her black hair and red lips, was the cause of it.

Feeling more than disappointed, Honey excused herself. Waltzing around the restaurant, she was a picture of solicitous charm. Waltzing around in her head was the same recurring thought: Why were all the best guys already spoken for?

Lindsey was supervising the bar. As usual, she dispensed drinks and opened bottles of wine swiftly and efficiently. She never mixed up orders and neither did she panic.

She was tipping a measure of Harvey's Bristol Cream into a schooner, the largest of the sherry measures. Honey knew without being told that it was for Mary Jane. She'd developed a passion for the very English drink. No doubt a little spirit inside would prepare her for the spirits she might encounter on her ghost walk.

'Your friend the bookseller has company,' said Lindsey, her eyes travelling to John Rees and back to her mother.

Honey rested her elbow on the bar and sighed. 'And there was I thinking I might get the opportunity to eat him alive.'

'Don't let Gran hear you say that.'

'She won't like it.'

'You bet she won't.'

The odd fact was that if the guy in question wasn't her own choice, Gloria Cross immediately eliminated him as a possible suitor for her daughter. It was strange, it was annoying and it was also plain bloody-mindedness. The game was to keep her daughter on her toes, not to lose her to someone over whom she had no control. So strong men were out of the question. Only the weak would prevail.

The fact was that if Honey *showed* interest, the man became suddenly unsuitable. Like John Rees. It had occurred to Honey long ago that her mother treated it as a hobby. Whereas other people collected stamps or went line dancing, she went searching for eligible men for her daughter; it passed the time.

Honey asked, 'So who's the supermodel?'

Lindsey checked the reservation register, running her finger down the page until she found the right time and name. 'Mr and Mrs Rees.'

'Oh!'

The restaurant was full and compliments to the chef were coming thick and fast. Honey knew she should have felt supremely smug that things were going so well tonight, but John Rees had punctured her balloon. She was almost glad when the customers thinned out and Mary Jane came tottering over to claim her lift to the ghost walk.

'I hope I'm not inconveniencing you,' she said, her bony fingers placed on Honey's arm. The weight of her hand was no more than a feather.

'Of course not,' Honey lied, her eyes sliding sidelong to Mr and Mrs Rees. Their heads were almost touching across the table. Their expressions were intense – not with desire, but with something else. They could have been talking about their marriage; they could just as easily have been disagreeing over the colour scheme for a new kitchen. Either was possible.

Mary Jane folded herself into the car in much the same way as she had into her seat in the restaurant – basically in three parts: lower legs, upper legs and torso. A finely crocheted grey cape was draped around her shoulders and fastened with a pin at the front. She chatted all the way, recounting how often she'd contacted Sir Cedric in the privacy of her room. By the time they'd reached Queen's Square and the Francis Hotel, Honey knew all about Sir Cedric's wives and which one Mary Jane was related to.

'Fanny,' she pronounced emphatically, '– Fanny Millington. Bob the Job actually located a picture of her; just a sketch, but enough to tell me she was a handsome woman. She bore Sir Cedric six children. His first wife didn't have any. Apparently she was fragile. I suppose we'd say that Fanny had good genes.'

'What about the third wife?' Honey asked, purely out of politeness. After all, Mary Jane did fly in from California every single year.

'I don't know anything about her genes. Apparently she ran off with the coachman and the marriage was annulled.' Beaming broadly, she shrugged her square, bony shoulders. 'Isn't family history just wonderful!'

Quite a crowd had gathered at the bottom end of Queen's

Square, just along from the Francis Hotel. Crocheted cape billowing in the breeze, Mary Jane strode to join the other tourists. The merry band chattered like magpies, quivering with excitement at the prospect of seeing what few had ever seen.

Honey turned the steering wheel, meaning to head back to the hotel, when Loretta Davies emerged from Charlotte Street at the top end of the square. She was wearing a white blouse and a black skirt – regulation uniform for a hotel waitress.

Honey hit the horn and downed the passenger-side window. 'Do you want a lift?'

Loretta opened the door and got in. 'Thanks. I've just finished my shift. Working helps keep my mind off things. I've made sure our place keeps going, but you just have to get out, don't you?'

Honey agreed with her.

Despite the uniform, three gold earrings dangled from Loretta's right ear. The white blouse was long enough to cover her belly button. Overall, she was fairly presentable.

It was now nine thirty. She calculated that Loretta had been on duty since mid-afternoon to be going home this early.

'Where do you work?'

'La Traviata.' She slid her feet out of her shoes.

Honey recognized the name of an upmarket Italian restaurant situated behind the world-famous Royal Crescent. 'Me feet are killing me. I've been on since two.'

'Poor you. I didn't know you worked in the catering trade. I presumed you did a bit for your mother and had something else – you know, like an office job.'

'Not bloody likely.'

The smell of trees bathed in darkness drifted into the car. So did the aroma of fast-food joints: hamburgers, kebab shops and taco bars.

Presumably she meant office jobs. She didn't.

'My mum likes things done her way. She gets Marge in to clean and do the laundry and ironing when it's busy. Especially now. I've hung around and looked after things, but it's only temporary. I had to get out. Honest I did.'

Her voice seemed to nosedive on the last two words. For

the first time it occurred to Honey that Loretta was not quite as confident as she made out. She was hurting. Under the circumstances, it wasn't surprising.

It took guts to ask the next question, but she forced herself. 'What did your mother say – you know, about your step-father . . . doing what he did?'

'Not a lot.'

Following Honey telling him what had happened, Steve Doherty had told Cora Herbert that her dead husband had raped her daughter. She'd been devastated, though not exactly surprised; in fact, she'd turned cautious.

Doherty's line of questioning had turned in that direction. 'It's understandable for a father to protect his daughter and to get angry if someone hurts her. So where's Loretta's father?' he'd asked.

'How the hell should I know?'

Of course Cora knew. But she'd guessed where the questioning was going. Her first husband had a motive to kill her second husband for abusing Loretta.

'She's protecting him,' Doherty had said, on the night he'd got her out of bed.

Honey had fingered her glass. 'So if he did it, why bury him in the rockery? Don't you think that's a bit close to home?'

'As good as anywhere. Close to where the incident took place. I reckon he panicked.'

'Are you saying that Cora was an accomplice?'

'She's denying it.'

She'd sipped at her vodka and tonic. 'I don't see Cora as a murderer. Bury him under our noses and we won't notice?'

'That's right.' He'd sounded and looked as though he'd uttered the last word on the matter.

Honey had risen to the challenge. 'Did you ever see that rockery? It was ludicrous. No one could help notice a change in its shape.'

He had shaken his head. 'Trust me. I'm a policeman.'

'I think you're wrong. I think someone wanted to shift the blame.'

He'd chuckled and ordered himself another pint. 'You've been reading Aggie Christie again.'

Ferny Down Guest House had been taken apart for evidence that Mervyn had been murdered on site. Cora and Loretta had been questioned for hours. There was no evidence. Nothing. Doherty had been gutted – hence the call to meet him at the Zodiac Club.

Now here was Loretta sitting beside her, and she was feeling sorry for Cora Herbert. The poor woman must be suffering more than her business.

They were fast approaching the Lower Bristol Road. 'I'll come in with you, if I may,' said Honey, '– just to see how your mum is bearing up.'

Loretta looked cautious at first. She'd fully expected her to say no. But she didn't.

'I suppose you can.'

To Honey's eyes Loretta was no longer the girl with the hard eyes and the blatant attempt to be sluttish. She was a little girl and vulnerable. How must it have felt to be raped by her stepfather and been too afraid to tell her mother? It didn't bear thinking about.

The porch light was still on when they got there. Loretta had a key. Honey followed her along the passage leading to the rear kitchen and the small sitting room adjoining the conservatory.

There was no one there.

'Mum?'

'I'm in here.' The response came from Mervyn Herbert's 'den'.

Cora was on her knees tidying up, repacking what the police had unpacked, and putting it away. Her backside wobbled against her meaty calves as she did it.

'I hope I'm not interrupting anything.'

Cora stopped what she was doing and glared. 'What do you want?'

'I saw Loretta and gave her a lift. I just thought I'd see how you were. It must have been quite an ordeal. Is there anything I can do to help?'

'Well you could start by finding a landscape gardener.

My rockery's a right shambles.' She turned back to what she was doing. 'Everything's a mess. Bloody coppers! Mucking my place up like this. I've got a business to run. It's got to be a bit tidy, you know.'

'Yes. I know.' She knelt down beside her on the moss-coloured carpet. 'Let me help you.'

Each watch was individually wrapped in old newspapers and repacked in a cardboard box.

'They look quite valuable,' she said suddenly.

'I wish,' muttered Cora. 'We'll let Jollys' find that out. The whole lot's going to auction.'

'I hope you get a good sum.'

Cora's response was mumbled and begrudging.

'Honestly, Mrs Herbert, specialist collectors who are looking for certain items might give you quite a bit more than you'd get at auction. I can ask around if you like. In fact, there's a certain name that springs readily to mind. You might know him. Or perhaps Mervyn knew him. He's called Casper St John Gervais?'

Cora shook her head in a vague manner as though she not only didn't know, but didn't really care. 'Never heard of the bloke.'

She'd had a similar response from Casper when she'd first seen the watch collection and wondered at the connection. 'I collect clocks, not watches,' Casper had said imperiously. 'And I never, ever frequent establishments along the Bristol Road!'

Honey pressed on. 'Do you think your husband might have known him?'

Cora shrugged and pulled herself up on to her feet. 'I don't know and I don't bloody care!' The flaps of the box were slapped firmly into place. Cora averted her eyes. 'I've got things to do,' she said with an air of finality.

Honey got to her feet. 'I'll see myself out.'

She paused in the porch outside the conservatory. Loretta was standing there swigging Coke from a can and staring out into the garden. There was something freshly vulnerable about the girl. There was also something about Cora's behaviour that made her ask a further question.

'Your mother was surprised that you told me about your stepfather raping you. Why was that?'

The teenage shrug again, the sort of shrug that's meant to signify indifference but in fact conveys deep concern. 'She didn't want me to.'

It was like a gate closing. Not much of an answer, but she sensed it was the only one she was prepared to give.

Outside, the night sky had blurred to slate-grey – that time in June and July when darkness never quite takes hold. Honey took deep breaths and looked up at the sky as she tried to clarify the clues and the people. Some said that a crime was like a jigsaw puzzle: one bit fitted into another. It was just a case of gathering up the right bits and putting them into the right places. *Trouble is*, she thought, *you have to find the bits in the first place.*

For a start, there was Loretta's father. His motive for killing Mervyn Herbert was understandable. But Elmer Maxted? Everything began with the lone American, here to trace his family tree. Surely Davies could not have had anything to do with killing him. Could he? The watches and clocks situation was also puzzling. Was it just a coincidence that Mervyn collected one and Casper the other?

She flicked open her phone and dabbed at Casper's number. It rang and he answered – quite quickly, as it happened.

'How well did you know Mervyn Herbert?'

He sounded taken aback at first, but quickly recovered. 'My dear girl, as I've already told you—'

'I don't believe you. So! Who are you going to speak to? – me or the police?' This was all instinct, a long shot. She sensed his unease. She'd asked quickly even before he'd had chance to say hello.

There was a pause, a period when she felt she could almost hear his brain ticking over. If she closed her eyes, she could even see his throat tightening.

'You'd better come on over,' he said.

'I will.'

Twenty-Five

Pamela Charlborough drank deeply from a lead-crystal wine glass and eyed her husband over its rim. The wine tasted good but did nothing to make him more appealing.

Once again she imagined him lying still and white instead of sitting at the same table with her, his hair almost white, his face mottled with broken veins. At least if he were dead she would get to keep the lifestyle and the wherewithal to maintain it. In her mind she blessed Sun Alliance and Royal Life. What a boon they were to modern living and the plight of the recently widowed. Unfortunately, she wasn't widowed. For better or worse – mostly worse – she was still tied firmly to Andrew.

She breathed deeply as the aftertaste of the wine tantalized her taste buds and fumed upwards into her brain. She opened and closed her eyes as she took deep breaths. Each time she opened them her gaze alighted on things in the room she would keep and things she would throw out once he was dead. It was something she'd done a thousand times, her mind changing as things were added or taken away from the house according to how Andrew's dabbling in antiques – most notably clocks – was going.

The stuff from the Far East would be first to go. Whoever wanted those dreadful bits of bamboo that threatened to fall over if you brushed too close? There was a table made of it, a coat stand and a matching umbrella stand complete with bamboo-handled umbrellas and walking sticks. She sighed. It was really all too much. The only flimsy things she adored were made of silk, edged with lace and extremely expensive. She still looked good in silky underwear. She smirked to herself. She looked pretty good out of it too.

She poured more wine as the pristinely white porcelain clock on the sideboard struck eight. Both her eyes and those of her husband went to it before looking at each other. A slow smile crossed her husband's face. He was laughing at her, crowing because he'd got it back and grabbed the money from her luggage.

Pamela simmered then snapped. She raised her wineglass in a mock toast. 'All right darling! You've got it back. Well bully for you!'

Andrew was drinking brandy. He swilled the amber liquid around his glass as he regarded her. His smile was contemptuous. 'Really, Pamela. You have no taste and your propensity for seeking out the more seedy side of society is really phenomenal. Fancy selling it to a second-rate clock dealer like Simon Tye. The man's a crook.'

'Necessity!' she snapped.

'You spend too much.'

Eyes wide and angry, she gripped her wine glass more tightly. 'You give me too little!'

Andrew's gaze went back to the newspaper he'd been reading. He usually read a newspaper when they sat down for the evening meal. It saved having to converse with her. Conversation was confined to necessary subjects – like money.

'My dear, I must have been mistaken. I thought it was cheap to live in Spain. That's why it suits cheap people.'

Pamela sprang up from her chair sending it toppling backwards. 'I'm not cheap, Andrew! I'm normal!'

Her husband raised his eyebrows and glanced at her over the day's headlines. 'Now don't lose your temper, darling. It emphasizes your wrinkles.'

The lead-crystal wine glass flew down the table. Andrew ducked. Now it was his turn to rise. 'You bitch!'

Pamela stood her ground on four-inch mules, the soles of cork, the uppers made of interwoven pink and blue silk.

Andrew was on her before she could run. The back of Andrew's hand hit her face and sent her flying across the table. Hair tousled, eyes blazing and blood trickling from her lip, she glared up at him, her fingers gripping the table edge.

'Why did I marry you?'

Andrew was disdainful. 'Hah! Why did I marry you is more to the point.'

Slowly, she righted herself and pushed her hair back from her eyes. 'But I know why you married me. I was the barrier between your first wife's family and you and Lance. If they probed too closely they'd find out the truth. As a widower you would still have attracted their attention and occasional visits. Marriage again put them at a distance. And I know, Andrew. He told me. The murdered man Elmer Maxted told me!'

His face paled. She knew she'd hit the mark. Clinging to the table edge, she arose from the floor her eyes shining. Now she was the one with power.

'I know what you did. I know about Lance and who he is – who he really is.'

Andrew's jaw tightened.

Blood trickled into Pamela's mouth when she smiled. For once it was her that was winning.

'I can ruin you any time I like. But it won't cost you much to keep my mouth shut. I like Lance. I wouldn't want to ruin his life.'

Andrew said nothing, his pale eyes darting between her, the drinks cabinet and Mark Conway. Unheard by his wife, Mark was standing in the doorway, listening and waiting. Andrew threw him an unspoken message to stay. Pamela, slightly the worse for drink, carried on with her tirade.

'Lance, the real Lance bled to death. Haemophilia – he had haemophilia. Only men suffer from it you know. Yet it's passed on to them by their mothers: The American told me Lance had it – or at least the Lance he knew. But our big, grown-up Lance doesn't have it, does he? Oh no, most certainly he does not. In fact, he's an extremely healthy young man. I wonder what his DNA would prove if they took swabs from you and him? But then, you already know the answer to that, don't you?'

'You're drunk,' Andrew said contemptuously.

Pamela laughed. With half a bottle of Chateau Talbot sloshing around inside her, she staggered to the door. 'Spain here I come! And I don't give a hoot if I've got to crawl there!'

Gripping the banister, she dragged herself up to her room. 'Spain, sun, sea, and sex – here I come!' She turned round when she got to the top. 'The sex especially,' she said, her eyes glittering with the desire to hurt. 'Good sex happens with young men, not old has-beens like you!'

Trevor, her husband's batman and part-time gardener was also at the top of the stairs.

'What the hell are you staring at?' she shouted, waving her arm and definitely meaning for her hand to slap his chest.

'Nothing, madam.'

'Nothing, madam,' she mimicked. 'Nothing, madam!'

Andrew stood quietly at the bottom of the stairs waiting for her to have the final word. He knew she would. She swayed slightly. He wished she would fall. She didn't. She hadn't finished yet. God, but he hated that smile.

'Be a good little husband, Andrew, and transfer some money into my account. Fifty thousand to start with.'

'I haven't got adequate funds.'

A cruel smile twisted her lips. 'Then sell a few things. Especially that clock! Yes! I insist you sell that clock in order to buy my silence. Now! Immediately.'

Although her vision was blurred, she saw the hatred on her husband's face. So what? She began to laugh then tapped Trevor on the shoulder.

'Your master awaits you – Fido!'

She swayed slightly before staggering off to her bedroom.

The door slammed. Sir Andrew beckoned Trevor to follow him. 'I need to talk to you.'

Wordlessly, Mark Conway followed where he led. The two men went into the dining room closing the door behind them.

'A rare example of a late eighteenth-century mantle clock. Can we start the bidding at one thousand pounds?'

Eleven thirty in the middle of an auction room was not the best place for asking questions and getting answers.

Honey assumed Casper had done it on purpose, especially since their meeting coincided with lot 75.

To her eyes the clock looked incredibly plain, but the tense atmosphere in the saleroom confirmed its importance.

'Its provenance is indisputable,' whispered Casper as though he were in pain.

'It's plain.'

The auctioneers voice filled the room. 'One thousand three, one thousand four, one thousand five . . .'

Casper was bidding. He did it casually, as though he didn't really care whether he bought the lot or not. But anyone who knew him was not so easily deceived.

'It is said to have belonged to Jane Austen's father – sold to pay for his burial.'

'I didn't know Walcot Street church charged that much, seeing as he's buried next to the road.'

It was a joke. The graveyard had been peaceful back then. Now visitors could almost do a drive-past, it was that close to the main A4.

Casper hissed at her to be quiet.

'Sorry. I'll wait for you outside.'

She slipped into the store opposite and purchased a chocolate muffin. Casper wasn't into eating in company, so it was a case of grabbing what she could and eating it before he came out.

The traffic was heavy around Queen's Square and the bin hanging from a lamppost received her food wrappers. By the time she was finished, Casper came strolling out of the auction house looking mighty pleased with himself.

'I take it you were successful?'

He nodded. 'Did you doubt that I would be?'

'I wouldn't dare.'

'Now. This fellow Herbert. He is, or rather was, very friendly with a clock-and-watch dealer named Simon Tye.'

'You never met him yourself?'

He shook his head. 'Absolutely not. But Tye did refer to him once or twice.'

Honey thought of the watches and described them to him. 'Do you think they could be stolen?'

He shrugged. 'Ask the police.'

'That's him,' Casper said, pointing to where two men were manhandling a grandfather clock into the back of a dark blue Volvo estate. 'I'll introduce you.'

Twenty-Six

She'd stood like an icicle, hardly able to take her eyes off the Volvo estate. Leaving Casper to drool over his purchase, she made her way to Manvers Street Police Station.

'Is this your car?' she asked the man introduced to her as Simon Tye.

Simon answered her a split second before Casper was about to butt in that he thought she was going to ask about watches.

'As matter of fact, no. It belongs to a friend.'

'Mervyn Herbert?'

He grinned. 'I know, I know. I should 'ave give it over to the coppers, but I was after this clock and me own jalopy is off the road.'

His blatant honesty astounded her.

'I wanted this clock,' he said on seeing her expression. 'The price was right, and for the mo I had the transport. OK?'

It sounded reasonable enough. But clues were stacking up. He'd known Mervyn. He'd known he'd collected watches. He also knew that his body had been found.

He caught her eyeing him with curiosity. 'Tell them I'll drop it round.'

His cheek amazed her. Her first priority had been to ask Doherty about the watches. Now she would first tell him about finding Mervyn's car.

The desk sergeant showed her into an interview room. He also provided her with tea and biscuits.

Honey sucked on a chocolate digestive that she'd just dipped into her tea. Chocolate muffin and chocolate digestive: not the healthiest diet in the world, but snatched on the hoof. That meant it didn't count towards consumed calories.

Through the window she could see the Georgian buildings at the back of Manvers Street. Her eyes travelled slowly over the back yards where weeds grew and stray moggies mated and fought with each other. Down under the houses were deep cellars. Some stretched out under the road, had rough workshops behind iron grilles. Some were damp, dark and musty. Others had been transformed into very nice basement apartments, or workshops and studios. The best abutting the main thoroughfares had become trendy wine bars and up-market restaurants.

Doherty breezed in.

'I saw Mervyn's car this morning.'

He stopped dead in his tracks. 'Where?'

She told him. 'A chap called Simon Tye said he was only borrowing it and that he would bring it in when he'd finished.'

'You're kidding!'

She shook her head. 'You'll catch him unloading a clock on the double yellow lines on the road closest to his shop.'

He immediately gave orders to have both the car and Simon Tye picked up.

'I take it from your lack of excitability that he wasn't too nervous about the murder.'

She shrugged. 'No, he wasn't. You can never tell though, can you?'

Shaking his head, he went on to tell her that forensic insisted that the number six ingrained on the rotten wood must refer to a house close to the river. But which house? Which street? There were a lot of houses and streets with access to the river.

Honey looked up suddenly. 'Does Simon Tye have a house close to the river?'

'I don't think so, but we'll check.' He eyed her as though not quite sure of what to say next. 'Tea OK?' He took a slurp of his own.

'Mmm,' she muttered. 'You sound as though you know where he lives.'

'He's known to us. A bit too sharp for his own good at times.'

It was Honey's turn to be thoughtful as she sipped her tea. The not quite sure looks continued.

Doherty suddenly surprised her. 'I wondered whether you were free next Wednesday evening? Who knows, we may have a need to celebrate.'

She shook her head. 'I'm not. I've been invited to an open evening at a bookshop.'

He looked crestfallen. 'Please yourself.'

'I will.'

She sensed that he wanted to ask her if she was going alone, but had curbed himself. However, something was brewing, and it wasn't just tea. He was fidgeting, rubbing his hands together, and his eyes were unblinking when he looked at her. It struck her as odd that he wasn't showing that much enthusiasm for pursuing enquiries regarding Simon Tye and the Volvo estate.

'OK,' she said, sensing he wanted her to ask what was afoot. 'You look as though you scored with a supermodel last night. What's up?'

'We've got him,' he blurted.

'And this is a celebratory tea?'

She raised her mug. It had a motif on the side saying 'I Love Bath'. She flashed that side at him.

'Nice to see that the police is promoting tourism, if only in a small way.'

'I'm being serious. Robert Davies is in custody. We found him living with a girlfriend on a narrowboat at Bathampton.'

'I'm pretty serious too. Why do you think the Hotels' Association is getting involved in police work? It's not because we've got nothing better to do.'

Doherty took another slurp and sighed with satisfaction. It could have been as much for the tea as for the case in hand.

'We can't celebrate just yet,' he explained. 'Not until I've got a full confession.'

Honey frowned. 'You haven't got any evidence.'

His cheeks did a funny sucking in and out, as though she'd slapped him on both.

To her great surprise, he slammed his coffee mug down on the desk. 'Well I think I'm the best judge of that,' he said, folding his arms more tightly than usual sending his muscles bulging more noticeably against his shirt. 'We're the professionals. You're only a liaison personage.'

Her eyes opened wide. 'A personage, am I?'

'A personage!'

Now it was she that slammed the mug down. She got to her feet, leaning on her knuckles so she was halfway across the table that stood between them.

Doherty flinched.

Honey had a husky voice at the best of times. Now it rasped out like the rattle of a machine gun.

'Why would Robert Davies kill an American he didn't know?'

Doherty's cheeks sucked in and out again – like bellows, but less effectively. 'We don't know for sure that he killed both of them. That's what we're going to ask him about: Mervyn Herbert and Elmer Maxted were about the same build, same height. We think the first killing was a case of mistaken identity – a text book case.' The smugness returned.

Honey sniffed. 'A bit overdramatic in my books!'

'Look,' he said, mimicking her stance. Both now rested their knuckles on the desk so that their noses were only inches apart. 'Trust me on this. Davies did both murders. I guarantee it.'

His eyes were pools of misty blue that too easily betrayed his thoughts. She'd ridiculed his judgement.

Honey straightened. 'Let's think this through. What about the watches? Were they stolen?'

'We've no record of them.'

'You haven't checked.'

'There's no need to!' He spread his hands and shrugged. Beyond him the backs of Georgian buildings glowed like honeycomb, one building very much like another because that was how they built things then: beautiful crescents, squares and terraces apparently erected absolutely identical and in pleasing symmetry. But they weren't. They were similar at the front, alterations having been done in the years between. The rear elevation of each and every building differed quite starkly from that of its neighbours.

'Steve, it doesn't make sense. How could one be so easily mistaken for the other? OK, I know they were the same height and build, but their features were so different, their hair colour for a start.' Honey considered it quickly. She'd only seen a passport photograph of Elmer Maxted, but she'd seen Mervyn Herbert. There were more differences than similarities. She told Steve Doherty that.

Doherty wasn't to be put off.

'Clothes could make them look similar.'

She shook her head reproachfully. 'It's been warm this month and neither would have been bundled up in a coat. People can disguise themselves if they're dressed for winter wearing scarves and mufflers and thick padded jackets, but hi there, just in case you didn't notice, it's summer.'

His face crumpled as though it was made of paper and she'd just bashed it. The hurt look turned to male petulance, a noisy agitated affair compared to the petulance of a woman.

'That's it! This is the end of our liaison. This is a murder inquiry and I don't need to tell you *anything*!'

She folded her arms. 'We'll let the Chief Constable decide that.'

'Blow him!'

'You're being childish.'

'I am not!

'You're not thinking.'

'Look! If you're a copper, you get a nose for felons like Davies. Believe me, he did it. The first victim was a case of mistaken identity. The second – well, I think we all know the reason for that. The bloke had it coming to him.'

'And the piece of wood? And the spice sacks? The wood had to come from somewhere, a house close to the river. And why spice sacks? Whoever killed these men had to have had access to a source. Otherwise, why not coal sacks or hay sacks, or even plastic bags?'

She could see from his expression that he really didn't want to go down that route at all.

'We'll cross that bridge when we get to it. I expect Davies got hold of them somehow.'

'I'd really like to see you again,' he shouted after her as she headed for the door.

She hesitated, wanting to turn and say, OK. Hurt pride made her keep heading for the exit. He wanted results. Quick results. Even though it would take time she wanted the truth. That, she supposed, was the amateur coming out.

Twenty-Seven

Honey knew what was coming. Her mother was folding table napkins. They weren't as good as they should be. Usually meticulous about presentation, it was obvious that her mind was elsewhere.

'Lindsey didn't come home last night.'

'Who told you that?'

Her mother pursed her lips disapprovingly. 'I went in to make her bed this morning, but didn't need to. It hadn't been slept in.'

Her mother had her own flat but made it her business to help out now and again. Sometimes she stayed over. Fortunately, all the rooms were taken at present.

'She slept at Sam's,' said Honey.

'Sam? Who's he?'

'She – Samantha.'

She wasn't too sure whether it was true. Lindsey had phoned and left a message on the answer phone saying she was sleeping at Sam's place. She didn't know of a female friend named Sam: no way she was telling her mother that.

The pinched lips straightened. 'That's all right then.'

Her mother's next subject was that Mary Jane was organizing a séance in the hope that Sir Cedric would manifest himself on a more visual plain. 'I think she's nuts,' said her mother. 'But there. What can you expect from a woman of her age?'

Honey glanced at her mother. If the truth be known, she was only five to seven years behind Mary Jane.

The phone burbled against her hip. She eyed the caller's number, didn't recognize it, but pressed 'receive' anyway.

'Hi. This is John Rees.'

Flip went her heart. The day was turning brighter. What was it Lindsey had said? Better to be desired by two men rather than one.

'Just a minute.'

Her mother tilted her head quizzically. 'Who's that?'

'It's private.'

She took the phone outside. Sun-dappled leaves rustled against a powder-blue sky. Even more perfect.

'I thought we needed to finalize things.'

His voice reminded her of the southern guys in Elvis Presley's backing group: the sort of huskiness that comes down the nose rather than out of the mouth. Her legs turned to jelly.

They arranged to meet at the George at Norton St Phillip, an ancient hostelry a few miles outside the city. An inn for close on a thousand years, the place was a living museum. Leather harness, old flintlocks, rusty farm implements and bright brass lanterns hung from every beam. A pile of leaflets stating that the hostelry had been brewing since the fourteenth century steadily dwindled. A Japanese group were in, cameras strung around their necks, faces full of enthusiasm. One after another they went to the bar, scrutinized the leaflets and took what they wanted.

North American accents blended easily with those from Canada, Australia, New Zealand and South Africa. French, Italian, German and Dutch gabbled alongside Japanese and Spanish. The place was busy – as usual.

'Wow! Can you beat this!' John exclaimed, head back and eyes wide with wonder. 'Everything is so . . . old! Don't you just love it?'

'It's been here a long time,' said Honey then felt guilty for making such a trite remark. She'd so badly wanted to make an impression, but what sort of impression was that?'

'Are you interested in history . . . ?' She stopped herself. 'Sorry. Of course you are. That's the whole point of the exhibition, isn't it?' If she'd been younger, she would have blushed. The thought was whimsical and fluttered around her mind pushing aside the remaining impetus to go knocking on doors bearing the numbers six and nine: at least for now. It wouldn't go away completely. She felt an affinity with Elmer Maxted. He'd come looking for his roots. She understood that. Daughter of an American father and an English mother, she'd floated between the two worlds, not knowing quite where she belonged. Once he'd blotted his copybook, her mother had blocked out her father's memory.

Like Geoff and me: could behaviour towards men be hereditary? She shuddered at the memory and likely consequences of her departed husband.

John was ordering food. She'd been running on automatic when she'd told him what she wanted: king prawn salad in cajun spices.

They were both driving, so they stayed with soft drinks. Once that was done, they got down to serious conversation – or as serious as it needed to be.

'So how long have you been running the hotel?' It was the question he was bound to ask.

'Two years now.'

'You must enjoy it.'

'Sometimes I enjoy meeting people. Sometimes I want to hide away from them.'

'Understandable. I suppose you don't get too much time off.'

'Not nearly enough. At least this police thing gets me out of the place. It's an interesting other dimension to the hospitality trade.' She surprised herself by burbling on about the murder case and what Steve had said, and what she had said. She stopped herself.

John didn't question whether she was married, divorced or widowed.

'I met your mother and your daughter.'

Honey grimaced at her drink. 'The sugar and spice in my life – though don't ask me which is which.'

'Your daughter looks like you. Your mother . . .'

She held up a warning finger from the side of her raised glass. 'Don't mention anything about broomsticks! OK?'

'I wasn't going to. I was going to say that she's quite a character.'

'That's a thought-provoking description.'

'Oh come on. You make her sound like Cruella de Ville.'

'No, my mother would never make a coat of puppies, though she might make a stew.'

He eyed her speculatively. Speculation and truth-seeking about her family was the last thing she needed.

'Only joking. She's just getting old and cantankerous,' she said lightly lowering her eyes as she sipped her drink.

Heaven help her if Gloria ever found out she'd said that.

Over plates of magnificently pink prawns speckled with spice, their conversation turned to the exhibition. She watched his lips move as he told her about the guest list. They were strong lips, supple with words. *And kissing,* she thought. *I bet they're good at kissing.*

He told her the names of the wines he'd chosen and the fact that his sister-in-law had taken charge of the catering. She wanted to ask why his wife, the ice-queen he'd brought into the restaurant, wasn't doing it, but it was none of her business. Keep to the facts, she thought to herself.

Be a pleasant girl, Hannah! Her mother's voice again. On this occasion she decided to take her advice.

'So what other historical artefacts have you managed to get hold of?'

He finished swallowing a particularly fat prawn before he answered. 'A suit of armour, a sedan chair and a clock: each represents a certain aspect of history. The suit of armour represents military history, the sedan chair represents the history of transport and the clock represents industrial history – the crowning glory of the Industrial Revolution.'

Tilting her head to one side so that her hair tickled her shoulder, she asked, 'So where do Queen Victoria's unmentionables fit in?'

'Simple,' he said, confidence shining like a slipped halo around his eyes, 'they represent women's rights, the march towards emancipation.'

Honey coughed into her drink.

John looked surprised. 'Have I said something funny?'

Regurgitating her drink and in danger of having it come

down her nose, Honey pinched her nostrils quite fiercely. It took a few seconds before she could answer.

'I can't quite see the connection.' It was difficult to control the giggles. She sensed he'd meant to make her giggle. Was her preoccupation with the Elmer Maxted case making her a dolly-dull-drawers?

He went on to explain. 'Big underwear. Big skirts. Women's movement was restricted by their clothes. Then came the twentieth century and – wham! – everything changed.'

'Though not very quickly.'

'OK, no, not very quickly, well not until the twenties, the Charleston and the flappers. But it happened. Women finally escaped big skirts, tight corsets and big underwear.'

It was strangely comforting to watch as he wiped up the juices with a piece of granary bread. 'Imagine all the things you wouldn't be able to do if you wore a big skirt.'

Honey grinned, shook her head and finished her meal. As she raised her glass to finish off the last drop, she caught sight of a familiar face. Loretta Davies saw her, pushed back her chair and marched over.

The smell of wine dropped from her mouth and her eyes were bright with too much of it. She was wearing an embroidered tunic and green leggings. Rings still adorned her fingers and dangled from her ears. Honey gave silent thanks that her pasty belly was covered.

'You know they've arrested my father.'

Honey half-rose. 'Yes, I'm so sorry, Loretta.'

'He didn't do it.' She shook her head slowly as she said it, each individual movement coinciding with each spoken word. 'He didn't,' she added defiantly, as though those two last words confirmed everything not contained in the evidence.

People cast looks in their direction.

Loretta was with her mother. Cora came across and took her hand. 'Come on, Loretta. You're making a scene.'

Cora paused, eyeing Honey over her shoulder. 'They've told me not to touch any of Mervyn's stuff until you lot take another look at things. Robert didn't do it. I know he didn't.'

Honey's eyes narrowed as she watched her go. The question of number six or number nine resurfaced in her mind. The merry moment between her and John was over – at least for this evening.

She wasn't aware at first that his eyes had narrowed and he was studying her.

'Judging by the look on your face, I guess we'd better call it a day,' he said.

Her eyes met his. She saw compassion there, even passion.

'Yes.'

Her gaze strayed to the heavy oak door shutting behind Cora and her daughter.

They needed support. She'd try to give it, but first things first. She had to go back to Charlborough Grange and ask if Elmer Maxted had visited the house. Not this afternoon: she still had a business to run. Tomorrow would do, and she didn't need to go alone.

'Are you doing anything tomorrow?'

John shook his head.

'Fancy a drive in the country?'

'Sure. Where to?'

'Charlborough Grange. Do you know where it is?'

'Sure. Of course I do. That's where the guy lives who's loaning me the clock.'

Twenty-Eight

A summer shower had come and gone. The sun came out and the main A36 that ranged out of Bath and up through Freshford was as wet and shiny as a docile river. A rainbow stretched from one side of the valley to the other. The road, the valley, the river and canal snaked towards it.

Honey felt a bit fraudulent about this being nothing but an afternoon drive. John explained that he was happy to take the opportunity to finalize arrangements for the loan of the clock.

Her phone rang just as they pulled up outside. It was Steve Doherty.

'Guess where Davies has been living?'

She didn't want to guess. From the moment she'd squeezed into the bucket seat in John Rees's Austin Healey, the real world and her concerns had folded in on itself – a bit like the way she'd folded into the seat.

At this moment in time she didn't care who had killed whom. The warmth of John's thigh was pressing against hers. Who cared that the day was warm? A little more heat of this type was perfectly acceptable.

She thought about hitting the 'busy' button. Doherty pre-empted her action.

'Honey? Are you there?' *Too late!*

'Go on. Hit me.'

'Prior to the narrowboat, Davies was living in a flat in Charlotte Terrace. Right next to the river. Number *Six* Charlotte Terrace! We've got him!'

She could imagine his face: the wide-open eyes, the smile fixed like that of a painted clown. No. Clown was wrong. He was a man doing his job in a strait jacket. He had rules and guidelines, the media and a demanding public to deal with.

'Did you find any evidence?'

That she had the audacity to ask the question surprised her. She could imagine his lips pursing as though he'd just sucked on a lemon.

'Circumstantial, but enough. See? I told you he was the right man.'

Doherty was cock-a-hoop that he'd found the culprit. Either he hadn't latched on to the note of misgiving in her voice, or he'd ignored it. The inclination to tell him she was still unconvinced played second fiddle today. He deserved support.

'Yes. You did.'

The connection was terminated.

'All set?' said John.

The young man named Mark Conway listened attentively as John explained why he was there.

'Ah, yes, sir. I am aware of the arrangement.'

They were shown into the conservatory and invited to sit on Lloyd loom chairs. Gratefully they sank into cushions covered in heavy cotton on which huge roses flourished. Mark went off to alert Sir Andrew.

'It's pretty hot in here,' said John, wiping the back of his hand across his forehead. He looked around pop-eyed. 'I suppose this is unchanged since Queen Victoria's time.'

'This place gives me the creeps. Don't you think those plants look like refugees from *The Day of the Triffids*?'

'They are a bit tropical.'

His voice deviated from the calm tone that she'd got used to.

'You don't like this place either, do you?'

He shook his head and gave her a direct look.

'I'm instinctive about places. I pick up vibes.'

'Please. No paranormal stuff.' She explained about Mary Jane. 'One doctor of the paranormal is more than enough!'

Charlborough made an impressive entrance just as John finished laughing, striding towards them, hand offered, his face a picture of patrician bonhomie.

He obviously favoured wearing the same colour from top to toe. Today he was casually dressed in pale-green lamb's-wool sweater and matching trousers. The collar of a checked shirt showed above the 'V'-neck of his sweater.

'My dear, Rees, how are you my dear fellow?'

'Fine, sir. I thought I would drive out and go over the final arrangements with you – if it's not inconvenient that is?'

'No, no, my dear fellow! Not at all!'

Perhaps it was the way John said it, or perhaps the way he looked, but Charlborough seemed unable to say no. He effused warmth and welcome, far different from when she had called here in Doherty's company. Doherty had attitude. So did she come to that.

When Charlborough's eyes turned to her, his smile tightened.

'This is Honey Driver. She collects antique clothes,' John explained.

Honey saw no point in denying the obvious. 'We've already met.'

They shook hands. Recognition clouded his eyes then was gone. His smile was tight, his grip limp.

'I came here in my capacity as liaison officer for the Hotels' Association. I asked you about Elmer Maxted.'

'Ah, yes,' he said with a stiff nod of his head. 'I seem to recall that you'd mislaid an American tourist.'

The terminology irritated. Her smile was as stiff and cold as his. 'He was not mislaid. He was murdered.'

'Ah! And the police have arrested the perpetrator?'

She couldn't help thinking he already knew this. News travelled fast – the 'old boys' network was rife with senior police chiefs and crown-court judges.

'They have arrested someone. Whether they make the charges stick is, as always, a different matter.'

'Quite so.' He turned immediately to John. 'Now, about my clock . . .'

Honey's gaze wandered to the gardens and grounds beyond the thick foliage and the stifling conservatory. A church spire pierced the sky above a row of rustling poplars.

The humidity, all for the benefit of the monstrous plants, was unbearable. She began dabbing at her glistening cheeks with the back of her hand.

'I'm sorry,' she said, interrupting their conversation; 'would it be all right if I went outside for some fresh air?'

For a moment she detected indecision on Charlborough's face, as he weighed up the consequences of granting or refusing his permission.

'Sorry for boring you,' John said as casually as you like. 'We're rambling into the realms of history.' He grinned across at Sir Andrew. 'Not everyone is as fascinated by the subject as we are. A little fresh air helps blow the cobwebs away, so they say.'

Charlborough's expression veered between arrogance and pained forbearance. 'Of course.' He turned to Honey. 'Please keep to the garden area. I have projects under way in the rest of the grounds.'

She didn't ask what projects, but the fact that places had been forbidden made her curious.

Her sweat cooled once she was out in the fresh air. Steps led down from the raised area outside the conservatory. Red-and-orange nasturtiums trailed from weathered urns. A balustrade of moss-covered stone ran around its perimeter.

Manicured lawns of epic size and decorous design swooped between the flowerbeds and trees, like a river running towards the sea. Unlike a river, these lawns ran up against a red-brick wall. The mortar joining the bricks was white and smeared, the bricks uneven and irregular, signs of age and ageing. An arched wooden door, the sort found in churches and medieval castles, dissected the wall just before it disappeared behind a laburnum. Nothing of a gardener, she vaguely remembered that laburnum flowers were poisonous. She made a mental note to check this, though goodness knows what for. Poison had not been used.

The door might not have beckoned so strongly if Charlborough hadn't ordered her – yes, *ordered* her to stay within the garden. But there it was: a cast-iron ring hanging there, waiting to be touched, turned and pulled.

It was probably locked, but it wouldn't hurt to try. The

door opened. There again were the huge greenhouses, thick with greenery, far more profligate than the huge specimens thronging the conservatory. And the size . . . a football pitch? At least. It was huge!

The roof curved like those on wartime structures, those now disintegrating under the onslaught of the years and the weather. Sandbags piled a dozen or so high protected its entrance. A shovel stood upright in a pile of sand beside a wooden fruit box – the sort used for storing oranges.

Just like the last time, no one was around. She wondered when they actually held these war games that people paid to fight.

The only sound was of birds and bees. Just as she'd hoped there were a few loose sacks on the ground next to the sand.

Sacks! *The* sacks?

She grabbed one and shook out the sand.

Holding it with both hands, she scrutinized its size. It looked too big. Just to make sure, she took a deep sniff. It smelled of new sacking.

Just as she thought about leaving, the door to the greenhouse made a wheezing sound. Humid air poured out to taint the freshness of a day after rain.

The fact that someone had come out with the tepid air did not register as quickly as it should have done. The sandbags were piled high and hid him until they were facing each other, each taken off guard, each unsure of how to proceed.

'You.' The same man as the time before. The man Sir Andrew had referred to as Trevor. Some kind of butler. Some kind of nightmare.

She brazened it out. 'Yes. I got a little hot in the conservatory. Sir Andrew said I could go outside.'

He had a square face, a down-turned mouth, deep-set eyes and shoulders that, although wide, totally lacked muscle definition. It was as though they had been cut out of stone and the sculptor had not as yet chiselled in the bodily details. Eye colour was hidden in the dark hollows beneath his brows.

Frightening! More so than before: like coming across Frankenstein's monster on a dark and dirty night, except that it was daytime.

She sensed that, for her own protection, she was the one who should first offer an explanation. She held the sack behind her back, letting it fall slowly to the ground.

'I'll make my way back now. I was promised a pot of tea.'

Not the entire truth, but close enough.

The man standing before her shifted his weight on to the opposite leg; either his tension was dissipated or he was about to make a grab for her. Discretion immediately became the better part of valour. Her legs jet-propelled her back to the door and the manicured lawns, the house and the overpowering heat of the conservatory. Hidden behind a sweet smelling bush, she took the opportunity to catch her breath, daring to look behind her when she was sure no one was following.

Sir Andrew had said that he was just a gardener tending the greenhouse. But the unease remained. Was it really only for war games, or was it something more sinister? Drugs were the obvious answer if she cared to take a jaundiced view of Sir Andrew. But what sort of drugs grew to that height?

'Better now?' asked John.

She forced a casual smile – the sort that worked well with pink cheeks and being slightly breathless.

Sir Andrew's eyes bored into her. 'I'm so glad you feel better.'

'Yes. Thank you.' She wondered if he had guessed that she'd disobeyed his orders, but wasn't given the chance to find out. The sound of a woman's voice seemed to splinter the beams of weak sunlight that had managed to shine through the canopy of plants.

'Darling, I didn't know we had visitors!'

Pamela Charlborough's hair was Helsinki-blonde. Her face was Bermuda-bronze. She wore a red silk dress that rustled when she walked and her perfume smelt of money. Her bare arms were covered in freckles and her toenails were painted the same colour as her dress and the high-heeled mules she wore. She was swaying slightly and carrying a very full wine glass.

'Another of your little soldier friends?' she asked in a raucous voice. 'My, but he's out of uniform! You should reprimand him at once, darling. Bend him over your lap, pull down his trousers and smack his tight little bottom!'

She suddenly noticed Honey. 'Oh! A little woman soldier, perhaps?' Her features screwed up like discarded paper. 'Don't I know you from somewhere?'

'Pamela!' The broken veins in Charlborough's cheeks spread over his face like a raging forest fire.

Lady Pamela looked surprised. 'Have I got the wrong end of the stick, darling?'

Sir Andrew's face was like thunder. 'Go away, Pamela!'

John was looking embarrassed.

Honey merely observed, feeling embarrassed at belonging to the same sex as the sun-tanned blonde.

Lady Charlborough's eyes narrowed once she was close enough to see Honey's face more clearly. 'Didn't you come here with that charming young detective? Yes! I'm sure you did.' She turned to Sir Andrew. 'Oh, my dearest darling, what have you been up to now?'

These two were far from being dearest darling to each other.

Sir Andrew looked daggers. 'Nothing! You're drunk!'

'Oh am I, darling? Then I'd better stop at once.' She laughed, took a few steps forward then poured her wine into a potted plant. The wine glass followed its contents, the bowl breaking from its stem.

Her husband was far from amused. 'Pamela! For God's sake, that's Waterford crystal!'

Smirking stupidly, Pamela Charlborough hid her mouth behind her hand. 'Silly me. Should not have said those dreadful things, should I? Naughty, naughty things.' She laughed again.

Although Charlborough looked thoroughly embarrassed, Honey found it hard to pity him. He was too smooth. The post of lord of the manor was ingrained in him. This was hardly the first trophy wife to end up feeling trapped and disappointed with the older, richer man she had married.

'I apologize for my wife's rudeness.' Sir Andrew's voice dropped an octave or two and his apology seemed sincere.

'We get on best when we're apart,' said Lady Pamela. 'In fact, I'm off to Spain tonight. My husband is footing the bill. Aren't you, darling?'

'That's nice for you. I hope you have a very nice time,' said Honey, her smile and tone as sarcastic as she could make it.

Pamela wagged a perfectly manicured finger. 'Aren't you presently playing at being a detective? I recollect you mentioned this when we met before.'

'Yes.' Honey maintained her smile. 'I probably recollect it more clearly than you do.'

The inference was obvious but took a while to sink in. Once it did, the insincerity of Her Ladyship's smile was echoed in her eyes.

'Well that's the way it is with trade, isn't it? I presume one has to do everything one can to make ends meet.'

Just when she was ready to floor Her Ladyship with a swift right hook, John stepped in. 'Where do you stay in Spain?'

His tone and smile were enough to charm the pants off a nun – and Lady Pamela was far from being that.

They left with arrangements fully made for the loan of the clock, and Lady Pamela inviting John to stay at her private villa if ever he came to Spain. Honey was ignored.

'Bitch,' muttered Honey once they were in the car and heading back to Bath.

'I think her husband is of the same opinion,' said John.

'A divorce in the making?'

'You bet. I've been lucky in that respect. My ex-wife is very convivial.'

The slim, gorgeous creature? Honey had to find out.

'Was that her . . .'

'In the restaurant the other night? Yes.'

Honey breathed a sigh of relief. He was just her type – and available.

'She sounds like a lady – which is more than I can say for Lady Pamela Charlborough.'

Twenty-Nine

There were garages converted from the original stabling at the rear of Charlborough Grange. The doors had been widened to take cars.

Mark Conway was servicing the engine on Pamela Charlborough's Mercedes Sports. He was slick with sweat, his T-shirt sticking against his skin. His hands worked quickly and efficiently. He knew what he was doing – was absorbed in it.

He smelled her perfume– expensive perfume, of course – before he saw her.

'Darling, you're coming to Spain with me aren't you?'

The bonnet was up and threw a shadow across his face. 'I'm wanted here,' he said without turning round.

He heard her heels clicking on the concrete, knew her hips were swaying provocatively as she sashayed towards him. His blood raced when she ran her hands down his back, tracing his muscles beneath the thin fabric of his T-shirt.

'I want you in Spain,' she said. 'I want you all ways and which ways in Spain.' His bare biceps were hard beneath her hands. She sucked in her breath. 'You have such a beautiful body, Mark.'

'I'm busy.' He tried to shrug her off.

She clung on. Her lips brushed against his neck. 'Imagine making love on a deserted beach or high on a cliff top overlooking the sea.'

Thoughtfully he wiped his hands on a piece of rag. 'Your husband might not like that.'

'I would like it,' she breathed. 'You know I would.' Her fingers travelled up to his jaw. 'I thought you loved me.'

He smiled. 'I've made love to you.'

'Whatever. It's enough for me. And I thought we'd agreed . . . you know . . . that afternoon. You agreed to get rid of him.'

'And how do I do that?'

'Fix his brakes,' she whispered. 'Make it look like an accident.'

Honey checked herself in the mirrored doors of the dining room. This evening she'd chosen to wear a white linen suit with a blue–and-silver rope belt. Casual but classy: her favourite words when it came to fashion.

'These earrings,' said Lindsey who had insisted on choosing her clothes with her, had made up her face and was now choosing her accessories. 'And this bracelet.'

'Whatever you say.'

Having someone make all the decisions was unbelievably wonderful.

'And remember to be home before twelve,' said Lindsey with a crafty grin. 'You won't change into a pumpkin or anything. I was just going to remind you to take your key just in case.'

'I promise I won't sleep over.'

Lindsey shrugged. Honey sensed a backing off because her daughter knew what was coming.

'So who's this Sam?'

Lindsey tutted and shook her head. 'You couldn't resist, could you? You had to ask.'

'Please,' Honey said. 'I worry about you.'

'Don't. Sam is a great guy. There's a lot between us. Just how much, only time will tell.'

Honey held up her hands in mute surrender.

'I'm off now.'

Her smile disintegrated on seeing her mother's reflection over her shoulder. She was dressed in Donna Karan and smelling of Chanel Number Five.

'And what shall I tell Mr Paget?'

That tone of voice! School reports came to mind. *Must try harder!*

'Mother, I've already told you, I'm not interested in Mr Paget.' Straight-backed and determined she headed for the door.

Her mother followed. 'But he's a dentist!'

She said it as though pulling people's teeth was tantamount to overseeing the International Monetary Fund.

Honey paused. 'And that, my dear mother, is reason enough not to be interested.'

'You can be very insensitive at times.'

'I'll look him up when I need a tooth pulled.'

Pouting her apricot lips and folding her arms, her mother stated, 'And what about Mary Jane's séance? Seven thirty she said.'

Honey closed her eyes. Typical of her mother: totally without warning, she'd leapt from one subject to another. 'I forgot!'

'Yes, you forgot, Miss Know-All!'

Her mother's reprimand was worse than having a tooth pulled. At least with a tooth there were drugs to counteract the pain.

Mary Jane was a delight, a truly valued guest, but in comparison with gorgeous John?

She opened her eyes. 'Mother, I have to go. This is important. I've accepted the invitation and have to attend. See?'

Retrieving the embossed card from her purse, she waved it in front of her mother's face.

Her mother's expression was unaltered. 'You don't fool me. I know why you're going.'

'But, Mother, I thought you wanted me to catch myself a man.'

Her mother sniffed. 'That doesn't excuse you. Mary Jane will be *very* disappointed.'

'I have to go,' Honey mumbled and headed for her precious exit through the bar, leaving her mother grim-faced and muttering about the evils of drink.

Union Passage is a traffic-free thoroughfare of specialist shops with narrow frontages, some unchanged since Beau Brummel was a lad. Street musicians and jugglers rub shoulders with tourists looking for a bargain and office workers looking for a lunch-time sandwich. Despite the shops selling Play Stations, mobile phones and computer graphics, it has retained its Dickensian charm.

Ideal for a bookshop, thought Honey walking with confidence through the gathering dusk on a balmy July night.

John Rees had been lucky enough to lease a shop still retaining an old fashioned frontage of art deco design. The theme of the framework supporting the window was taken across the glass in the form of a transparent Beardsley woman. Typically she had flowing tresses and gown, her willowy arms framing the central display.

The shop door was open. A hum of conversation and the tinkle of glasses drifted out. Hopefully the night air would drift in. Few shops boasted air conditioning and although linen was cool, it creased easily.

Making up in depth for what it lacked in breadth, a throng of people jostled like a queue, wine glasses held tightly to chest. Cut-glass voices droned on about the meaning behind an author's work or the reasons why women were forced – *forced* – into wearing corsets.

'It was a man's way of keeping a woman submissive,' the dreaded Audrey Tyson-Dix was imparting to a politely attentive John Rees.

Honey stood on tiptoe to ensure that their eyes met.

He smiled, swiftly introduced Audrey to someone else and eased himself in her direction. He managed to grab a glass of wine en route.

'Glad you could come.'

'It's a tight squeeze,' she said. As she said it, a woman with a bookshelf bosom and belly to match squeezed between them. Despite the fact that she'd eased through sideways, Honey still ended up with her wine glass pressed against her nose.

John grabbed her hand. 'Follow me.'

Holding her wine glass high, she did as she was told.

'There's steps here,' he said over his shoulder.

Three steps. 'And some more.' Another three.

Eventually, they were at the back of the shop and had

room to breathe. John nodded to where the crowd was thickest. 'Never mind the culture, you can see what they've really come for.'

Sadly, he was right. The wine and food had been placed on a table at the front of the shop on the lowest level. That was where the crowd was thickest.

She smiled up at him and clinked her glass against his. 'There are always exceptions.'

He smiled back. 'I'm glad to hear it. Would you care for a look at the exhibits?'

'OK.'

First stop was her own property.

'Yours, of course.'

'Not literally,' she said, shaking her head. 'They might have been OK for Queen Victoria, but I wouldn't be seen dead in them.'

'Passion-killers.'

'Definitely. I barely saved them from one of my waitresses who presumed they were a tablecloth. My mother calls them 'harvest festivals'. All is safely gathered in.'

'Can't say I'm surprised.'

Her eyes strayed to Sir Andrew's clock. John followed her gaze.

'He insisted I insure it.'

Honey frowned. 'I've only met the owner a few times, but already I get the impression that it's the love of his life.'

John tilted his head to one side as he observed it. 'Not exactly. Apparently he idolizes his son, Lance, so I hear.'

'Is that so? I haven't met him.'

'I get the impression he's at Harvard, though unwillingly. It was his grandfather's wish and a provision in his Will that Lance finished his education there. The old man left all his money to his daughter, but when she died everything went to him. Seems he was only a kid at the time, not much more than a baby.'

'I wonder what she was like in comparison to Lady Pamela.'

'A bit more of a lady?'

'I would think so.'

'I understand wife number two has now left for Spain.

Sir Andrew phoned me earlier. He's promised to show up later.' He shrugged. 'Whether he will or not . . .'

Honey's gaze slid sidelong to the horde of hungry guests. 'He'll have to squeeze himself in.'

John looked at his watch. 'He did promise.'

'Well I doubt that he's accompanying his darling wife to Spain. I think he must hate Spain as much as he does her.'

John shrugged and took a slug of wine. 'He was living there when his wife died in a car crash – head on, just her and the boy: Luckily Lance survived.'

They moved slowly along the exhibits: the books; memorabilia; lace mittens, bonnets, old tools etc.

'Look at these,' he said, indicating a few sheets of newspaper preserved behind glass. 'Do you know, it's only in the last hundred years or so that newspapers were available to everyone? Facts were shouted out by town criers and passed from mouth to mouth. Truth could be mighty distorted between source and target audience back then.'

Honey squinted to read the tiny print of the oldest newspaper he had there. 'It's a wonder any news ever got through.'

John nodded. 'Great battles and occasions; it all got through OK. My dad kept old newspapers covering the war years. He used to bring them out now and again just to remind himself of what he'd gone through.' John's voice took on an aura of sadness. 'It's surprising how reading an old newspaper can jog the memory.'

'Yes,' she murmured, squinting to read the tiny print. 'Old newspapers can be . . . That's it!'

John frowned at the glass she'd shoved into his hand.

'I have to go.'

'Was it something I said?'

'Yes,' she groaned, touching his face with her fingertips. 'John, would you think I was too forward if I told you that I wanted to take you to bed?'

He shook his head. 'No.'

'Oh, that's wonderful. But I can't hold you to that just yet. There's something I've got to do. Can you keep it warm for me? I can't say I'll be back tonight, but imminently. What do you say?'

'That's good for me.'

He looked happy when she kissed him on the cheek. It was all she could do for now.

Every step to the shop door was painful, not just because it was slow but because business was overriding pleasure. She had to get to where it had all began, and clocks had nothing to do with it.

She didn't hear him following her. She wasn't meant to. That was the good thing about wearing trainers. OK, your feet might end up stinking, but no one heard you following.

He saw her take her phone from out of her pocket and tap in a number. Judging from the brief moment the phone was next to her ear there was either no signal or the battery was flat.

He'd expected her to return to the hotel. Instead she headed for the taxi rank outside the Abbey.

Swearing beneath his breath, he eyed the number of people still strolling around, recording their visits to the city on digital camcorders and cameras. His eyes wove with her through the crowds and watched as she got into a taxi.

A text came through to him on his own phone. He read the message quickly. He was wanted. It wouldn't take long. He'd catch up with Honey Driver later.

Thirty

Lady Pamela Charlborough snapped shut the clasp of her Gucci handbag and summoned all her bravery. She turned to her husband.

'My car's broken. Mark will have to drive me to the airport. I've booked a hotel. He can stay overnight.'

Her husband took quick strides across the room, caught her wrist and squeezed hard.

Fear creased the pumped out flesh around the botoxed lips as she struggled. 'Stop it! Stop it! You're hurting me.'

He tightened his grip.

'Good. I want to hurt you.' He smiled at the thought of her feeling pain, the discomfort as her veins filled up with trapped blood.

He brought his face close to hers.

'Let me go!'

'Darling,' he said between grinding teeth. 'How can I let you go my little darling, you who think you have the right to dispose of my possessions even before I am dead, things that I prize, things that have been in this house for years?'

'I needed the money!'

Sir Andrew's hand encompassed her neck. His thumb pressed on her windpipe. She began to choke and tugged with both hands at his fingers, her eyes wide with fear.

He still held his brandy glass in his other hand. The feel of her squirming excited him. Her mouth was open. He knew she was trying to scream but no sound came out. He was holding her neck far too tightly for that. The wine glass snapped in his hand. Pamela's eyes almost bulged out of her head, partly through lack of breath, partly through fear.

He brought the jagged edge of the stem close to her

face. She closed her eyes. When she found nothing had happened, she opened them again. She mouthed the most profane words she knew, yet no sound came out. But he understood. She could see from his eyes that he had understood. It had been years since she'd looked up into his eyes at this close a range. He looked as if only part of him was in the room. The rest was somewhere else.

He relaxed his grip on her neck. Staggering and gasping for air she ran for the stairs.

Once the bedroom door was safely locked, clothes and shoes and toiletries flew into her luggage. Lingerie was wound into balls; shoes were shoved haphazardly amongst delicate laces, silks and cashmere.

The locks were fastened. Passport and essentials were thrown into a tan leather bag with the famous Gucci symbol on the side. Her cell phone fell on to the silk and satin counterpane.

Chest heaving, she stared at it. Revenge was like an ice-cold knife between her ribs. It was not in her power to destroy Andrew, but she could make things difficult for him – swine as he was.

She phoned the police, asked for whoever was in charge of the case and told him that the murdered American *had* visited Charlborough Grange.

'It would be very worthwhile if you questioned my husband.'

Doherty noted what she said. 'We do already have someone helping us with our enquiries. I'll let you know if we need to speak to you or your husband again.'

Frustrated by his answer, she slammed the 'disconnect' button. Someone had to be interested.

Her! The hotel-liaison person! She'd left her card.

Honey answered on the fourth tone.

'My husband lied. The American was here,' she said once the initial introductions were taken care of.

'That's interesting. Thank you very much.'

Lady Pamela's mouth remained open. This was not the response she'd hoped for – from either of them.

'Interesting? Is that all you can say?'

'Look, I'm a bit busy at the moment, but if you'd like to jot down all you remember . . .'

'Surely what I know deserves a little time?'

'All right. Tell me something.'

Pamela paused. 'Elmer Maxted. Do you know where he died?'

Honey sighed. 'As far as they know, he was killed in the cellars of one of the houses with access to the river. They think the house he was murdered in was numbered six or nine.'

'I see.'

'What did you want to tell me?' asked Honey.

'Never mind. I'll put it in a letter.'

She slammed the phone shut. Razor-thin, it slid from her hand and into her suitcase.

Nothing was going quite as she'd wanted it too. Even her car was refusing to start. 'Give me an hour and I'll take a look at it,' said Mark.

'Half an hour!'

He turned his back on her temper. 'An hour!'

'Mark, I think you should come to Spain with me.'

He glanced at her, then looked away. He said nothing.

She wanted to say so much, but couldn't. He might not approve of what she was about to do.

The maid had left today's *Bath Chronicle* on the dressing table. The headlines caught her eye: SUSPECT RELEASED. She read on. The police had raided the wrong house, the wrong terrace. What was more, the suspect they had arrested had been released due to lack of evidence. She shivered.

Her room was an oasis of tranquil pale lime and deep pink. She sat herself at her desk, took out a pad and began to write. Once finished, she read what she had written. Her fine eyebrows arched with satisfaction. Yes. This would do the trick.

Frances Tolly, the housekeeper, came in to tell her that Mark had failed to fix her car.

'Then tell him to get the Rolls out, and tell him I need a driver,' she added. 'I'm not driving that bloody great thing!

He'll have to stay overnight at the airport hotel.' *And come with me. Yes, he must come with me!*

Pamela smiled at the prospect. Perhaps it was just as well that the sleek little Mercedes would not start. The thought of Mark's youthful body sent a shiver of excitement down her spine. There was so much potential in that young man. She'd tempted him into having sex with her. Now she must persuade him to get rid of Andrew.

Frances turned to go.

'Wait a moment. Can you post this for me, Frances? It needs a stamp.'

'Of course.'

After sealing the envelope, she passed it to the maid.That, she thought, closes the last chapter in a loveless marriage. They'd get divorced and she'd get her share and that would be that.

Her luggage was transferred into the trunk of the Rolls-Royce. Trevor was driving. She would have preferred Mark, but he'd gone on an errand. She didn't look back as they drove off. She never wanted to see the place again.

The main gate loomed up before them. Suddenly, Trevor stopped the car.

'What's wrong?' she asked frantically.

'There's something wrong with the brakes. We'll have to go back.'

'My God!' She shivered. *If I don't kill him, he'll sure as hell kill me.* 'Thank goodness you noticed, Trevor.'

He swung the car round and headed back down the drive.

Trevor left the car running whilst he went into the garage to find what he needed. When he got back out the car was gone. He ran round to the front of the house. Nothing. No car to be seen.

Arms hanging listlessly at his side, he shrugged and walked back to the house. She'd probably wanted to drive herself. It wouldn't be the first time she'd shot off to meet a secret lover. He didn't care which it was. He had the greenhouses to contend with. He had war games to prepare.

Thirty-One

Cora's hands shook as she placed the cereal packets along the sideboard in the dining room, the granola next to the bran flakes; the cornflakes next to the Rice Crispies, then the Weetabix, the Shreddies and the Sugar Puffs.

Things wouldn't be done like this at the Green River, but in a guest house it was perfectly acceptable. The lines were straight, the crockery gleamed and the cutlery sparkled. None of this seemed enough for Cora. Again and again she realigned the packets. Her hands shook and for once her fingers did not reach for cigarettes.

Honey tried to contain her excitement. She might be wrong about the newspapers being the key to everything, but her instinct told her otherwise. Her instinct also told her to tread carefully; be nice.

'It must be very difficult – losing your husband and trying to keep things going.' Two husbands actually, and when it came to charm and reliability, both were interchangeable. She didn't add anything about Mervyn having abused his position as stepfather to Loretta. How would I feel, she wondered. A pair of large pinking shears – the heavy and very sharp sort that dressmakers use – popped into her mind: something else she mustn't voice!

'Our Loretta's a help. She's given up her other job to give me a hand.'

'That's good of her.'

Cora stopped the obsessive moving of cereal packets and glared at her. 'She's a good girl! I won't have anyone saying anything else. Neither will Bob.'

Robert Davies! The impression came over loud and clear

that she and her former husband were shoulder to shoulder in this.

'You don't think he killed Mervyn?'

'Of course he didn't! Though at times he was tempted mark you!'

Honey shook her head. 'No. I don't think he did either.'

'That copper does.'

Honey knew Cora was referring to Doherty. 'It has to be admitted that your first husband did have a motive for killing your second husband. But why the American? It doesn't make sense to pin that one on him as well.'

Cora shook her head emphatically. 'He didn't do it! Neither of 'em!'

Sitting at a table with an instant coffee, Honey watched as Cora resumed her fussing along the sideboard, straightening servers, smoothing the lace-edged cloth covering the polished wood. The intricacies of the case slid around in her head – a bit like pieces of Scrabble; a bit like Cora rearranging the cereal packets. That's what she was doing, only mentally and not with coloured cardboard.

Move that bit there, this bit here, and approach from another angle. She could have come straight out and said, 'Hey, can I have a look at the old newspapers those watches are wrapped in.' Best to tread softly, she'd decided. *Softly, softly catchee monkey,* or in this case a motive and a murderer.

'Do you think Mervyn was capable of murder?' The question was out before she could put on the brakes.

Cora was like a figure on a TV screen when someone hits the pause button on the video. She didn't seem surprised, more confused, as though the thought had never, ever entered her bleached-blonde head.

Eventually, she came to herself. 'Mervyn was a first-class creep, and that's putting it mildly! Bob was never like that. Never!'

She picked up a duster and began flicking it at imagined specks around the bay window. The windows rattled as a heavy truck trundled past heading towards Bristol.

'But him murder that nice Mr Weinstock? No. Like our

Loretta said, Mervyn invited him into his den. He didn't do that very often I can tell you. Even me and our Loretta weren't allowed in there.'

Something clicked in Honey's brain. Cora had just called her first husband Bob. No! Could it be Mary Jane's Bob the Job?

'Did er . . . Bob . . . meet Elmer?'

Cora stiffened.

'Bob the Job?'

Cora leaned on the sideboard when she turned round. Her doughy figure turned doughier.

'So. You know about it. That was his interest, you see. He started doing it in prison years ago. He'd put adverts in magazines about helping people trace their roots, and they'd write to him. Got hundreds of replies he did.'

Though her mouth was dry with excitement, Honey curbed her enthusiasm. She didn't want to alienate Cora. The poor woman had gone through enough.

'Is there any chance that you and Bob might get back together?'

Cora shrugged. 'There may be – if we get through this bother, that is.'

Honey put down her coffee mug. 'So. Tell me about Mervyn's watches. He was quite a collector.'

'That's right. Rubbish most of them, from car boots and junk shops. But that was his hobby. Mended them and got them going he did.'

Honey tapped thoughtfully at the rim of her coffee mug as though a road through all this had only just come to her. 'Do you think I could have another look in there?'

Cora made a whistling sort of noise as she drew in her breath. 'The police said it wasn't to be disturbed. I got told off for clearing it up.'

Honey played her ace. 'You never know. I might pick up on something that the police have overlooked. Who knows, it might help your first husband get off the hook. And then, who knows, the two of you might have a future together.'

Cora pursed her lips as she thought it through. 'Why not?'

'But we won't tell the police. Right?'

'Coppers! What do they know! Come on.' She flung down her duster.

Mervyn's den smelled of dried rubber and stale beer. The blink of a computer terminal caught her eye. The unit was old and smudged with dirty finger-and-palm prints. Having a frugal attitude to energy waste, she turned the screen off and looked for the box.

Cora had placed it beneath the ancient desk on which the computer sat. She pulled it out. As she unwrapped the contents from their newspaper, she became aware of Cora watching her from the doorway.

Wishing she had a camera, she placed each one on top the desk. None of them looked particularly valuable, but you could never tell.

'Do you have a camera?' she asked Cora.

Cora disappeared and came back with the required object. There was enough film to include most of the watches if she put three or four together in one shot.

Pretty soon she'd done the lot. The idea was to show them to Casper. He would know if they were valuable. Cora could do with the money.

One of the newspapers tore as she started to rewrap each watch as she'd found it. Her hands shook. Various headlines caught her eye. They were interesting, some downright dramatic, but what exactly was she looking for?

The tragedies of the world were there in black and white. Robberies, murders, and children left motherless following a fire. The odd thing about the papers was that they weren't local to Bath. On the contrary, they'd been published in Ireland. She read on. One of the boys had been abducted and never seen again. The other had been given a home by a wealthy landowner in the south-west.

Honey sat back on her haunches and sighed. 'These newspapers are next to useless.'

Cora misunderstood. 'I'll go and fetch some more.' Cora turned to go.

'No. Best not,' said Honey. 'The police might get uppity about us disturbing things.'

As far as she could see, the newspapers said nothing. The sudden idea at the bookshop wasn't as good as it first seemed. It couldn't have been them that had led to the murder of two men of two different nationalities, and probably two different dispositions. Except . . .

There was a son . . . he'd survived an accident in which his mother had died. Not like these two loves, she thought eyeing the orphans whose mother had died in a fire.

One of the boys looked quite a bit older than the other. The younger one looked to be about the same age as young Lance would have been when his mother died.

She frowned. And this means something. But what?

Once the watches were rewrapped, Cora went with her to the front door.

'It's a nice night,' said Honey.

Cora sighed. 'It'll be a better night once all this is sorted out. It's unsettling having people think you've done away with yer husband. Bad for business.'

Honey wasn't so sure. Having a murdered husband found in the back garden attracted the ghoulishly curious. A murdered American was a different matter. The national press had got hold of the story. OK if it had stayed local, but national could syndicate the news to international. She thought about this more deeply as she walked back along Bristol Road. She got a taxi as far as Widcombe Basin.

'I'll walk from here,' she said, got out and paid the driver.

She took a left along the towpath enjoying the smell of water, the colours of a narrowboat moored in the lock. Lights from the restaurant of a nearby hotel lay like fallen stars on the water. The night was clear, veins of purple stretching from the western sky, the air just cool enough to invigorate the brain without chilling the skin.

She passed a troop of tourists undertaking yet another ghost walk. The tour guide, a leggy chap wearing learned glasses above an acne-covered chin, was sounding awestruck.

'There are many legends and many buildings supposedly haunted by a "Grey Lady". One of the most famous has to be the one who haunts the Theatre Royal.'

A low murmur of interest rustled through the listeners. 'Have you ever seen her?' someone asked.

'I didn't exactly see her,' said the guide, his eyes brilliant behind the wire-rimmed specs. 'But I did feel her presence. It's a bit like turning round quickly and fancying you've just seen someone out of the corner of your eye.'

Perhaps it was the tone of emphatic belief that made Honey do just that. Someone ducked into a doorway. A ghost? No. She'd caught a glimpse of white trainers. Ghosts didn't wear white trainers – did they?

Swiftly she joined the crowd following behind their guide like a clutch of spring ducklings.

Someone nudged her elbow. 'Have you ever felt someone was trying to get in touch with you from the other side?' The woman spoke in a thick New York accent.

Honey grimaced. 'Mostly my bank manager when I've gone on the wrong side of my overdraft facility.'

Thirty-Two

The sun streamed into the dining room of the Green River Hotel. The clattering of cutlery against crockery drowned the sound of butter knives grating against toast. Guests conversed across white damask tablecloths and the smell of grilled bacon and fresh coffee drifted like a friendly wraith around the room.

Mary Jane sat at her usual table in the farthest corner – her favourite spot. From there she had a panoramic view of the breakfast room and everybody entering it. Her head bobbed to one side when she caught sight of Honey, and a starburst of wrinkles spread out from her lips as she smiled.

Honey raised the coffee pot. 'Coffee?'

Mary Jane's smile remained as she nodded. Her eyes stayed unblinking on Honey's face. 'He's been watching you,' she said in a hushed voice.

Honey had been about to ask her what she wanted for breakfast: Mary Jane's statement pulled her up with a start. Her first inclination was to ask if he wore white trainers. Instead she kept it simple.

'Has he now?'

'Yes. I think it's you he's interested in. Do you ever notice him?'

She guessed where this was going: Mary Jane's long-dead ancestor. Mine host must grin and bear it. And dead residents were so much less trouble than the living ones!

Anna had not turned in for work this morning. Nor had Rosie, a stalwart of the fifty-plus generation who had rarely, if ever, let her down.

Logic told her that both had good excuses for not coming in. Rosie phoned in pretty sharply. She'd slipped the length of the stairs on her backside and had gone to see her chiropractor. Anna had stayed too long in the bar with Smudger the night before. Logic told her that she was still in bed – probably with Smudger. Unfortunately, being able to work out the mysteries occurring in the lives of her staff didn't get the breakfast out. Dumpy Doris was cooking breakfast whilst she and two girls on work experience waited on tables. Such was the glamour of the hotel trade. Flying by the seat of your pants was more like it!

Mary Jane's chirpy take on the paranormal was amusing but sometimes irritating – like now.

'I saw you waltzing along the Royal Crescent the other day. He was right behind you.'

Sir Cedric no doubt. 'And I thought he never left the ancestral home.' Still smiling, Honey waltzed off to the next table with the coffee pot.

Mary Jane leaned backwards, cricking her head to an awkward angle. 'I don't mean Sir Cedric. I mean the guy who looks like that film star who ended up getting butchered in *Gladiator*.'

Being hit with a baseball bat couldn't have been worse. She just about controlled her shaking hands. Smiling, she put the pot down on the next table. 'Help yourselves,' she said to the four Australians sitting there.

Pulling up a chair, she leaned over the table and looked up into Mary Jane's wise old face. 'Make my day. Am I being pursued by Russell Crowe? If so, I'll slow down and let him catch me.'

Mary Jane went all vague. 'It might have been *Spartacus* I was thinking of. You know: fair-haired and a broken nose.'

Honey's elation vanished. Kirk Douglas and a Zimmer frame came to mind.

'I think you are. Now this guy – he wasn't wearing trainers, by any chance?'

As she considered the question, Mary Jane's pink lips pursed on the rim of her coffee cup. A perfect pink imprint was left behind.

'I didn't notice his feet. Just his face.'

'Ugly?'

She meant ugly as in dangerous. Visions of police mugshots clicked through her mind.

'Bland,' said Mary Jane after much consideration. 'But then, I might not have noted his features in detail. I wasn't concentrating too much on him. I was watching the sheep feeding on the grass in front of the Royal Crescent.'

Honey frowned. 'There aren't any sheep grazing in the Royal Crescent.'

Mary Jane's expression of total belief was undiminished. 'Not now, but there used to be.' She nodded at a picture on the wall of the Royal Crescent as it had been in the eighteenth century.

'See? If you go to the Crescent and narrow your eyes, you can see them gambolling there just as they used to.'

'Amazing.'

Mary Jane caught her arm before she could leave. 'Before you go,' she said, her voice falling into a deep whisper. 'I thought you should know that Sir Cedric reckons your life is in danger. He saw blood and a lot of trees – like a forest, he said, only worse.'

'Really?'

'The other night at the séance. He came through, you see. He was terribly specific. You should have been there.'

In the past she had always taken Mary Jane's prophecies with a pinch of salt. Recent circumstances had had their effect. Suddenly she felt vulnerable.

'Perhaps that's what comes of being a detective,' she said with a hint of sarcasm. 'Jane Marple,' she added with a laugh that she thought sounded convincing.

'I'm sure that's got something to do with it,' said Mary Jane. 'And that's why I've decided to assist you.'

Visions of Mary Jane, dressed head to toe in a pink kaftan and silver sandals, floating into Manvers Street Police Station came to mind.

'I think I'm supposed to do this by myself.'

Mary Jane nodded emphatically. 'Along with that cop with the dodgy hair colour. Yeah. Sure. I know. But that isn't what I meant.'

She sat back as though about to deliver a eulogy fit for

a king. 'I have a private income, thanks to my dearly departed mother, so I've decided to move in here permanently.'

Honey's jaw dropped. 'You're not going back to California?'

'Why should I? I've found my roots and I'll be buried here in the land of my forebears. What could be better? Can we agree a special rate?' The shrewdness of age shone in her eyes. No doubt the funeral parlour would be tied into a discounted deal when the time came.

'Leave it with me.'

Uncertain about the advantages of having the gangly woman as a permanent guest, Honey gathered up greasy plates and headed for the kitchen.

Her mother was putting the bacon away and Clint, complete with cobweb tattoo, was dealing with the washing-up.

'Hannah,' said her mother once the fridge door had slammed shut, 'Mr Paget tells me you have not returned his calls.'

Honey grimaced. Each time her mother's dentist had called, she'd got someone to tell her she was out. The Eastern European Reception girls were quite wonderful at it. Trying hard not to giggle, they adopted thicker accents than they actually had and pretended that their knowledge of English was very poor. Amazing how obliging they could be for the sake of unrequited love.

'Mother, I'm rather busy at the moment.'

'You sound just like your father. He was always busy.'

'That figures. He ran a multi-million-dollar industry,' she muttered whilst scraping bits of sausage and bacon rind into the bin.

'And left me almost destitute!'

'Hardly that. He allowed you what he could. After all, he only *managed* the company.'

Her mother grimaced. 'Keep your voice down. Think of my image.'

Honey rolled her eyes. Rumours that her mother's former husbands had all been millionaires were exactly that:

rumours – carefully created rumours put about by Gloria Cross herself. Image, as she insistently reminded her, was everything.

'Well there you are! No one could blame me for finding solace in the arms of another man! Nothing can beat good and frequent sex for keeping a woman looking young. You should do more of it yourself.'

Honey blushed.

The jaw of Clint, their part time washer up, dropped like a lump of lead. A soapy plate slid from his fingers. The sound of it smashing made Honey jump. The top plate from the greasy pile followed it.

Gloria Cross jerked her chin at the smashed plates. 'Two plates. That's bad luck. Everything should come in threes.' A hand encased in pink rubber reached for a plate.

'No!' Before the deed could be done, Honey had grabbed it with both hands.

'Plates cost money.'

'Yer mother may have a point,' said Clint, his shaved head wreathed in steam from the dishwasher. 'It's Friday the thirteenth today. Unlucky for some,' he said with a smile and winked.

What with Mary Jane deciding to move in and now this!

Accepting she was surrounded by weirdoes, she shook her head and left the kitchen.

Making out bills in Reception and dealing with the morning mail would make things right again.

It didn't!

The quality envelope smelling of perfume intrigued her. It did more than that once she'd opened it.

Honey stuffed the letter back into the sweetly scented envelope and addressed the girl on reception. 'The bills are done, the phone's quiet and I'm off out,' Honey told her.

'And if anyone wants you?' asked a surprised looking Olga, her cheeks pink with youthful energy.

'If they want to reserve a room or a table in the restaurant, write it down. If it's a man and he sounds reasonably endearing, give him my cell-phone number.'

'And Mr Paget? Your mother told me he wishes to marry you.'

Honey saw the grin on Olga's face. 'Tell him I've gone to work in a leper colony.'

Thirty-Three

A stilted silence hung over the incident room and the aroma of stewed coffee clogged the air. Coffee got colder in half-full cups and no one seemed to have much of a laugh in them. Even in the direst of circumstances somebody usually camc up with a corny gag or dry pun to break the dire circumstances of the occasion.

Clutching the letter from Lady Charlborough, Honey peered in through the glass door at the glum expressions and lacklustrc postures. Some personnel were slouched in their chairs, others bent over their desks, heads resting on arms. Steve Doherty was using a pencil to tap at a Santa Claus mug.

Now was the time to take the plunge. The door swung wide open. A few pairs of eyes looked up to see what noisy so-and-so was disturbing their grief.

'Our person from the Hotels' Association,' said Steve, his chin still rcsting on his hand, his elbow resting on the desk. The corners of his mouth were wedge side down.

He flashed her a Grim Reaper grimace before shifting his glance on to something less unsettling. He chose the paperclip dispenser.

Honey sensed discomfiture – severe discomfiture.

'Don't tell me. You've had to let Robert Davies go and you're peed off about it!'

Steve's overly wide mouth twisted into a snarl. 'You come to gloat?'

'No.' She held up the letter. 'I've come to give you this.'

'What is it?'

'A letter from Lady Pamela. It explains a lot.'

He eyed it suspiciously.

'It won't bite you. Though she might have taken her teeth to you given half the chance.'

A wave of sniggers circled the room.

Doherty glared. 'You lot got nothing else to do? How about a bit of door to door? Better still, traffic duty. Savvy?'

The others in the room turned back to their individual tasks: sieving evidence files, playing spider solitaire and drinking tea.

Doherty straightened as he took the letter. As his eyes devoured the words, his dour expression brightened. 'So! She's accusing this bloke Spiteri of being a psycho.'

'Hmmm.'

'What's "hmmm" supposed to mean?'

'I thought she'd accuse the person she hates most.'

'Her husband?'

She made that *hmmm* sound again. 'Someone dedicated to her husband. And with the right address.'

Doherty waved the letter. 'This is enough for me!'

Sensing a shift in mood, a few of his team eyed him like dogs about to be let off the leash.

'Braden,' he barked.

A dark-skinned female detective with shiny black hair, bolted upright.

'Get a fix on a bloke named Trevor Spiteri.'

'Yes, guv.' Her fingers pounded the computer.

'Fleming?'

The man named Fleming was already on his feet, hanging over Doherty as though ready to snaffle up every word.

'Get a warrant!'

The excitement was tangible. Honey could almost taste the change in mood. It was as though she had entered a different room, certainly not the one she'd come into just a few minutes ago. Everyone was animated. Everyone was keen to replace one arrest with another.

She glowed in their praise.

'You're one of the team!'

'We got him now!'

'You're a doll.'

The corners of Doherty's mouth went sunny side up. 'You'll be wanting a job here before long.'

'Let's not get silly. Though I did prove myself right.'

His eyes said, 'Bitch!' She didn't give a hoot. She told herself it wasn't gloating, just setting the record straight.

'Don't rub it in.'

'You owe me.'

'Dinner?'

'OK. But more than that. I want to come with you. I want to be in on the arrest.'

He hesitated.

'You owe me,' she repeated.

'OK. And hopefully he'll be there.'

His attention jerked to the glossy-haired woman. 'So what do we know, Braden?'

Glossy-hair leaned back from her console. 'Grievous bodily harm – ten years back. He's ex-army. Born in Warminster . . .'

Doherty jabbed a finger in her direction. 'Print it off!'

Honey took a deep breath. Today had started weird. Now it was getting weirder.

Charlborough's batman lived at number six Rathbone Terrace, a stone's throw from Charlotte Terrace where Robert Davies, 'Bob the Job,' lived. As with others in the city, its cellars went under the road and had doors opening on to the river. In the past the rich dudes who'd lived in the houses had moored shallow leisure craft here. The rich dudes were gone now, the elegant houses divided into equally elegant apartments, rented at roughly the same price per month as each house had cost to build way back. She wondered if Trevor Spiteri wore white trainers.

'Got it!' Fleming shouted, an arrest warrant flapping in the air. Up went the cheer. Cars were organized, the plan discussed. Honey ran out behind them, her heart thudding with excitement. Without waiting for a specific order, she got into the car beside Doherty.

He opened his mouth to form the words, 'Shove off.' He seemed to have second thoughts and changed his mind. With a screech of wheels they were out of the car park and on to Manvers Street, Doherty aiming the car like a missile homing in on the target.

The terrace was not as elegant as some in the city, its architecture originating at the beginning of the nineteenth century. Gone were the Palladian pillars each side of a wide door, the carved pediments over long, light-filled windows. The refined features had been replaced by the more businesslike style of a swiftly moving industrial age. Aprons of black and white quarry tiles sloped from threshold to pavement in front of each house, worn down by a thousand footsteps.

Car doors slammed in unison. Uniforms and plain-clothes officers tumbled out.

'I'll take the front door with you two.' Doherty pointed a crooked finger at two of the passengers of another car. He turned to Honey. 'You get around the back with these two. And keep out of the way.'

Hair flying and face flushed, Honey followed the two policemen, the heels of her black suede boots scattering gravel behind her.

They came face to face with a blank wall. The two policemen looked baffled. One lifted his helmet and rubbed at the redness left behind on his forehead.

'The guv'nor must 'ave got his facts wrong, miss. There's no entrance round here.'

The river bounded the rear of the houses. The side wall prevented them from going any further. There was no back alley, no way of slipping from one back yard to another.

Honey glared in the direction of the river. Doherty hadn't wanted her to come. He'd got his way. Words were unnecessary, which was just as well. Doherty's name was mud.

Back in Rathbone Terrace heads were appearing at windows, figures at doors. As insistent as plague, speculation crept from one flat, one house, and one doorway to another. By word of mouth it passed the black railings protecting the drops to narrow basements. Sash windows shaded with Venetian blinds or the braids and tassels of traditional design flashed past.

She barged through the cordon at the entrance to number

six. The entrance was narrow. Four uniformed bods were plenty to keep the curious at bay.

'Nobody's allowed in,' said a young fella with a ginger moustache.

'I'm not a nobody.'

He threw out his arm and inadvertently brushed her bosom.

'You touched my breast. That's sexual assault!'

He went beetroot-red.

'I didn't mean . . .'

Braden, the dark girl with the glossy hair, chose that moment to come running out.

Honey homed in on her. 'What's going on?'

'I'm sorry, Honey. Spiteri's barricaded himself into his flat. Steve – DI Doherty is talking to him. He says that until this is resolved, no one is allowed inside.'

The sound of a sash window being pulled up preceded a head appearing out of a third-floor window.

The two women looked up.

'I suppose that's him,' said Fleming.

Honey agreed.

'I'll jump if you smash my door in,' Spiteri shouted.

Honey recognized the hushed voice coming from a broken voicebox.

'We only want to talk to you,' Fleming shouted back.

'If I jump and hurt myself, I shall claim police harassment,' Spiteri shouted back.

Honey couldn't resist. 'You might not be able to claim a single penny.'

'Name one reason why I couldn't.'

'The fall might kill you. Your head and guts could be splattered on the pavement or speared on the railings.'

Even from this distance, Honey perceived his perplexity, the horror of having reality spelled out to him. To jump or not to jump? No contest.

Feeling slighted, Honey tackled Braden. 'He sent me round the back purposely.'

'Um. Yes,' said Braden, fluctuating between loyalty to Doherty and disgruntled sisterhood.

'He's a pig!'

Fleming managed a lop-sided grin. 'We all are, aren't we?'

Honey folded her arms. 'That isn't what I meant.'

'He's miffed,' said Braden.

'He's toast,' grunted Honey.

After confirming that she was definitely not to be allowed in the house, Braden summoned more assistance through her radio.

Honey found herself melting into the small crowd of watchers as though she never had been of any consequence. Mentally she was sticking pins into a real-life Doherty. She'd been part of the investigation and now she was not.

She hardly noticed the dusky young woman in the business suit come out of the house next door. Only when she spoke did it occur to her that the woman moved like a panther, silently, swiftly and with instant impressiveness. She came beside her that quickly.

'What is going on?' Her voice was as dark as her hair.

Honey turned and took in the details. The crisply white collar of a starched blouse lay flat against the lapels of a navy-blue business suit. She carried a briefcase – or perhaps it was a laptop. The heels on her shoes were businesslike, built for day wear. It was easy to believe that at night those long legs appeared even longer in four-inch heels. She was beautiful.

'The police are trying to arrest the man next door.'

'But not very successfully.'

'Par for the course.'

'Do excuse me for saying so, but I got the impression you were with them.'

Honey grimaced. 'So did I. I think they decided that I'd outlived my usefulness.' Blurting all to a stranger seemed ridiculous, but she couldn't help herself. 'I got that evidence. Not them.'

This is silly. Stick to the facts. She vaguely remembered that line coming from some old TV show made in the fifties. Or was it the sixties?

The lovely lady from next door tutted and shook her

head. 'Poor Mister Spiteri. And only just back from visiting his family.'

Honey's response was offhand. 'Really?'

'Yes. He was away most of the summer and has only been back two weeks.'

Two weeks? Honey turned to face the informant. 'Is that a fact?'

The young woman's complexion was to die for. Honey felt a tinge of jealousy for her youthful skin, dark eyes and confident manner. The perfect teeth flashed pearl-white. 'I was told this by a nosy parker that I know very well – my own grandmother, in fact.'

Thick lashes flickered as she checked her watch. 'If you wish to confirm this, go into my house and up the first flight of stairs. My grandmother is home. The rest of the family are out at work all day. Don't tell her that I called her a nosy parker, but I can confidently assure you she can tell you everything that happens in this street. She doesn't get out much and therefore sees everything.'

Out of gratitude, Honey felt a need to show interest in such a helpful young woman. 'Your family is in business?'

'My parents, along with other members of the Patel family, run various businesses. My brothers and I have professions.'

'And what is yours?' Honey asked, adopting the warmest of smiles.

'I'm a tax accountant.'

Honey's smile froze.

The young woman saw her look. 'I said tax accountant, not tax inspector.'

'Ah, yes,' said Honey, taking a deep breath and fanning her face with her hand. 'Thank goodness for that.'

'Please. Tell my grandmother that Zakia said you should speak to her. Like a lot of elderly people, she has an obsession with security.'

The property, like many Georgian houses, had once been home to just one family and their servants. Now it was divided into individual homes for the members of one family.

After the third knock at the Patels' door, it opened inches

and a pair of dark eyes appeared over the tight restraint of a brass security chain. The perfume that wafted out through the gap was instantly recognizable: Chanel. Exactly like her mother.

'Mrs Patel? I'm working in conjunction with the police. Your granddaughter, Zakia, suggested I speak with you.'

'Will she get to work on time?'

'I see no reason why not.'

'Oh. That is good.'

Her dark eyes darted from Honey's head to her toes and back again before the door closed, the chain rattled and the door reopened.

'Please. Come in. I will put the kettle on. You'll have to excuse the mess. I'm researching my thesis for a degree with the Open University.'

'Oh, really. What subject are you studying?'

'Computer Science, though I am not sure I have picked the right aspect. I'm more interested in stripping them apart rather than understanding the mathematics and the science of the subject.'

Surprised, Honey raised her eyebrows. 'You mean you can actually take a computer apart and put it back together again?' Technology was not Honey's forte. Anyone who understood the things was a genius; a saint if they wanted to strip them apart.

Mrs Patel grinned. 'Oh, yes. I can strip it down, thanks to my grandson's instruction.' She frowned as a thought occurred to her. 'The trouble is that neither of us are any good at putting it back together again.'

Mrs Patel was dressed in a swathe of rich green silk banded with gold. Grey hair spread like a halo framing her face. She was elegant and oozed confidence. Nothing, thought Honey, had ever been allowed to stand in the way of anything she'd ever wanted to do.

'Come. Follow me. We will make ourselves comfortable.' She limped towards the right as she led her to the back of the house overlooking the river. 'This is my private little flat where I go when I wish to be away from the family,' she explained. Her eyes shone as she spoke. Arm outstretched, she indicated a row of family photographs including one of Zakia wearing mortarboard and gown and clutching her degree. Pride shone from Mrs Patel's eyes.

Honey guessed she wasn't often in this room – at least, not when the family were home.

'Sit here. I will make tea.' She limped off into the adjoining kitchen. The sound of a kettle being switched on and crockery being laid out rattled into the living room.

The Georgians had liked rooms with high ceilings and big windows to let in the light. This one was no exception. A bentwood rocker packed with silk-covered cushions was placed in front of the high window. Beyond the yard was the river.

'There is where I sit and watch the world at the back of the house,' she explained, returning with the tea. 'Sometimes I watch the world at the front of the house. I have another chair just like this one in front of that window.'

'You have very nice views. I bet you see all that goes on.'

Mrs Patel sighed, her fine wrinkles deepening, as they appeared to fold layer on top of layer. 'I see a lot. Sometimes it is very interesting. Sometimes it is tiring. I sit here a lot, you know. It is my hip, you see. The pain interferes with my studies. I am waiting for an operation. I am waiting until the end of the month and then if I have not got an appointment my son says he will pay for me. I can get it done in France if I have to.' She rubbed her hip as she said it.

'I hope you get it sorted soon,' said Honey politely. 'Let me help you with the tea.'

'That is very kind.'

It was Mrs Patel who made herself comfortable as Honey made the tea and brought the tray into the room.

On crossing the room she again glanced out of the window. There was a clear view between the trees to the parapet at the rear of the yard and the river.

'I wish I had a view like this.'

Mrs Patel smiled and nodded as she eased herself back into her chair after taking her tea.

'It is a joy. I see all life from here, even though I find difficulty getting around nowadays. There is little I miss.' She suddenly looked worried and the smile dropped from her face. 'No one has complained about me being a nosy parker, have they?'

Honey smiled and sat on a leather chesterfield, which was red and a bit saggy in the middle. A blue-and-red silk shawl with soft gold fringes was thrown across its back.

'No, Mrs Patel. In fact, because of your habit – and your pain, you might be of some help in solving a murder.'

'A murder!' Her face brightened. 'A real one? This is a real case, not just for television?'

Honey thought of poor Elmer Maxted and Mervyn Herbert. 'I'm afraid this is for real.'

Mrs Patel clapped her hands. 'All the years of watching murder mysteries and now I am actually witness in a real-life murder.'

'That is so.'

'So,' said Mrs Patel, her face beaming, 'how can I help you?'

Leaning forward, Honey rested her elbows on her knees and clasped her hands together in front of her. 'I understand that Mister Spiteri next door has just come back from abroad. Is that right?' Fearing she might frighten the old girl, she spoke softly, but clearly.

'Is he a suspect? What did he do? How did he do it?'

Mrs Patel, despite her obvious age, didn't appear to be deaf, frightened or put out by the possibility that a murderer lived next door. On the contrary, she seemed to relish the prospect.

Honey had to disappoint her. 'I actually think that his guilt or innocence rather depends on what you've got to say.'

Mrs Patel's mouth dropped open. Her brown eyes glowed with excitement. 'Do go on, do go on!' Mrs Patel was the witness a good policeman dreamed of: clear-headed and totally committed to giving a good account of all she knew.

'Was Mister Spiteri away for some time?'

The correct answer would win Spiteri his freedom and Doherty a big slap of mud on his face.

There was no bated breath about it; Mrs Patel was out with the answer. 'He came back about two weeks ago on a Thursday at about five in the morning. I don't sleep that well, you see. That's the trouble with getting old.'

'And how long was he away?' Her heart thudded against her ribs. Everything depended on the answer. If Spiteri had been away at the same time as the murders were committed, then he was in the clear. Doherty was not. She found herself praying for the right answer.

'He was away for about two months visiting his relatives on some island in the Mediterranean. It's near Sicily, I believe.'

A map of the Med surfed through Honey's mind. 'Malta?'

Mrs Patel nodded. 'I think that is the name of it. He did tell me this but I was never very good at geography.'

'Fantastic!' Honey clapped her hands. She couldn't wait to slap the details around Doherty's dumb face.

Mrs Patel smiled. 'I am so glad I was able to help. Although he looked a little intimidating, he was really quite a nice man. So friendly. Not like the other man who used to stay in the basement flat. You would never think that they worked together for the titled gentleman.'

Honey's feet had been itching to be up and away, confronting Doherty with the fact that Spiteri could not have murdered the two men. Mrs Patel's nosiness was reaping rewards beyond belief.

Her legs turned to lead. Her voice sounded far away. 'What other man was that, Mrs Patel?'

'Not Mr Spiteri – him of the Desperate Dan jaw. If, like my boys, you ever read the *Dandy*, you would know what I mean.'

The *Dandy* was a children's comic from years ago. There had been a hero in it with a lantern jaw. The description matched that of Trevor Spiteri, the man she'd looked up at in the greenhouse at Charlborough Grange.

'This other man – would you recognize him?'

'Of course.'

'You definitely saw him arrive next door?

'Most definitely.'

Honey got to her feet. 'I have to tell the policeman next door. Will you come with me to confirm this?'

For someone with a dodgy hip, Mrs Patel got to her feet in double-quick time. Her enthusiasm had more effect than state-of-the-art robotics. 'I am right with you!'

'I'll take these into the kitchen for you,' said Honey reaching for the tray.

'No! No!' Mrs Patel pushed the tray back on to the table. 'Never mind that. This is the most exciting thing that's happened to me for years. Come on. We must hurry.'

Honey paused. 'Mrs Patel, I can't thank you enough.'

The dark eyes sparkled impishly. 'I used to be a journalist, you know. I used to gather and write factual features on a freelance basis. That is why I am so sure about times and dates and the comings and the goings. Besides, I keep a diary.'

Honey stiffened, her eyes round with hope. 'A diary?'

She nodded. Her smile returned but was coyer than it had been. 'I like to write down what I have seen. Sometimes I write a line or two of poetry about the night scene – you know, the lights and everything, people hurrying by, lovers strolling, the river – anything that catches my eye.'

'May I see it?' Honey asked. She rubbed her palms together. They were clammy and stuck together.

'If it helps at all. There,' she said. Her finger pointed to a book bound in pink plastic. Red plastic lips stood proud of the cover. It sat on top of a brass-topped table, the sort that's no more than a big plaque on turned legs. 'If you don't mind getting that for me,' said Mrs Patel.

Honey did as she was told and passed the diary to Mrs Patel, who in turn passed it back to her. She took it with both hands.

The fluidity of the writing was far more beautiful than what she had to say. Her entry for that date read almost like a shopping list. There were times of the comings and goings of her son, her daughter-in-law, the postman and even the traffic warden and what colour cars he'd booked. Mr Spiteri's coming home was entered.

Just as she had stated, there were a few lines of poetry

added that reflected what she had seen that day: 'Green leaves, black road, grey river swirling swiftly by. People walking, people talking, green, green grass and crisp blue sky.'

'May I borrow it?' said Honey.

'Of course.'

Mrs Patel followed her down the stairs. At the bottom Honey turned to make sure she was all right.

'I am fine,' said Mrs Patel, her face glowing. 'Just wait until I lock my door.'

Having been at the back of the house, it came as something of a surprise to see that the police presence next door had diminished.

Honey addressed a remaining constable. 'Where is everyone?'

'Gone back to the station with the accused.'

Honey swore under her breath. Doherty and everyone of importance had flown the nest.

'Just the lab boys remaining,' the constable added as a man in a white jumpsuit pushed his way across the pavement.

After finding that her phone batteries were flat, Honey sighed and turned to Mrs Patel. 'I'm sorry but we'll have to go to the station and report this.'

'No worries,' Mrs Patel said brightly.

Honey's gaze slid between the two front doors, the number six of next door, and the number 7 of Mrs Patel. She frowned. After that, the numbers leapt from 7 to 9. Number 9 had a For Sale notice outside. The frontage of seven was wider than each of the properties to either side.

'Where's number eight?' she asked.

'We are six, seven and eight,' answered Mrs Patel.

The door of number 6 was still open to allow the comings and goings of the forensic people.

'I would dearly love to look inside that basement flat,' said Honey, eyeing the stone steps leading downwards.

Mrs Patel began rummaging in the tan leather handbag she had insisted on bringing with her. 'I have the keys.'

'You do?'

Though a recent acquaintance, nothing about Mrs Patel

should have surprised her, but the old girl was still capable of springing the unexpected.

'My other son owns next door. I keep the spare keys.'

At this juncture it occurred to Honey that rather than press a judge to issue a warrant, Doherty would have better served his purpose by knocking next door at granny's place. Mrs Patel was a matriarch of the highest order.

After deliberating about whether they should impede the legitimate key holder, the police watched as they descended the steps.

'It has its own private entrance,' said Mrs Patel. She winked. 'Very discreet.'

The basement flat consisted of two bedrooms, a bathroom, a kitchen and a ground-floor living room. A pair of French doors opened on to a tiled patio at the back.

Even after modernization and treatment for damp, some basements retained a mouldy smell. Not this one. Painted white and lit by recessed spotlights, the flat was crisp and clean. Perhaps too crisp, too austere. There were no books, no magazines, no television set or the slightest evidence that anyone sometimes lived here. And yet they did.

Honey sniffed. The smell was familiar – not greasy bacon or chemical cleaners like you find in old bedsits: perfume, very expensive perfume, hung in the air. She'd smelt it before. Mrs Patel's saucy wink and comment suddenly made absolute sense.

'What was the name of the man who used this flat?'

'Mr Conway.'

Honey recalled the polite young man who'd brought the tea. 'Did you ever see the woman he came here with?'

Mrs Patel rolled her eyes suggestively. 'Oh, yes. Very blonde and trimmed with gold. Expensive, though slightly less than tasteful. Best described as brassy.'

Honey took a deep breath. 'I couldn't have described her better myself.'

Lady Pamela Charlborough. It couldn't be anyone else.

'So! It was a love nest.'

'Indeed.' A concerned frown crossed Mrs Patel's cheery

face. 'Just the one woman, of course. It is not a knocking shop, as they say.'

Honey shook her head and controlled the grin. 'No, of course not.'

'He did not always come with her. Sometimes he came alone.'

'What did he do there – when he came by himself?'

'Mostly he used the workshop. Through there.'

She pointed to a door beneath the stairs. 'It leads to the cellars. He makes heads from plastic and clay. He told my son this when he began renting the flat. My son said he could not do such things here, so he must use the cellar.' Spreading her arms, she indicated their pristine surroundings.

'I shouldn't think so,' said Honey agreeing with her.

'I do not like dolls,' Mrs Patel said suddenly.

'He made dolls?'

Mrs Patel jerked her chin like a duck prodding at a suspicious weed. 'Heads. He made latex heads for his boss.'

Honey suppressed a shiver.

She managed to keep her tone pleasant, as though she hadn't thought of the heads in the greenhouse, which, of course, she had.

'How come you managed to get a look at them?'

'He wanted something to cover them with. He asked my son if he could save him the small sacks the spices come in. My son did this and asked me to give them to him.'

Sacks! So whoever made the latex heads for the war games used spice sacks to keep them clean. And got them from Mrs Patel's son.

Honey shivered. She'd been barking up the wrong tree thinking the sacks might have come from Jeremiah's market stall. And they hadn't come from the pile outside the greenhouses either. They'd come from Mrs Patel's son and were used to cover latex heads. Perhaps the murderer had got so used to covering latex heads with the sacks, that he'd not been able to resist doing the same with his victims.

Finding out the truth about something as perplexing – and stupidly simple – as those sacks was like breathing frosty air. It wasn't just refreshing, it invigorated.

'So,' she said, trying hard to control her racing heart, 'when's he expected back?'

'He's not. As you can see, my son is selling both this house and number nine. Mister Spiteri had agreed to move out at the end of the week. He's been offered accommodation with his employer, who I believe is moving abroad. In the meantime my son offered Mr Conway the basement of number nine in which to keep his heads. I did not see him move his things there, but I presume he did.'

'Like rats leaving a sinking ship,' Honey murmured.

She phoned Doherty from Mrs Patel's phone before leaving but was told he was interviewing.

She should have guessed. 'Tell him he's got the wrong man.'

'I wouldn't dare,' said the female voice on the other end.

No, thought Honey. Steve the stubborn policeman; he had to find things out for himself.

Thirty-Four

Doherty was being stubborn.

'You need a search warrant for number nine.'

'No I don't. I've got our man.'

'No you haven't. He was abroad at the time.'

'He'll have to prove it.'

'He will. There are witnesses.'

She hoped the sound of the phone being slammed down burst Doherty's eardrum. Stubborn cuss!

For the rest of that day, she played the same game, refusing to take his calls, pretending she was out, doing anything rather than speak to him.

Lindsey caught her cleaning the glass in the front door. 'You don't have to do that.'

'It's surprisingly therapeutic.'

'You're taking long enough.'

'You bet I am.'

Three times she'd sprayed the glass, and three times she'd polished it.

'How's Sam?'

Lindsey grinned. 'Coming on nicely. By the way, I told Grandma you were practically engaged.'

The polishing stalled. 'Why?'

'She wouldn't stop asking me questions about the other night when I slept at Sam's.'

'So I was thrown to the lion.'

Lindsey looked contrite. 'I needed to do that. She wouldn't let go.'

Honey smoothed Lindsey's hair back from her forehead. 'Poor darling. I'm sorry about that.'

'Don't be. It's not you giving me hassle. It's her. Grandma

would have been great in the days when young girls were presented at court.'

Honey shrugged. 'You had to guard your back.'

'Thanks for understanding. She's still on about the carpet though. There was nothing I could do about that.'

Honey's gaze went through the glass to the white trainers standing on the other side of the street. Her stalker was getting braver, though doing his best to hide behind a green wheelie bin.

'Does he look familiar to you?' she asked Lindsey.

Lindsey took a bite of the cold toast she'd snitched from kitchen leftovers and shook her head. 'What's he doing?'

'Following me. I think.'

Lindsey frowned. 'Perhaps he's a hotel inspector from the tourist board or something.'

Honey blew a mental raspberry. 'Hotel inspectors don't wear Lee Cooper jeans and white trainers.'

Lindsey peered out of the window. 'How do you know they're Lee Cooper? Have you seen his butt?'

'They just look that kind of quality, and no, I haven't seen his butt.'

'By the way, Doherty called.'

'The jerk! Was he apologetic?'

'I wouldn't say apologetic. Try contrite.'

Honey glanced at the gilded face of the long-case clock. 'Isn't that a difficult word for this early in the day?'

'I was in early last night. I suppose reflective might be a better word than contrite.'

Honey punched a fist into the air. 'He's let Spiteri go. I win!'

'He asked you to phone him. He'd brought Sir Andrew in for questioning and was now looking for Mark Conway.'

'Ah!' Honey tapped her smiling lips. My, but it was good to be right. She became aware that Lindsey was giving her the incisive *What have you been up to, Mother?* type of look. Honey knew it well. She often used it to stump her own mother.

'He wanted to solve this case all on his Jack Jones,' said Honey.

'Alone! But he didn't.'

'No. His call means that he's been out to Charlborough Grange, but Mark Conway wasn't there.'

'Right. And you know where he is. Yes?'

'No. But I want to.'

In her mind she was the Lone Ranger hunting down the baddy alongside a bumbling lawman. The truth was that crime wasn't quite like that at all. *Leave it to the professionals*, said a small voice in her mind, *you know it makes sense*.

The trouble was that there were *two* small voices. The other one was feeding her ego, telling her, *Sure, babe, of course you can do it. You're cleverer than him!*

Was someone lying or was it sheer pride and arrogance urging her on? Whatever! She was game for it.

'What are you doing now?' asked Lindsey. Not for the first time in her life she sounded nervous of her mother's intentions. The way her chin was jutting reminded her of the time they'd lived in a brand new house in a village. The locals had opposed the development. They'd also insisted that a footpath still ran through the back yard of the house they'd bought. One day Honey had caught their ringleader relieving himself against a bush she'd just planted.

He'd done it three days on the trot, insisting he was entitled.

On the fourth day her mother had been ready with a piece of brown paper smeared with thick, dark molasses. Taking him unawares, she'd slapped the brown paper on to his exposed loins. The stuff was a devil to remove without help. His wife would have had to help him. Likely as not, he'd also had to explain how molasses had got tangled in his pubic hair.

The footpath problem went away.

Honey was heading for the door and the man across the street. 'I want a word with you,' she called out as she ran across the road, weaving in and out of the cars.

Horns blew. Brakes screeched to a halt. She ignored the

truck driver whose expletives did nothing for cultural heritage. Her attention was fixed on the man in the trainers. She'd half-expected him to leg it, but he didn't. Instead he seemed to come all undone, shifting his stance and drawing his hands from his pockets.

Flight or fight: that was the choice he was facing. Flight meant darting off through the evening-rush-hour traffic. Fight was facing a middle-aged woman who'd obviously made her choice.

'You've been following me,' she said, fists curled over sweaty palms and resting on her hips.

He had chocolate-brown eyes and corn-coloured hair. Mid-twenties and made to be admired. What was more, she'd seen him before. It would come to her, but first the explanation.

He was dithering, still thinking about legging it.

She stiffened her stance. 'Well!'

'I didn't mean to frighten you.'

'So! Apologize!'

'I'm sorry.'

He looked into the distance. That was when she realized who he was: a little older now, but definitely the young man in a photograph.

'You're Lance Charlborough.' She frowned. Why would he follow her? Why had she never seen him in person at the house?

'I found out,' he said, as though those three little words answered everything she might wish to know. 'I found out that my real mother died in a fire.'

Suddenly she knew what he meant, or at least where this was leading. The article in the old newspaper pointed in the right direction.

'How?' she asked.

'Mark had always tried to keep the truth from me. He's older than me. He wouldn't let anyone hurt me. No one.'

'Mark Conway.'

He nodded.

The truth dawned. 'Don't tell me . . .'

I will. We're brothers. He's older than me. When our

mother died, he looked out for me. I was too young to understand. But I do now. I really do.'

There was an intense look on his face. Mark Conway's character was melding together like layers of papier-mâché. He'd *lived* for his brother. And anyone who hurt him? The opposite, she guessed.

'So! What happened?'

Lance swallowed as though he were having trouble coming to terms with what he'd learned and what he wanted to say.

'Our father couldn't cope when our mother died. He abandoned us. Sir Andrew took us in. He'd lost his son. He wanted another. A lot of money was involved, but it wasn't only that. He was devastated. His real son was a haemophiliac. He died in a road accident and apparently Sir Andrew was devastated.'

Honey drew her hand across her breast. She had been going to give him one hell of a tongue-lashing. But not now. His pain was tangible.

'How did you find out?'

'She told me – my stepmother. She got it from the American. Apparently the first Lady Charlborough was his sister-in-law.'

'Cousin-in-law actually. And your father – Sir Andrew. Does he know that you know?'

He nodded. 'He does now. I think there's a lot of money involved.'

You bet!

'When I left home a few weeks ago, my father – Sir Andrew – cried out after me that he'd make everything right – that there was no need to worry about my inheritance.'

He shook his head. His eyes seemed to melt with moisture. 'But it isn't my inheritance, is it? Not really.' He shook his head. 'I never knew anything about it until she told me. Mark knew, but he'd kept it from me. He'd protected me. He's always protected me.'

Despite his age, Lance Charlborough had a waif-like quality about him. She felt instantly sorry for him. In his formative years, he'd been lulled into the false security of a different identity.

Suddenly she had an urge to cuddle him, just like she had Lindsey as a child. *Hold off*, she warned. *Once you kiss his ear and lean against his six-pack, a story at bedtime is right out of the window.*

No cuddle, but second best. 'Come and have a coffee.'

They went to Starbucks. Over cappuccino he told her that he'd got a job as a voluntary prison visitor. That was when he'd met Robert Davies – Bob the Job. It was him that had done the tracing and come up with Elmer Maxted, related by marriage to Sir Andrew's first wife. Lance had contacted him. He'd insisted on coming over right away. Lance had begged him not to use his real name, just in case his adoptive father sussed what was going on.

'I wish I hadn't started this. I feel so guilty about Elmer getting killed.'

'Do you think your father did it?'

The chocolate pools looked into hers before he nodded. 'But I couldn't turn him in. I love him as a father, so I couldn't do that, no matter what he's done.'

She thought of her mother and nodded. 'I know what you mean' – though unbridled matchmaking hardly ranked alongside murder.

'I wanted to know what was going on, so I followed you.'

'Why not follow the cops?'

He shrugged. 'They're the professionals. They might have noticed me.'

It hurt. But never mind, she told herself; you're proving them all wrong. The professionals adhered to strict guidelines. Her enquiries were less stringent and carried out between the shenanigans of a domineering mother and a dozy dishwasher.

They parted company once she'd promised she would let him know when someone was arrested. He gave her his phone number, but no address.

'Just in case you cave in under torture. I don't want my father – my adoptive father – to know where I am.'

Your father's liable to torture me? She didn't voice the comment, just in case it was true.

After he'd gone, she felt a need to talk to someone about the nuances of the case, but not the police. They were busily looking for Mark Conway, Lance's brother.

She phoned Casper. He answered within seconds.

'What now?'

'I thought you'd like to know what's going on in the world of crime-fighting.'

'Not really, my dear. I just want things tidied up for the sake of next year's profit ratio. I trust you are swiftly putting this problem to bed. Are you doing that, Hannah?'

Only a man like Casper could sound so like her mother.

Her mood was reflected in her tone. 'Well you know what they say, Casper: if you want a man to do a good job, get a woman to do it.'

He made a snorting sound. Disdain was Casper's middle name.

She carried on, wanting to tell someone involved – even if only on a moderate level – all that was going on.

'The police arrested the wrong man. His name's Trevor Spiteri.'

'That's a foreign name.'

Full marks there. 'Being foreign isn't a precursor for guilt.'

'That's a matter of opinion.'

'I think I should tell you I'm being followed.'

'A psycho?'

She paused. Lance was far from being a psycho, but he was insecure, a little sad.

She explained about the basement flat and the expensive perfume. She also explained about the newspapers. 'It all ties in. Lance wrote to Elmer, who was murdered because he knew it was virtually impossible that Lance was still alive. Drugs to speed blood-clotting weren't so widely available then. Mervyn was showing Elmer his watch collection, but his attention was drawn to the old newspapers. First the report of a fire, and then the photograph of father and son at a social event – plus Mark Conway. The two boys were doubles for the two boys whose mother had died in the fire. Both Elmer and Mervyn put two and two together.'

'And now?' Casper's tone was only slightly less disdainful than it had been.

'I'm going to try and speak to Lady Pamela. She's a cow, but I think she's willing to drop her husband in it.'

'Not a happy marriage?'

'Far from it.'

After that she phoned Doherty again. 'The next-door neighbour kept a diary of the comings and goings in Rathbone Terrace.'

'And?'

'I think I know where Mark Conway is.'

'I want that diary.'

'I'll bring it to you, but not yet – not until I'm satisfied that every stone's been unturned.'

Thirty-Five

It might have been sheer instinct that made her swerve into the car park in front of the church. On the other hand, it could have been fear. Confronting Charlborough filled her with dread.

She watched whilst two women armed with bunches of gladioli, roses, lupins and delphiniums disappeared through the arched doorway. Keeping the church clean and placing flower displays in dark little alcoves took on a sudden – and safe – attraction.

Why do you suddenly want jam and Jerusalem? she asked herself. *Because being a detective isn't like doing a crossword puzzle. There's people involved and some of them are downright dangerous.*

Summer was in full swing, the trees groaning in the breeze with the weight of dark-green leaves, the grass bowing in waves.

Once the coast was clear, she got out of the car, locked it and followed the path through the churchyard.

She passed along the side of the church and around the back, where the grass was longer and the earth lumpy, as though those buried were trying to sit up.

Wispy heads of uncut grass tickled her legs. She shivered, and not just because of the grass.

As she ventured further into the older part of the churchyard, marble gave way to pock-marked stone. The names of the departed had flaked away. Lichen blemished the faces of granite angels and ivy smothered the last breath from a rose bush planted on a child's grave. In the distance sunlight flashed on the windows of Charlborough Grange.

Honey took a deep breath. 'Let's go beard the lion,' she murmured.

Swiftly, before she could change her mind, she climbed over the stile. The footpath led her beside the canal before veering off towards Charlborough Grange.

The smell of wood smoke curled lazily up from a well-stacked bonfire. There was no one in sight.

The huge greenhouse lured her onwards. She remembered the heads, the very ones Mark Conway made from wax.

The sandbags were still piled around the entrance. The door made a sucking sound when she opened it. The humidity gushed out like a warm wave.

Outside was bright daylight. In here it was dark and smelled of rotting leaves. Within seconds her clothes were stuck to her back.

'Anyone here?' she called.

There was no neat path down the middle, no trays of seedlings waiting to be planted. Huge leaves fanned out from plants whose more natural habitat was Borneo, Sumatra; anywhere further south and east than north Somerset.

This was a jungle. It was the only word to adequately describe it. The sudden sound of insects, the calling of monkeys, and all the other strange noises associated with a tropical rainforest burst into being.

Her hair clung stubbornly to her face as she looked this way, that way, half-expecting something monstrous to leap out from between the fronds of tropical lushness.

'Is anyone there?' she shouted again. She told herself not to waste her breath. Who the hell was going to hear her above the din?

Bravely she made her way beneath huge leaves, stepped over thick roots. A flash of colour to the right caught her attention. An orchid – just one. For some stupid reason she was curious to know whether it was in a pot. She stepped closer, the thick foliage closing behind her.

Perhaps it was a tree root she fell over, or perhaps a stone. Whatever it was threw her off balance. She fell heavily to the ground.

'Damn!' she muttered.

She peered up through the thick vegetation. There was no movement of monkeys or birds. She tried to listen for anything other than the animal sounds. But they couldn't be real. She could see no animals. The sounds were on tape and someone had switched them on.

With trembling fingers, she parted the leaves and peered out.

She saw him at once.

He crept low, his footsteps not making a sound. His face was blackened. He wore fatigues, carried what looked like an AK47 under one arm. His hand rested on a long leather sheath hanging from his belt.

Honey swallowed. Good God, had she stumbled into a real war game?

She couldn't be sure who it was. She assumed it was Charlborough.

Discretion being the better part of valour, she melted into the undergrowth. The soil she slid into was soft and damp. She inwardly groaned at the obvious. Footprints would be seen.

She sank back as far as she could without making a noise. What would Charlborough – if it was Charlborough – do if he caught her?

Swallowing fear was like swallowing cornflakes without milk. They stuck in her throat. But should she be afraid? she asked herself. Was it for certain that Charlborough had done the dirty deed? He was protective of his adoptive son. And Mark Conway had been having an affair with her ladyship. She guessed Lady Pamela had made the running. She was that type.

She advised herself that she was condemning him without good reason.

More rustling ensued around her. Another figure joined the first one. She heard someone sigh. 'Christ, I've had enough of this.'

Peering cautiously through the undergrowth, she saw the recent arrival take off his balaclava.

'Still, it has been quite a team-forming weekend,' said the other man.

This was great! She didn't recognize either of them.

'Gentlemen!'

They looked taken aback to see her emerging from the bushes.

'Are you with us?' asked the johnny-come-lately.

'No. I'm with the tourist board. We're doing a survey on customer satisfaction. Are you totally satisfied with your weekend here?'

She dragged Mrs Patel's notebook out of her bag just to make the lie look a little more authentic. It was very pink and she tried to hide the plastic lips on the cover with her hand.

'I'll just make a few notes,' she said as more weekend soldiers tumbled out of the bushes. 'How do you rate the course on a scale of one to ten?'

She pretended to note down the series of numbers called to her. 'Thank you,' she said, shoving everything back into her bag. 'You've been very helpful.'

All thoughts of confronting Andrew Charlborough went out of her head. Hot and sweaty, she ran all the way back to the canal.

The sobbing branches of a willow tree dipped into the water. The grass beneath it looked soft and green. Heart pounding, she flung herself beneath its shade. As she did so, Mrs Patel's notebook fell out. The red plastic lips looked incongruously out of place amongst the greenness.

Having been invited to read the poetry and Mrs Patel's diary entries, she'd forgotten to do so. Birdsong and the sound of a brightly painted narrowboat heading towards Bath made her want to linger. Castles, roses and impossibly blue birds decorated the vessel's full length. The bright colours even outdid the cover of Mrs Patel's diary. But the cover made her smile. It was fun – probably just like the diary.

'Nice day,' she called out. 'Lovely boat.'

'Thank you.'

She looked in the direction the narrowboat had come from. There was a white yacht moored fifty yards away. The sign fixed to the wooden decking it was fastened to said, 'PRIVATE MOORING. CHARLBOROUGH GRANGE'.

Sir Andrew owned a luxury river boat. It was shiny fibre-glass and stainless steel. It must surely have a large engine, another mechanical device for Mark Conway to look after.

She picked up the diary and began to read. It was strong stuff – at least as far as the case was concerned.

Mrs Patel reported Mr Conway coming in but not going out. She also mentioned activity at the river's edge – someone clearing out their cellar and boats coming and going. The dates were clear. Honey frowned. Mrs Patel was very observant. She described what looked like a rolled-up carpet or a piece of furniture being turfed out into the river. Her phraseology reflected her obvious indignation. It looked to come from number 9, she had added.

'But number nine's empty,' murmured Honey.

She lay back in the grass. The peace of the old canal was disturbed by yet another boat. It didn't sound like a narrow-boat. Opening her eyes, she raised herself on to one elbow and looked. The river cruiser was white and long. Its owner/captain stood proudly at the wheel. A blonde woman accompanied him. They were both in their fifties, just about the right age for indulging their dreams. Of course, if you were rich enough . . .

Suddenly she sat upright. Sir Andrew Charlborough could afford to indulge himself. The canal, not the river, ran through the grounds of Charlborough Grange. Via a series of lock gates, the canal led into the river . . .

She dialled Steve Doherty's number. 'Have you interviewed Mrs Patel?'

'Honey!' He sounded pleased to hear her. 'Yes, I have. Very interesting, but we need a bit more. Best of all would be finding Mark Conway.'

'He's our man. I told you. He killed both men.'

'We confirmed with Sir Andrew that his wife had been having an affair with Mark Conway. He didn't seem unduly worried about it.'

'Did she deny it?'

'She wasn't there. Her husband says she's gone back to Spain.'

'And he's not worried about that either.'

'You're not surprised?'

'You only met her once. I met her twice.'

'She wasn't that bad.'

'She was blonde, Steve, and you're a man which means you're biased.'

'We're trying to find Mark Conway,' said Doherty.

'He's in number nine! It's empty! Mark Conway was used to slipping in and out unnoticed and I know how he was doing it. Sir Andrew has a boat. Mark Conway maintains it just like he does the cars. Anything mechanical he said.' At the other end of the phone, Doherty felt as though he'd been stranded on a roller coaster and now he was swooping down to the terminal. He shouted over his shoulder. 'Get hold of the key holder.'

Thirty-Six

It was eight o'clock in the evening. A mist was rising from the river when they eventually got the keys. The estate agent, annoyed at being dragged away from potential clients, had insisted on accompanying them.

'Go carefully! This is a very valuable property,' he cried as they pushed against the door once the key had turned. 'It has great development potential!'

'Search the whole house,' Doherty ordered. Four burly detectives rushed into the ground-floor hall.

The estate agent had a shiny tie and a surly attitude. 'I hope you don't expect me to accompany you. There's no electricity on, you know,' he added.

Docherty grabbed Honey's arm. 'Not you. This is police business.'

'No way! I've been with this case all the way through. You can't blank me out now.'

'Yes I can. I'm a policeman.'

Doherty was about to follow his men until he noticed Honey leaning over the railings looking down into the basement courtyard. The rusty hinges on the iron gate creaked as she pushed it open.

'Oy!'

Instead of following the uniforms, Doherty raced after her down the slimy green steps. The small courtyard wasn't big enough to swing a cat – even a kitten, but it still smelled of cats' pee. The door to the cellar area had glass panels of multi-coloured diamonds.

It wasn't locked. Doherty pushed it open.

'I say again, the electricity is not switched on,' said the estate agent, leaning over the railings above them.

Doherty switched on his flashlight. 'No need to concern yourself, sir; boy scouts are always prepared.'

'So are girl guides,' said Honey, and did the same.

They passed into gloom, the light from their torches picking out the fact that whoever bought the place had a lot of work to do. Nevertheless, they were likely to make a fortune. This was probably the last house on the block ripe for conversion to flats.

A passageway led to the rooms at the back. He opened a latched door and discovered the steps down to the lower level. They moved silently, surprised at hearing so little evidence of the big-footed men exploring above them. At the bottom of the steps was a small hall. Honey raised her hand to her nose. The smell of damp and mould was overpowering.

Doherty moved off to her right. Just as they'd supposed, there was an opening in the stonework between number 6 and number 7.

Doherty motioned for her to stay behind. She did as she was told, though not because he'd ordered her. She'd heard something and fancied he had not.

The light from Doherty's torch moved away. Her own began to dim. Drat. Why hadn't she thought to recharge it?

Telling herself that she wasn't in the least bit nervous, she moved sideways and thought she passed through a doorway, but couldn't be sure. Was she in number 9 now?

It was dark. Doherty and his flashlight were far away.

She guessed she was in one of the small, square cellar rooms close to the river. This was where provisions had been kept in years gone by. Not now. Now there was only decay and damp and darkness.

Like a cloak it surrounded her. She moved sideways, thinking she heard someone, something.

The smell of mud and a rush of air told her she wasn't far from the river now. There was still ground under her feet, so she couldn't possibly fall in, she told herself. All the same, she took great care. Not until she could see the orange lights shining from the other side of the road did she sigh and manage to switch her torch back on. It was probably only a rat she'd heard earlier. She flashed her torch in front of her and sucked in her breath. Was that rats she could see moving about on the river? If they were, they were a strange shape and very large.

Her foot brushed against something. She flashed her torch downwards and her mouth went dry. The flashlight caught a pair of staring, dead eyes. This was not one of the plastic heads she'd found in the war-games greenhouse. This was real, the flesh blackened and falling away from the face. The earrings were gold. *Pamela Charlborough was not in Spain!*

Her stomach churned. She put her hand over her mouth and almost dropped her torch. Just then the source of the sound she had heard earlier revealed itself. Despite her height, his arm was around her neck. Her legs buckled as he jabbed his knees into the backs of hers.

'Let . . .' she began. It was all she could say, he was holding her so tightly.

'Do you see them?' he asked, his voice excited, his whole body seeming to tremble. 'Do you see my trophies? My father told me how to kill. He served with Sir Andrew in Malaya. Did you know that? The Gurkhas used to cut off their enemies' heads. My dad learned how to do it from them. And Sir Andrew – him too.'

She gagged. His arm was tight against her throat. A cold chill ran down her spine. Even before she felt it against her neck, she knew it was coming.

'This is my friend,' he said.

Because the steel blade rested on her neck, he loosened his grip on her throat. Obviously he guessed she'd be too scared to do anything silly. He was dead right.

'I'm not a police officer,' she said, trying not to sound frightened. 'My name's—'

'I know what your name is. You're just like the others. You want to upset everything. Can't have that, can we?'

She closed her eyes, prayed it would be over quickly, then thought of her mother and Lindsey. Which one would have to identify her?

She fought the terror. *You are not going to panic.*

Easier said than done.

'Please!' Her voice sounded small.

She managed to peer over his arm. She could see the river and the waning light of sunset glowing around the opening and the city lights across the river. She prayed for Doherty to come. He was *bound* to come.

Fifty yards away, Doherty's flashlight had failed. Muttering to himself, he edged his way back over the slimy flagstones.

The walls crumbled silently as he felt his way back to where he'd left her. The muted light from the world outside was shining ahead of him. He saw them silhouetted against the light and held his breath.

Was that his own heart he could hear? Be quiet, he wanted to say, but no words came.

Frozen to the darkness, his heart went out to her. His first thought was to rush Conway. No! She'd be dead by the time he got there. Somehow he had to catch Conway off guard and get him away from her. But how?

He knew she'd seen him. Hopefully, Mark Conway had not.

In the little light there was he looked for anything that might help him push the pair apart. There was nothing on the walls, nothing on the floor. There were iron hooks and bars ranged along the ceiling. Before refrigeration this had been where meat was hung. One of the bars hung from the ceiling like a giant pendulum.

Doherty was only of average height. Honey hoped he was strong enough. She could imagine the sweat running down his face as he calculated its weight and how hard he'd need to swing it. Everything depended on him getting it right.

Judging by the consistency of the walls, the ceiling would be equally crumbly. The iron bar was at least twenty times the weight of the biggest pendulum he'd ever owned. But at least it was a guideline. All the same, she knew that somehow she had to swing Conway round so he'd get the full impact. Too short or too far and she might be hit.

Doherty looked from the hanging iron to Conway, who

seemed oblivious to any small noise – even the sound of heavy footsteps above his head.

Honey listened as he muttered about Charlborough and what he'd done.

'He was my brother, you see. Our mother was dead. Our father didn't want us. That's what hurt the most, but Andrew made up for that. He gave us a home – as long as Shaun became Lance. That was the deal.'

'And he paid your father off,' she said, looking beyond him and praying she'd get the timing right.

'That's right – very handsomely; but then, look what Sir Andrew was gaining.'

Honey swallowed. The knife was sharp against her throat. The tiniest movement or the wrong word and her crisp white shirt would be the wrong shade of pink. And yet she had to move, and not just a little – violently, so that he was facing Doherty.

She braved herself to ask a few more questions. 'Do you hate him for that?'

'Of course not. He's treated us well.'

'Does Lance know that Sir Andrew is not his real father?'

'He didn't! Not until she told him. That bitch! That harlot!' His arm tightened around her. 'I won't have anyone – *anyone* – spoil his life. And she did. Though I tried to be nice to her. I really did.'

Honey thought of the crisp, clean love nest. 'Yes. Of course you did.'

'First that American trying to upset the applecart, and then that slimeball Herbert begging for money.'

'He tried blackmail?'

'Yes. That's the only way his sort ever gets money: by leeching off others.'

'So you buried him in the rockery, hoping that Mrs Herbert's first husband would be blamed.'

'That's right! Lance had been having a fling with that little slut Loretta. He told me all about it.' His laughter echoed off and around the damp ceilings.

'Bob Davies deserved to be blamed. It was his fault that the Yank came visiting in the first place. Him and his stupid hobby. Maxted had the money to check things out. Detecting was his hobby. He didn't need to do it. But he wanted to see the boy, and then that stupid bitch told him the truth.'

Mark told it all. The gaps in the jigsaw began to fall into place. The real Lance had inherited haemophilia from his mother. He had died in the same car accident in which she had died. Sir Andrew hadn't been too well off at the time and was determined to hold on to the fortune his wife had brought to the marriage. Without an heir it would have reverted to his wife's family. So he'd bought – it was the only way she could describe it: *bought* – Shaun from his father. The deal was struck on the condition he took Mark as well.

'So a kidnap was contrived, the boy never found.' Honey's voice shook.

'That's how it worked. Shaun – Lance – never knew any different.' He paused. She felt his body tensing and guessed what was coming next. 'Until now.'

'But you killed Lady Pamela. Surely she was trying to protect you?'

'And make sure she got her husband's money. That's why she accused Trevor and not him. Bitch! Dishonest bitch!'

Doherty was reaching out, trying to get hold of the bar without being seen.

Honey licked the sweat off her lips and tensed her muscles. Doherty was almost ready. His fingertips touched the rough metal before he gripped it tightly. It wasn't easy, but he tried to control his breathing. Counting helped, not just because it made him concentrate on taking long, shallow breaths so that he wouldn't be heard, but also because he was heaving back on the iron bar, pulling it back as far as possible before he let it go. He closed his eyes. Was there any alternative? He knew there wasn't. It was now or never.

With almighty effort, he heaved it back as far as he could, then let it go.

The pendulum swung. Just as it reached its farthest point, Honey jerked from the waist. Conway was taken off balance. To regain his hold on her, he had to face Doherty.

The iron swung and hit him full on.

Honey was flung sideways as the force of the iron sent Conway crashing towards the water. She lay winded, breathing in dust and dirt, feeling soreness on her cheek.

Doherty ran to her.

'I'm all right,' she kept saying in a squeaky voice that sounded nothing like her own. 'I'm all right.'

'She's all right,' he called out to the other figures moving in the gloom.

'Is he dead?' Even to her ears, her voice hadn't quite gone back to normal.

Doherty glanced towards the dark bundle lying still on the floor. 'With the side of his head missing? I should think so.'

Honey rejected his offer to help her to her feet. 'I'm OK.' She looked down at her favourite suit and groaned. 'Why did I choose white?'

'Because you're contrary and won't be told anything.'

'Luckily for you! If the death sentence was still available, poor old Bob the Job would have swung by now.'

He frowned. 'Who?'

She shook her head. 'Never mind.'

Thirty-Seven

A guy wearing a lop-sided toupee and a carnation in his buttonhole smiled in her direction. For a split second his shiny shoes pointed in her direction. His course altered the moment John Rees appeared.

'Have you had a good day?' he asked once the drinks were on the bar.

She nodded. 'Good enough. My daughter hasn't told me she's pregnant, the chef hasn't sliced off a customer's ears, and no one's set the curtains alight with a double sambuca.'

He nodded affably. Being affable as well as good-looking was definitely one of John's things. She told herself he was exactly what she needed; nothing too macho or too much of a lad with the ladies.'You seem good – you know, kind of relaxed.'

She licked a dewdrop of wine from her bottom lip. She couldn't stand wastage.

'I am. Tonight I'm wearing my relaxation hat.'

'Do you have many?'

She counted them off on her fingers. 'There's my father-confessor hat – people tell you all sorts of details about their private lives over the bar. Then there's my 'the customer is always right' hat. That's the one I reserve for the loud-mouth who insists on his consumer rights when a greenfly lands on his salad. Then there's—'

'Whoa! And what about your amateur-detective hat?'

The sound of her sigh seemed to echo through her body. It was lovely to feel relaxed from top to toe.

'It was a case of brotherly love and family factions.' She lifted her glass. 'It's all over now.'

'So how do you intend to celebrate?'

'My favourite would be to buy something really old, silky and outdated from an auction. Jollys' held a clothes auction yesterday, but I couldn't make it. Shame. There were some good items going under the hammer. But never mind: I'll catch the next one.'

John smiled. 'It was a good auction.'

'You went?'

He nodded.

'Lucky dog!'

'I was. I bought you a present.'

He reached down to the gap between their bar stools. 'Here,' he said. 'I saw this and thought of you.'

She started to undo the black plastic bin bag he'd handed her.

'Stylish wrapper,' she mused.

He shrugged. 'It was practical.'

Her fingertips touched something familiar. A thrill shot through her. Honey smiled. Whalebone running through crisp lace and soft silk feels like nothing else in the world. She peered in and saw red satin trimmed with black lace: probably French, just like the one she'd missed on the morning when Casper had summoned her to his office.

John's hand covered hers. 'Best if you didn't get it out in here. People might get jealous.'

She grinned. 'A corset. Should look nice encased behind glass with the rest of my collection.'

The look he gave her was almost serious, certainly unsmiling. 'In my opinion it's the corset that should do the encasing. What do you think?'

A slow smile spread across her face. 'Read my mind.'

The hollow sound of a phone ringing in the deep recesses of her favourite Gucci handbag cut the conversation short. But the inclination remained.

'Mother!' Her smile was stiff and barely patient.

'Hannah, I've arranged for Mr Paget to meet you in the bar of the Francis Hotel at nine o'clock. Are you far from there?'

'I'm sorry, Mother, I am. I'm in Bradford-on-Avon,' she

lied. 'I'll have to take a rain check, I'm afraid. Can you tell him that?'

The response was grumbled.

The echo of another phone trilled from the other end of the bar. The guy with the toupee answered the call, shoved the phone away and ordered a double whisky.

'So!' said John. 'A bottle of champagne is very well deserved.'

She leaned closer to him. 'A bottle of champagne, a four-poster bed and a red satin corset.'

Her phone rang again. This time it was Doherty.

'Hi! We're partying, having a right humdinger of a celebration. Fancy joining us?' He hesitated before saying the words she wanted to hear. 'After all, you put so much into this. I need to show my appreciation.'

'I'm sorry, Doherty. Not tonight.' She smiled at John. 'I'm inspecting the facilities at a prominent Bath Hotel.'

'Never mind. Another time? Just the two of us?'

'Always willing to oblige.'

She snapped the phone shut. Blue eyes and stubble. Why was that so attractive? She also liked the way Doherty's hair flopped over his forehead, and that lop-sided smile. She hadn't realized she was so deep in thought until John's voice broke through.

'Shall we take a rain check too?'

She jerked her head up. 'What?'

He smiled at her. 'Look. I wouldn't want to rush anything.'

She bent her head, fiddling with her phone as she thought things through. Suddenly the four poster and all the trimmings didn't seem quite as attractive as they had done.

'I'm sorry.'

'Don't be. I wouldn't want to rush things.'

But Doherty would, she thought as she left the bar. Damn him for phoning, for being lustful, masculne and annoyingly attractive. Damn her feet for heading towards Manvers Street and a party that she just had to be a part of.